PRAIS NOVELS

"A very detailed and intriguing start to a new series."
—*Fiction Vixen Book Reviews*

"Rising superstar Harrison ventures into darker territory with her chilling first book in the Game of Shadows series. Harrison's mythology and world-building skills are on clear display . . . No matter what the genre, Harrison should be an auto-buy!" —*RT Book Reviews*

"I love good world building and Harrison is a master at it."
—*The Book Vixen*

"Dark, fun and devious." —*Bitten By Books*

PRAISE FOR THE NOVELS OF THE ELDER RACES

Lord's Fall

"The series remains one of the best in paranormal romance."
—*Dear Author*

"I have a lot of love for this series. In a genre that is ridiculously overpopulated, this series is a standout for me."
—*Fiction Vixen Book Reviews*

Oracle's Moon

"Grace's human limitations are pushed to the edge as she learns to wield her new powers. Series fans and new readers alike will cheer her on." —*Publishers Weekly*

continued . . .

"Harrison's flair for developing rich and well-rounded characters anchors the thrilling action and intense emotions found within her books. Harrison provides proof positive she is fast becoming a major star of paranormal romance!"

—*RT Book Reviews* (Top Pick)

"A delightful romantic urban fantasy."

—*Alternative Worlds*

Serpent's Kiss

"A perfect blend of romance, action and drama."

—*RT Book Reviews* (Top Pick)

"I am hooked on the amazing world of the Elder Races."

—*Romance Novel News*

"Thea Harrison's Elder Races novels are my current addiction."

—*All Things Urban Fantasy*

"The author deftly weaves a fantastical romance that spans generations . . . A delightful read with intriguing potential for many more highly anticipated tales."

—*Night Owl Reviews*

Storm's Heart

"Vividly sensual love scenes and fast-moving action sequences are the main reasons I love this paranormal series . . . Ms. Harrison takes us once again into an intriguing tale of love and suspense."

—*Fresh Fiction*

"[Harrison's] world building has simply grown, become richer, more dynamic, more unique and altogether fantastic."

—*Romance Books Forum*

"[Thea's] world-building skills are phenomenal . . . A very sexy tale with a hint of action and adventure and highly memorable characters."

—*Romance Novel News*

Dragon Bound

"Black Dagger Brotherhood readers will love [this]! *Dragon Bound* has it all: a smart heroine, a sexy alpha hero and a dark, compelling world. I'm hooked!"

—J. R. Ward, #1 *New York Times* bestselling author

"I absolutely loved *Dragon Bound*! Once I started reading, I was mesmerized to the very last page. Thea Harrison is a master storyteller, and she transported me to a fascinating world I want to visit again and again. It's a fabulous, exciting read that paranormal romance readers will love."

—Christine Feehan, #1 *New York Times* bestselling author

"I loved this book so much, I didn't want it to end. Smoldering sensuality, fascinating characters and an intriguing world—*Dragon Bound* kept me glued to the pages. Thea Harrison has a new fan in me!"

—Nalini Singh, *New York Times* bestselling author

"Thea Harrison has created a truly original urban fantasy romance . . . When the shapeshifting dragon locks horns with his very special heroine, sparks fly that any reader will enjoy. Buy yourself an extra-large cappuccino, sit back and enjoy the decadent fun!"

—Angela Knight, *New York Times* bestselling author

"Thea Harrison is definitely an author to watch. Sexy and action packed, *Dragon Bound* features a strong, likable heroine, a white-hot luscious hero and an original and intriguing world that swallowed me whole. This novel held me transfixed from beginning to end! I'll definitely be keeping my eyes open for the next book in this series."

—Anya Bast, *New York Times* bestselling author

continued . . .

"Full of tense action, toe-curling love scenes and intriguing characters that will stay with you long after the story is over. All that is wrapped inside a colorful, compelling world with magic so real, the reader can feel it. Thea Harrison is a fantastic new talent who will soon be taking the world of paranormal romance by storm."

—Shannon K. Butcher, national bestselling author

"Fun, feral and fiercely exciting—I can't get enough! Thea Harrison supplies deliciously addictive paranormal romance, and I'm already jonesing for the next hit."

—Ann Aguirre, national bestselling author

"An outstanding blend of romantic suspense and urban fantasy." —*Booklist* (starred review)

"Utilizing vivid characterization, edge-of-your-seat danger and an intriguing alternate reality, Harrison crafts a novel that grabs you from the first sentence and makes you bitterly regret that the book must end."

—*RT Book Reviews* (Top Pick)

"The writing is just superb . . . This world is really fantastic—exciting, very sexy and humorous. Fans of paranormal romance must read this book." —*Smexy Books*

Berkley Sensation Titles by Thea Harrison

Novels of the Elder Races

DRAGON BOUND
STORM'S HEART
SERPENT'S KISS
ORACLE'S MOON
LORD'S FALL
KINKED

Game of Shadows Novels

RISING DARKNESS
FALLING LIGHT

Falling Light

THEA HARRISON

BERKLEY SENSATION, NEW YORK

THE BERKLEY PUBLISHING GROUP
Published by the Penguin Group
Penguin Group (USA) LLC
375 Hudson Street, New York, New York 10014

USA • Canada • UK • Ireland • Australia • New Zealand • India • South Africa • China

penguin.com

A Penguin Random House Company

FALLING LIGHT

A Berkley Sensation Book / published by arrangement with the author

For information, address: The Berkley Publishing Group,
a division of Penguin Group (USA) LLC,
375 Hudson Street, New York, New York 10014.

ISBN: 978-0-425-25510-0

PUBLISHING HISTORY
Berkley Sensation mass-market edition / February 2014

PRINTED IN THE UNITED STATES OF AMERICA

10 9 8 7 6 5 4 3 2 1

Cover art by Judy York.
Cover design by George Long.
Interior text design by Kristin del Rosario.

Chapter One

WHEN MICHAEL KILLED the two unconscious men that lay sprawled in the overgrown grass, he did so with quick, efficient slashes across their carotid arteries.

Their spirits were already gone, destroyed by the most dangerous entity on earth. They had become drones that only looked like men, soulless vessels that enacted the Deceiver's wishes.

Understanding what had happened to the men hadn't stopped Mary's expression from filling with pain when she had examined them. She had still held out hope that there was something she could do for them. Michael had watched her gaze turn dull when she realized the men were beyond her help. She cared about everyone. That fact lay at the essence of her healing.

Michael didn't care for total strangers the way Mary did. All he felt was tiredness and a grim sense of relief as he straightened to watch the bodies bleed out. When he was certain that they were, in fact, finally dead, he limped over to the area where Mary had said that she had dropped her gun. He found the nine-millimeter, then turned to take one last look around at the area surrounding the small, rustic cabin.

More bodies littered the clearing. More casualties of the millennia-old war that he and the others had fought.

In this latest confrontation, the Deceiver had come much too close to capturing both Michael and Mary. He had shot Mary, and he and his drones had wounded Michael several times. Only by the sheerest luck and an insane gamble had they managed to survive and send their old enemy scrambling in retreat.

The strong morning light fell into Michael's eyes, blinding him. The bright yellow haze filled his mind, and his head swam. For a moment, he felt disconnected from his body, half in another realm, sensing as if from a distance how his physical wounds throbbed.

The knife wound in his upper thigh was the worst. It ached like a son of a bitch. The knife had scraped bone. He was lucky it hadn't severed an artery. When Mary had bandaged them in the cabin, she had stitched and bound the knife wound tightly. It stanched the worst of the bleeding, but he could feel that the bandages had already grown heavy and wet.

He had other wounds that were not physical but spiritual in nature, claw marks from the swarm of dark spirits that had attacked him, and from when the Deceiver had almost destroyed him.

He didn't remember what had happened, only what Mary told him. He had been unconscious at the time, but he could sense the damage running through him like a series of dark fault lines. He felt as if he took the right kind of blow, a blow filled with power and not mere physical strength, his spirit might shatter.

He needed to get off his feet and give the leg wound a chance to stop bleeding. They needed to leave this place before the Deceiver could regroup and try to come after them again. Michael suspected that the Deceiver would pull back, gather reinforcements and regain his strength rather than go after them again right away, but they couldn't take any chances. At the moment, they were too vulnerable to fight off another concentrated attack.

This cabin was isolated, a few miles away from Wolf Lake, deep in the Michigan National Forest. Once, it had been a useful hideaway, but now that its location was known, its usefulness as a safe house was gone. When they left, they wouldn't be returning.

He turned to limp toward Mary who leaned against the passenger door of his car, a nondescript, battered blue Ford with a transplanted BMW engine that he maintained meticulously.

While she waited for him to finish his grim task, she tilted her face up, eyes closed, to the bright morning sunlight.

The sight of her struck him powerfully, almost like another physical blow. She was small and slender-boned, just five-foot-two, with bright, aquamarine blue eyes, honey-colored skin and thick, layered tawny hair that curled crazily if left to its own devices.

She was gorgeous and almost a stranger. He had only known her for a few days in this life. They had been lovers for a single night, but they had been soul mates for millennia.

As he approached, she opened her eyes to look at him. She looked as exhausted as he felt, her lovely eyes circled with shadows and her soft, full mouth bracketed with lines of pain. Her jeans were streaked with dirt, and she wore one of his flannel shirts. It was massive on her, and the tails came down almost to her knees.

The Deceiver had shot her in the shoulder. Michael had bound her arm in a sling. Then he helped her to roll up one sleeve past her slender wrist, while the other sleeve remained empty.

When he reached her side, he tucked the weapons in his black canvas bag in the backseat. Then he couldn't resist touching her. He leaned over to kiss her. She cupped the back of his head, stroking his short hair as she kissed him back.

He took her free hand. "Listen to me. We're both hurt, and Astra's strength is depleted."

Astra, his old childhood mentor.

Astra was also the leader of the original group of seven that had left their world six thousand years ago to pursue the Deceiver when he had escaped their prison and fled to Earth.

In order to follow him, the group had needed to die as the Deceiver had died, in an arcane ritual filled with alchemy and power. The ritual transmuted their souls. As they died, they left their world and joined the Earth's natural cycle of death and rebirth, where they lived and died as humans did, over and over again.

Astra had come to help Michael and Mary in astral form when they fought their latest battle with the Deceiver, but astral projection took a lot of power. Fighting in astral form took even more power, and they couldn't expect any more help from her anytime soon.

Mary's hand squeezed his, her expression sharpening with concern. He realized he had fallen into a fugue.

He told her, "Thanks to the damage you did to him, the Deceiver has to take time to recover too, but we don't know how much reinforcement he has nearby, so we can't stop in one place again. I can drive for a while, but you need to concentrate on healing yourself. Nothing else matters. Heal yourself so you can take over driving, because soon I'm going to need your help. Do you understand?"

She nodded. "Yes."

"Good."

He lifted her hand to kiss her fingers, and she curled her fingers along the lean edge of his cheek as she studied him with a worried gaze. He opened the passenger door for her, and after she had slid in, he walked around the car and eased into the driver's seat.

Just before he tried the ignition, they shared a quick, tense glance. They were deep in the forest, miles away from any kind of help, and they were both injured. If the Deceiver had found any time to disable the engine, they would be in a shitload of trouble.

She whispered, "Come on, start."

He turned the key, and the car purred to life. The engine sounded as smooth as it had the last time he had tuned it. "Now we need to make tracks," he said. "We've miles to go before we sleep."

"Miles to go before I sleep," she said, her voice slow and tired. "That was a Robert Frost poem, right? Some poet wrote that, anyway."

He shook his head and wished he hadn't, because it made his head throb worse than before. His heart beat in heavy, hard slugs, and his mouth felt hot and dry. "Whoever it was, I've got a bone to pick with him."

"At least we're alive and together," she pointed out.

He shifted the car in gear and pulled onto the gravel drive. "And at least we get another day or two. And maybe more." If he had anything to say about it, they would have a hell of a lot more.

"That's a veritable wealth of minutes," she said.

She echoed what they had said to each other last night, in the intimacy of tangled sheets, as the firelight died and rising darkness conquered the room.

Despite the seriousness of their situation, one corner of his mouth lifted. He said, "And that's a staggering fortune in seconds."

"Hey." She flicked his arm lightly with her fingers. "You never did steal any flowers for me, you know."

It had been his final promise to her nine hundred years ago, when they had last met, in other bodies and other, long-ago lives. He would steal flowers for her in the spring. She would learn how to milk a cow, and they would make love all winter long, at his country home outside of Florence in Italy.

They had never gotten the chance to do any of it. They had both died a few moments later.

He set the memory aside. That tragedy had happened a long time ago. Now they had found each other again, and he would be damned before he let any of this slip away.

He gave her a smile. "I'm with a woman who is developing a memory like a steel trap. I'll have to get right on that."

Her lips curved in response, although it didn't banish the worried expression in her gaze. "I'll hold you to it."

He had to drive south to connect with a road that would take them back east toward U.S. 131. Even though they traveled on two-lane country roads and there was no other vehicle in sight, he still took no chances and pulled the car to a sedate halt at a stop sign. The last thing they needed was to call attention to themselves.

As the car rolled to a stop, the morning sun spilled at a slant through the driver's window, stronger than ever as it hit him in the eyes. The light, heavy and gold, blinded him.

He disconnected from his body again.

The falling light.

He and his mate lived in a city topped with graceful white spires. Their sky was crowned with two suns, and the falling light turned their days endless and golden. They were creatures of power and fire, born at the same moment and destined to journey through life together.

She stood tall and slender, and her large, silver eyes were filled with the beauty and mystery of her soul. That mystery called to him. He could empathize with her but never truly fully understand her. The colors of her emotions were like a symphony. She was as fierce in her devotion to her healing as he was to his warrior nature. The rightness of that, the completeness, balanced and sustained him.

Their people did not die of old age. They did not know death, unless it happened by accident, through illness or by war.

Or until a criminal brought it to their city. He murdered

innocents who stood in the way of his crimes before he was captured and imprisoned.

And then escaped.

When the call came to find those who would go in pursuit of the criminal, Michael didn't hesitate to approach his mate about volunteering.

Are you sure? she asked. *If we go, we can never return home.*

The details of the transmigration spell had been explained meticulously to them. They would die. Their souls would leave their world, and they would have to transform in order to travel to an entirely new, strange place.

The spell was the only way they could reach the other world where the Deceiver had fled. There could be no return. If they chose to transform, they would literally no longer be the same creatures, while all the alchemy that made such an extreme journey possible would remain on their home world.

Still, the Deceiver must be stopped.

It is worth the price, he said.

At the time, he could not know that they would keep paying and paying.

"Michael," Mary said.

As he blinked the sun out of his eyes, he got the impression that she had called his name more than once. They still sat at the stop sign of an empty intersection, the car idling quietly.

A tight band circled his wrist. He looked down. She had taken hold of his arm in a strong grip.

Mary's expression was tight. "You blacked out."

"No, I didn't," he said. "Not quite. I had a memory resurface, that's all. It's okay, I'm all right."

He could tell by the doubt in her eyes that she didn't quite believe him, but there was nothing she could do. They didn't have any other choice. They had to get moving.

"Did you remember anything important?"

He smiled a little. "I remembered what you looked like a long time ago."

Her tight grip relaxed. "Promise me that you'll pull over if you have to."

"Of course."

With obvious reluctance she let go of him to settle back into her seat and close her eyes. He found his sunglasses tucked in the glove compartment of the dashboard. He slipped them on, blocking out the sun and the details of the events that had happened so long ago.

The past was no longer relevant. Their future was uncertain at best. The present was all they had.

It was time to make the most of it.

Accelerating gently, he turned onto the intersecting road. They traveled east until they reached the highway. Then they turned north.

They had to join Astra and combine their strength before the Deceiver got the chance to attack them again.

Then finally, finally, they would take down that bastard once and for all.

ALL TOO AWARE of Michael's injuries and his grim, dogged endurance, Mary did as he directed and focused on healing her own gunshot wound so that she would be able to help him and take over driving. She was tired and in pain, and not thinking as clearly as she would have liked, so she fumbled the job at first.

When the Deceiver had shot her, she had a crisis-driven epiphany. Shock, pain and instinct had driven her awareness into her own body, and a floodgate of ancient memories had poured out, like golden treasure from a secret, inner chamber. Somehow she had staved off shock and started healing her own body.

How had she done it?

She remembered quite well the experience of having the epiphany, but replicating what she had actually done was a different matter. She needed practice before she could do any kind of healing very easily.

The color red had initially triggered the memories. As soon as she recalled that, it did so again. Her perspective shifted, and she saw the interior of her own body as a warm, glowing red vibrancy like live coals, except for the wound. That area was a dark, jagged hole.

She sank her awareness deep into herself. The entry wound was small and located just under her collarbone, but the bullet had flattened to inflict more damage where it exited than where it had entered. The scientist in her grew fascinated as she studied the area. She could see and sense where the initial healing had already begun.

The first time she had worked on healing herself, she had been in imminent danger as she confronted the Deceiver who had stolen her ex-husband's body. She had shoved commands into her own flesh with all the finesse of a bulldozer. This time, she nudged more gently.

Once again, her body responded. Veins fused, and torn flesh knitted together. As she watched, she realized she was only accelerating what would have happened naturally over the course of time. It didn't erase the damage that had been done to her, or cause her body to return to the state it had been in before she was shot. She would have to exercise her shoulder and arm carefully to stretch and condition the area, and she would retain the scar. . . .

Maybe there was a different way to promote the healing so that she erased the scar, but if so, she couldn't remember it. Hopefully the more she used this newly recovered skill, the more memories would return.

For now, though, she didn't care that her skin puckered in rough circles at the entry and exit points, or that her shoulder felt stiff and sore as the last of the wound knitted together. She also noticed other, less urgent imperfections in the glowing, scarlet landscape of her body—various scrapes and contusions she had collected over the last few, very eventful, days.

Those wounds were minor, so she ignored them. Michael needed help more than she needed a few bruises healed. As she studied her handiwork, she felt an immense satisfaction and a sense of completeness.

She had always known she was a healer. This was how she healed.

As exhilarating as the experience had been, it had depleted her body's resources. She needed a quick nap before she was safe to take over driving. So she coaxed herself to sleep, and as she had done so often over the last few days, she drifted into another dream.

Chapter Two

ASTRA HAD SIMPLY done too much.

Somehow, nine hundred years ago, the Deceiver had injured Mary so severely, she hadn't reincarnated for generations. Astra had spent that time playing cat and mouse with the Deceiver while she reconnected with Michael every lifetime she could, and she searched for clues to what had happened to Mary.

If Astra could have destroyed the Deceiver by herself, she would have done so long ago. But she couldn't. They were too well matched in strength. She needed the others to fight by her side in order to overcome him.

In this lifetime, Astra and Michael had become convinced that Mary had finally been reborn. They had searched for her for years, but they only managed to get the occasional glimpse of her in the psychic realm.

A few days ago, events had finally come to a head. Mary had torn that old spiritual injury wide open, and Astra had leaped into an astral projection in order to try to reach her.

Then the Deceiver had drawn Astra into a dream to show her one of his executions. Only hours after that, she had thrown herself into another astral projection to join Michael and Mary as they fought off the Deceiver and his forces. She had fought in the battle for as long as she could before she finally had to drop out.

Now, after her prodigious expenditure of energy, Astra slept as her elderly, fragile body struggled to rejuvenate. The ancient, alien part of herself was always awake, always aware. It drifted patiently in the darkness of her mind.

That part of her could sense the rest of the battle that consumed the others. Even from a distance, their fight lit the psychic landscape. Astra watched and did nothing, because there was simply nothing more that she could do.

So she gathered her psychic resources. As soon as she had regained enough strength, she created the delicate web of imagery, illusion and desire that made up a dream sending. When it was complete, she loosed it in the direction of the one she targeted. Then she waited.

Some time after the battle, the one she waited for drifted into sleep. Astra felt her dream sending activate. She reached along the web she had woven. When she touched the mind of the sleeping one, the dream had already begun. She eased into it.

Her dream body found itself standing in the middle of a spacious, tiled hall. She walked down the length of it, passing rows of columns as she looked around with curiosity. The ceilings were high and vaulted, and thin sheets of carved marble covered the walls. There was no imagery anywhere in the carvings, just interlocking patterns of such delicate complexity that the cool, hard stone resembled lace.

It was daylight, and the dream carried a sultry heat. She could hear the silvery sound of splashing water nearby and followed the sound. She came upon a courtyard filled with a small, immaculate garden fragrant with a brilliant profusion of colorful flowers. A marble fountain carved with gracious dimensions spouted water in the middle of the garden.

A young woman, dressed in a simple homespun cotton tunic and trousers, sat on the edge of the fountain. She was too thin, her quiet face carved with stress, thick hair captured in a dark blond braid at the nape of her neck.

As Astra approached, the young woman turned wide, sky blue eyes toward her and said, "For some reason, I keep coming back to scenes from this lifetime. Even though I've healed, I must not be finished with it after all. You must be Astra."

"Yes," she said.

"I thought I recognized you. I'm Mary, if you didn't already know." Mary studied her with frank curiosity. "Michael said you were old, but you look like a young woman."

"My body is old, although I don't, thank God, have to be old in my dreams."

"A few days ago, when you came to me, I was in the Grotto on the university grounds at Notre Dame."

"I wondered where you were," said Astra. "I knew you were some distance from me, but somehow still local, and certainly not as far as overseas. Of course things are different in the psychic realm than they are in the physical world. You were also too confused and distressed to be able to tell me anything concrete."

"When you appeared, I actually thought you might be the Virgin Mary. I was pretty disappointed you weren't." Mary's shoulders lifted in a wry shrug. "No offense."

Astra laughed. "None taken."

"Has Nicholas arrived yet?" Mary asked.

Surprised, Astra's dream body stilled as her mind raced.

Millennia ago, when she had first been born on this earth, she had developed close ties with the people of the First Nations. She had taught them ways of the spirit in the hopes that they might become her allies in her fight against the Deceiver. *PtesanWi*, they called her. White Buffalo Calf Woman.

Over the years, she continued to maintain a connection with a select few of the First Nation elders. Nicholas's father, an Ojibwa elder named Jerry Crow, was one of her most recent allies. Together she and Jerry had trained Nicholas, who for a human was unusually strong, both in mind and body.

The boy had fulfilled all their hopes. He had become a Green Beret and worked his way to the head of the Secret Service detail assigned to protect the President of the United States, where he stood guard against more than mere physical threats. Attuned to the spiritual realm, Nicholas had been their defense against the Deceiver attempting to make the President into a tool to enact his wishes.

A few days ago, Nicholas had been assassinated. Jerry and one of his grandsons, Jamie, had traveled to her house to give her the news. Even now, Jerry lay in one of her guest bedrooms, laboring for his life. After a life filled with too much smoking and stress, Jerry's heart was finally giving out on him.

He needed to be in a hospital, but he had expended all of his strength in coming to tell her about Nicholas's death. Astra's place was in such a remote location, if Jerry tried to get to a hospital now, the trip alone would probably kill him.

While Astra was not primarily a healer, she had some skills. She knew that she could heal Jerry. It was, just barely, within the realm of her abilities, but she couldn't afford to expend the precious energy it would take to save him.

Not when she was so depleted, and not when the Deceiver was so close and such a danger to all of them. And especially not when destroying him was the sole reason she had come to this earth.

But she couldn't see how Mary could be aware of any of that.

Eyes narrowed, she asked, "How do you know of Nicholas? Did Michael tell you about him? If Michael is hoping that Nicholas might be of any assistance, I'm afraid I have bad news for you. Nicholas was murdered a few days ago."

"Yes, we know," said Mary, surprising her again. "We don't know very many details, but we do know that he was killed. His ghost came to help us—or at least he helped me, when I was running in the woods. We asked him to make sure that you were all right."

Astra relaxed marginally. If Nicholas's ghost had come here, he would have sensed Jerry's ailing presence in her house, and he would have gone to his father.

She would check to make sure once this dream had run its course. For now, she sat beside Mary, on the wide edge of the fountain.

"If he promised to come, then I'm sure that he will show up soon," she replied simply. "He is too canny to be caught by the Deceiver's allies and traps." She ran her fingers through the cool water as she looked around. "This is a lovely place."

"For the most part, I think this was a lovely life until the end. Maybe that's one of the reasons I keep coming back here in my dreams." Mary looked at the rosebushes. "The woman who was my mother in this lifetime loved this garden. My father put in the fountain just for her, and this was her favorite place in the world."

Astra smiled at her. "It's not hard to see why. How did you heal yourself?"

Mary's gaze returned to her. "Which time?"

She took a breath. "Ah. So you were hurt in the battle?"

"Yes. Michael and I were both hurt. Michael was almost destroyed." Mary's mouth worked. Then her thin, young face went carefully blank. She said, "We're not doing very well right now."

Astra said in a gentle voice, "I could sense that Michael had taken some damage. If I could do anything more to help you, I would."

Mary's wide blue eyes pinned her. "He said you ran out of strength."

Astra showed her a mental image of her cold, frail physical self as she huddled on her narrow bed. "My body is very old. I am already working to prevent death as it is, and over the last few days I've expended a lot of energy."

After a moment Mary said, "I see. I guess I still held out some hope that you might be able to help us. I'm sorry."

While Mary struggled with her disappointment, Astra slipped with subtle dexterity into the illusion of the younger woman's dream body. While Mary's physical body might be some distance away, Astra could still examine her spirit, which looked whole and bright. She really did indeed seem to be fully healed. Astra slipped away again before Mary noticed.

"So how did you heal the first time?" Astra asked. "When I saw you in the Grotto, your spirit wound ran down the length of your torso."

Michael had already told her how Mary had summoned an Eastern dragon for healing, but suspicion had become Astra's oldest and dearest friend. She wanted to see for herself if their stories matched.

"I called for help," Mary said, looking down as she pleated the edge of her tunic. "It was something that I had learned to do in this life."

She raised her eyebrows. "I see. No wonder you keep coming back here in your dreams."

"Yes."

She leaned forward to put her hand over Mary's. She sensed the younger woman's inner withdrawal although her dream body didn't move. "Mary, listen to me. I sensed earlier when you and Michael had stopped to rest at the cabin. I thought at the time that it was a dangerous decision, and then the Deceiver almost took you both. You must not stop again. There are things I can teach you, and things you need to help me do. We must not let the Deceiver keep the three of us from reuniting."

"That's what Michael says," Mary said. She lifted her gaze. "We won't stop again."

"Good," said Astra, sensing truth.

"I must go," Mary said suddenly. "I meant to take only a little nap after I healed my shoulder. Michael's still injured. He needs me."

"Of course." Astra stood. "It is so good to see you again, Mary. It has been far too long. I have missed you. Please come quickly."

Mary stood as well. "We will. We are."

Astra nodded and thrust gently out of the other woman's dream, traveling back to the cool quiet well of her own mind.

I am not in control of her, Astra thought. And Mary does not show the absolute dedication to our cause that we all need, especially now when the Deceiver is so close at hand.

The realization was jarring. Astra had been confident of Michael for so many centuries. For lifetimes. His rage at the disappearance of his mate ran so deep. But now that he had found Mary, she was beginning to skew his motives.

They were starting to fight for survival, not for the Deceiver's destruction.

Astra must be prepared to kill them both when they arrived.

Chapter Three

ALMOST AN HOUR after battling Michael and Mary at the cabin, he was still flying high on adrenaline and anger. The energy he had taken from the people he had killed at the country diner buzzed along his nerves. The sensation would fade after a few hours. Until then, it was better than any drug, and he should know. He had tried them all.

Heroin, cocaine, methamphetamine, crack, LSD, ecstasy, PCP. Marijuana did nothing for him. Smoking it made him hungry and even more paranoid than usual. He just didn't see the point, although he was rather fond of opium.

It was so easy to enjoy drugs when he had no lifelong commitment to any one body. Nicotine? He loved it. There was nothing quite like that first cigarette right after he took over a new body. Taking a drag of smoke into virgin lungs was better than sex.

When he experimented, he was always careful not to overdose. After all, for him, the point of using drugs was recreation, not a desire to escape his life. He didn't want to accidentally die and have to start life all over again as a real baby, not knowing his own true identity. That would leave him too vulnerable to his enemies.

But none of the drugs, not even his favorite, coke, could hold a candle to the experience of taking human lives. He drank them down like they were the finest of liqueurs. If gold had a taste, he imagined that was what a soul tasted like.

Pure life force. It was the most valuable commodity in the universe. It was also the easiest resource to harvest, and the best goddamn high there ever was.

He wished he could drink down the life force of his old enemies the way that he had discovered he could do with humans. Imagine what kind of high that would be—revenge and sustenance all at once. He'd tried once or twice, the rare times he had been able to capture one of them. But he had never discovered the knack for it. Either their spirits were too strong or they were too like his, and his desire remained nothing more than a frustrated fantasy.

He was aware that he was rambling a bit and not with very much relevance or clarity. Making an effort to rein in his wandering thoughts, he ran through the list of what he had accomplished since he had fled from the cabin.

By now, the Michigan state patrol would have discovered the massacre at the Northside Restaurant. His drone at Quantico would have initiated contact with the state police to insure that the FBI would take over the homicide case. With his drone in position to target the search, by this evening, one of the most intensive manhunts in the history of the United States would be under way for Michael and Mary.

While the knowledge was very sweet indeed, he couldn't afford to relax and wait to let the authorities bring in his prey. For a survivalist like Michael, there were a lot of places to hide in the countryside, and Michigan had so much freshwater coastline, it was going to be a nightmare to try to patrol the borders.

Also, he knew very well that Michael and Mary were

working hard to join Astra in whatever hole that bitch was using as her current lair. They were stronger together than when they were apart. Even though there were now only three of his enemies left, as long as Astra joined anyone that came against him, he knew that even a small group could be enough to bring him down.

He had to try to stop the three from reuniting if he possibly could, otherwise he might spend the next several decades—the rest of this generation—on the run. If that happened, he knew from experience that the balance would only begin to swing in his favor again when Michael's and Mary's current human bodies grew old and frail.

Old age was not a friend to his enemies. Their spirits became trapped by the limitations of their failing meat. That was the drive behind his original search to find a way to leap from human host to host, so that he could stay forever youthful, forever strong.

Deep in thought, he drove to his latest temporary headquarters in a motel room in Grand Rapids. He had just unlocked the door and was entering his room when his cell phone rang.

He glanced at the number. It was his drone at Quantico. He kicked the door shut and answered it.

"Oversight for the case has moved to DC," his drone said. "I've insisted that I want to remain involved, so headquarters complied by assigning me to head the task force."

He twitched a shoulder impatiently. Sometimes working with drones was an exercise in irritation. They might be under his total control, but that control came at a cost. Drones lost a certain initiative or essential drive that independent people with souls retained.

But contracting jobs out to independent humans, or even partnering with them, meant that he could never be absolutely sure of their loyalty. It was always a judgment call which way to jump with a project.

"Martin, what did I tell you about bothering me with

unimportant details?" he said. "You remained in charge of the case. That's all that matters."

"Well, yes and no," Martin said, sounding apologetic. "My point is, I'll be working with outsiders from DC. Some of them will be joining me in the field, so there will be witnesses to anything I do. It's a complication and might slow things down. It'll be harder for me to plant evidence and direct the search."

"Well then, you'll just have to introduce me to your coworkers," he said. "You know how I love to meet people."

One good handshake was all it took. If he met a human in person, he could turn him or her into one of his drones. The procedure took energy and depleted him for a while, but needs must be met. This mission was too important to allow any interference from outsiders. For this, he had to retain total control.

"Understood," Martin said. "In the meantime, we've been discussing initial steps. Michigan is a logistical nightmare for a manhunt. Even if we enlist help from the National Guard, there is no way we can cover all of the state's borders, especially the coastline."

"I'm well aware of that," he snapped.

"We have to prioritize the hunt somehow," Martin told him. "Do you have any orders or preferences on how we do that?"

He tapped a front tooth with his thumbnail as he thought. Mary had lived in St. Joseph, which was located in southeastern Michigan. A few days ago, she had crossed the state border to go to Notre Dame, in northern Indiana, where two of his drones had tried and failed to kidnap her.

Then she and Michael had met up somehow, somewhere. It didn't matter how the two had found each other. He knew that Michael and Astra had been searching for Mary just as he had been, and twinned souls had a knack for connecting with each other.

Soon after the two had reunited, he had found them

through a little dark spirit who brought him news of their location, for a blood price. They had gone to ground in a cabin that was not far from Michigan's western coast, and it was significantly north—almost halfway up the Lower Peninsula.

Perhaps Michael and Mary had only gone in that direction because that was where the safe house was located. But if Astra's location were somewhere entirely different, say for example further south, would they have risked adding so much more mileage to their trip by going in the opposite direction—especially when they knew he was hunting for them?

He didn't think so. That meant they were traveling north for a reason. And with him so close on their heels, they would have only one overriding reason. Astra.

He said, "Concentrate your resources along the western and northern coastline of the Lower Peninsula. Set up a roadblock at the Mackinac Bridge. We don't want them to cross over to the Upper Peninsula if we can avoid it. If they reach the national forest up there, it will be even harder to ferret them out. And make sure the state patrol understands they need to maintain an aggressive search on all the main highways."

"Yes, sir," said Martin.

His mind switched gears, and he remembered another avenue of research he wanted to pursue.

Nicholas Crow had shown himself to be an adept in things of spirit that most people knew nothing about. That was why he'd had Crow assassinated.

He had done it to clear his way to meeting the President—and shaking the President's hand was a goal that remained near and dear to his heart. Ironically, though, now that Crow was no longer an obstacle, he didn't have time to orchestrate a way to meet the President and either turn him into a drone or take over his body. He would just have to conquer the Commander in Chief some other time.

But Crow still interested him, after the fact of his death.

How had the man learned the things he had learned? And why had Crow chosen such a targeted career path that led him to head the Secret Service detail that protected the President? Who Crow was, the totality of the man, seemed so . . . specific.

Long ago, Astra had scattered her teachings throughout the First Nations, sowing knowledge of the spirit realm throughout all the peoples who migrated over continents and multiplied like rabbits. Ever since that time, he never knew when something might pop up to plague him.

Had Crow learned what he had known from one of his elders? Or was it just possible that Astra herself had a hand in teaching him?

"One more thing," he said. "I want you to dig into Nicholas Crow's background."

At least there was one good thing about his drones. When he gave an order, they never asked why. They simply did as they were told.

Martin said, "Certainly. There will already be a couple of detailed dossiers of him on file. Not only did he have the highest level of security clearance, but his murder is getting an aggressive investigation. What level of information are you looking for?"

"I want to know everything," he said. "I want to know what Crow liked to eat for breakfast. I want to know where he was born, where he grew up, and where he went to school. I want to know who he fucked when he was a teenager, and every lover he's had since then. I want names of friends and family members, all the important people in his life, and where they live."

He had learned a long time ago to leave no stone unturned. As busy as he was these days, it still might be very productive to interrogate a few of the people from Crow's life.

Martin said, "I'll have my staff compile the available data, and I'll get it to you as soon as possible."

"Excellent." It was a good start. If the information currently on file didn't have enough detail to satisfy him, he would have Martin's people dig further. "When are you coming to Michigan?"

"I'll fly into Grand Rapids this evening."

"Contact me when you get here." He punched the disconnect button.

That was when he looked down at his hands, really looked at them for the first time since the cabin, where Mary had killed his former host by inducing a heart attack and forced him to leap into the body of his nearest soldier drone. Even though he was in an entirely different body, just remembering the battle caused a phantom pain to ghost through his chest.

He ignored it and turned the hands over. They were broad and callused, with thick wrists and chunky finger joints. Wiry ginger hair coated the back of the hands and arms.

His lip curled as he inspected them. This was not at all the type of body he preferred to inhabit. He typically chose young, handsome hosts with well-toned bodies, and he had a particular preference for blue eyes. People responded so well to blue-eyed handsome young men.

There might be a certain brute strength sewn into this meat, but there was no style or elegance at all to it. Oh, look, there was even more of that awful wiry ginger shit coating the backs of the fingers.

Dirt crusted the edge of the fingernails.

Surprise and revulsion held him frozen.

He had put that filthy thumbnail in his mouth. Actually his mouth was part of the new body attached to that filthy thumb. He ran the tongue over the teeth. They felt crusted and dirty.

The last of the floating high from the restaurant murders left him abruptly. He crashed and became completely aware of his connection to this disgusting flesh.

Growling, he threw the phone on the bed and stormed into the bathroom to confront his image in the mirror.

Muddy green eyes looked back at him out of a boxy face that had a lumpy nose shaped like a potato. It had clearly been broken at least once before. His host had a short buzz cut that did nothing to disguise the fact that his hairline was receding. He bared his teeth. They were prominent and yellow.

Ugly. Ugly. Ugly.

He punched the mirror. A starburst of cracks shot across the surface, destroying the reflection. Then he snatched up toothbrush and toothpaste and brushed the body's teeth furiously until the gums bled. When he had finally finished, he tore off all the clothes and showered in water so hot it made the body's skin redden.

He ignored the discomfort, just as he ignored the pain from his—NOT HIS—the body's cut and bleeding knuckles. He didn't have any drones with him. He didn't have the time to search for a suitable candidate to use as a replacement. He also couldn't afford to expend any energy on migrating to yet another new host. For the moment he would have to suck it up and suffer some time in this monkey suit.

"I owe you for this one, cookie," he whispered to Mary.

He could add it to a very long list of grievances that was thousands of years old. To tell the truth, he just never got tired of being angry.

The old proverb had gotten it entirely wrong. Revenge was not a dish best served cold.

Revenge was a dish best served with all the passion and ingenuity one could muster.

Chapter Four

AS SOON AS Astra had appeared by the fountain, Mary realized she was dreaming. She knew that every word they spoke to each other was as real and true as if they physically stood in the same room together.

When they finished talking and Astra disappeared, she woke up.

Afternoon sun spilled into the car. Her nap had been much too short, and her body groaned with the accumulation of tiredness and the bruising. Her left shoulder felt especially stiff, the muscles aching, but the gunshot wound was really and truly healed. She poked at the area in wonder.

She caused that to happen. A smile broke across her face. She stripped off her bandage and put the flannel shirt on properly.

Then she turned to face Michael. The visual impact of him was a shock to the senses. He was a tough-looking, tall man, broad in the shoulders and chest with lean, toned muscle. His dark hair was too short to be tousled, but a new growth of beard dusted the hard planes and angles of his face and gave him a slightly disheveled appearance. He carried himself with a hard, bright soldier's confidence, and his presence filled the interior of the car.

She wondered if the sense of shock came because they were still so new to each other, almost strangers, or if she would always feel it when she looked at him. She suspected she would always feel it. She had seen the tiger that lived in his skin.

He had slipped on a pair of sunglasses and drove with one hand on the wheel, while he leaned his head against the other hand, his elbow propped against his door.

He looked haggard and remote, locked into some private world she couldn't reach. There was an ashen tinge underneath his tan. She didn't like the look of it.

"Okay," she said, her tone careful. "I'm better, and I'm ready to help."

"Good. I'll pull over as soon as I can." He spoke tersely, his face hard and expressionless.

She frowned. She had a nickname for his capacity to shut off all emotions: Mister Enigmatic. For a short while, she had thought they had banished that part of him, but it looked like Mister Enigmatic was back and doing well. She reached out to him, intending to lay her hand on his arm.

"Don't," he said, his tone abrupt. "Don't touch me right now."

This was not the lover who had been in her bed last night, who had whispered to her so tenderly as he moved inside of her.

She recoiled and sat in hurt silence until he signaled ten minutes later and pulled into a rest stop. He pulled the Ford into a parking space some distance from the other cars, killed the engine and dropped his head back against the seat. His body went lax, and he heaved a shuddering sigh.

Mary studied him. The difference between his earlier tension and this utter wretchedness worried her even more. Ignoring his earlier rebuff, she put a light hand on his shoulder and reached out with her senses.

Pain and exhaustion buffeted her through the tactile contact. She sucked in a breath.

"Well, shit," she said. He had stayed in a clench just to keep driving, while she was preoccupied with immature hurt feelings. She tugged at him, but he was so big and heavy, she couldn't budge him. "Come here."

He half-leaned, half-fell toward her. She removed his sunglasses, tucked his head onto her shoulder and held him tight. He put his face in her neck. "Get into the driver's seat," he muttered. "We need to keep driving north. Let me know when we reach Petoskey."

Anger flared, quick and hot. "I'm going to help you first. You need to be healed."

He slid into telepathy, the contact thin and minimal. *I don't have the energy to argue with you. We've got to keep moving.*

"Shut up," she said between her teeth. He reminded her of an abused animal that didn't expect or ask for help, because it had no concept of gentler things like compassion or tenderness. She felt the urge to slap somebody. Instead she stroked his short, black hair. "I know very well that we've got to keep moving. I will get us on the road *in a minute*."

Someone tapped on her window.

She startled and twisted. A middle-aged woman peered into the car, her expression concerned. A man stood waiting nearby, holding a dog on a leash. Mary rolled her window down partway and raised her eyebrows in inquiry.

"Excuse me." The woman spoke in a pleasant soft Virginian accent. "My husband and I were just walking our dog, and I couldn't help but notice—are you two all right?"

Michael had barely stirred at the intrusion. It was a measure of how depleted he had become. Mary could sense he had slipped into a half-conscious state. Her mind raced as she thought through their options.

"No," she said. "We're not. He's sick and I don't want to leave him. Would you mind doing us a favor?"

"Why sure, sugar," said the woman. "We have a cell phone. Do you need us to call 911?"

She shook her head, her thoughts strangled with uncertainty. Should she say she was a doctor? No, that seemed too distinctive, although the situation itself was already distinctive enough that they would already stick out in the woman's mind.

It was too late to fret about any of it now. She said, "Thank you, but I can drive him somewhere quicker than an ambulance could get here. I need you to do something else, please, if you would."

The woman didn't hesitate. "How can I help?"

Mary slid one hand along Michael's wide-muscled back to the pocket of his jeans, located the bulge of his wallet and pulled it out. A quick, discreet peek at the contents revealed several thousand dollars in large bills, and around fifty-five dollars in smaller denominations. She pulled out a twenty and a ten, and handed the money to the woman.

"I don't want to leave him. Would you mind going inside and buying all the Gatorade and bottled water you can? I hope there's a way to get change. When we pulled in, I didn't notice if this rest stop has a snack shop or just vending machines."

"Gatorade and bottled water." The woman's hand curled around the money but her voice had become uncertain.

It was clear the woman thought she was acting oddly. Mary didn't blame her. She glanced at Michael lying slack in her arms. Hell, the whole thing looked odd.

She tried to look as sincere as she could. "We thought his fever had broken and it would be okay to keep traveling until we got to our hotel. Now it has spiked again, and I think part of the problem is that he's gotten dehydrated. It may take me at least a half hour to find an urgent-care clinic. I want to get some liquids into him right away before I leave. If you don't mind."

"Of course I don't mind," said the woman, her uncertainty vanishing. "Do you have aspirin or Tylenol, or do you want me to see if I can buy any of those little travel packets?"

In spite of her worry, Mary smiled at the other woman's kindness. "I have a bottle of Tylenol in my purse."

"I'll be right back," the woman promised.

Mary watched her approach her husband, say something to him and hurry toward the nearby building. She shook her head. Her improvised explanation still seemed flimsy to her. She hoped the other woman didn't think too hard about it.

"This has got to be the road trip from hell," she muttered.

Feeling a surge of protectiveness, she cradled Michael's big, heavy body close. She rested her cheek on top of his head and sank her awareness into him. He was still bleeding sluggishly from a couple of the more serious wounds. He had a nasty bone-deep gouge in his thigh.

The Deceiver had attacked them on more than one front, not only with a troop of well-trained fighters but also with hundreds of dark spirits in the psychic realm. When Michael had taken physical wounds in the fight, the dark spirits had swarmed over him. They took advantage of the opportunity his injuries gave and drained him of energy.

The damage he had taken from the swarm seemed fairly shallow. Her main concern with those wounds was there were so many of them. To her mind's eye, they looked like dozens of claw marks. What disturbed her most were the almost imperceptible shadows that ran like fractures through his energy. Normally his spirit had an indomitable quality, a sense of boundless strength, but now there was something vulnerable, almost breakable about him.

Fresh from the lessons she had learned from healing her own body, she found it was the work of a few minutes to stop his bleeding, enhance his body's own natural pain inhibitors and pour a lavish amount of her own energy into him.

She was spending strength she could ill afford to spare from her own overtaxed resources, but they were stronger when they could work together as a team. She didn't know where they should go after they reached Petoskey, and Michael wouldn't be able to tell her if he was unconscious. Besides, he had scared her when he had leaned over and collapsed. She hadn't yet had a chance to recover from the last time he had scared her, when the Deceiver had taken him.

It was hard to leave healing him unfinished, but she did. She concentrated on cradling him close for a few more stolen moments. This might be all the reaction time she got after their recent brush with destruction, so she would have to make the most of it. She rubbed her face against his soft, short, dark hair until the woman approached with her arms full of Gatorade and bottled water.

"There was a snack shop, so I was able to buy plenty," the woman said.

"You are an angel," Mary told her. The woman handed cold bottles to her through the window. There were eight twenty-ounce bottles, three of them water. Pleased they had so much of the sports drink, Mary set the bottles on the passenger floor.

"Here's your change."

Mary shook her head even as she opened a bottle of Gatorade. Distracted, she said, "Please keep it."

"I can't keep your money, sugar." The woman held her hand insistently through the window.

Mary looked up, her attention caught by the woman's genuine distress. She glanced around their shabby, cluttered car, then back at the woman, noticing the woman's expensive clothes and carefully tended appearance. She gave the woman a crooked smile and held out her hand for the money. "Thank you for everything."

The woman lingered. "My husband thinks your best bet for finding an urgent-care clinic is to go back to Cadillac. You remember passing through? It's just fifteen minutes south on the highway."

"Yes," Mary lied. "I was thinking of Cadillac too."

The woman glanced at Michael. "Well, my name is Charlotte. My husband, Jim, and I will be over by the picnic tables for another half an hour if you need any more help."

"I'm grateful for what you did," Mary said. "There isn't

anything more we need. I'm just going to get some Gatorade down him before we leave. Thank you again."

"You're welcome. God bless."

Mary's eyes flooded with sudden dampness. She blinked them back as she watched Charlotte and her husband walk away. She had been so braced in survival mode, so busy dealing with one horror after another, that the simple kindness of a passing stranger almost broke her composure. Then she thought of Michael suffering without complaint, rejecting her overture until the car had stopped, and she wanted to yell or hit something.

"Okay, Michael," she said gently. His heavy unconsciousness had eased into sleep. Even though she hated to disturb him she gave his shoulder a brisk shake. "Wake up. I'm not going to start driving until you get some of this Gatorade down. If you want me to drive, you've got to wake up and drink this."

She felt his awareness surface before he stirred. "How long have we been stationary?" His voice was slurred.

"Only for about ten minutes." Helpless to resist, she gave in to impulse and pressed a kiss to the hairline at his temple.

He lay sideways against her. He passed his free arm around her waist and pulled her against him, the muscles of his bicep rigid as he held her tight. "You were supposed to keep going."

Irritation flared. "How was I supposed to do that with you passed out in the driver's seat? It's not like I can move you by myself. I know we need to keep on the move. You and Astra don't need to keep reminding me."

He let go of her and pushed himself upright. He scanned the scene. He still looked desperately weary, but his gaze was alert. "You talked to Astra?"

"I took a short nap after I healed myself," she told him, her tone truculent. She handed him the Gatorade and he drank it in thirsty gulps. Then she opened a bottle for herself. It was a black cherry flavor and tasted little better than the sugared water she had forced down at the cabin. She drank it anyway. "She came into a dream I was having. We talked."

The strong muscles in his neck moved as he tilted back his head and finished the bottle. "What did she say?"

She hesitated as she thought of the frail, elderly body Astra had shown her. Whenever Michael talked of Astra, he seemed to think that uniting with her would be an asset, but Mary wasn't so sure.

Still, she was unwilling to disappoint him as much as she had been disappointed, so she spoke with caution. "Only that we needed to get to her as soon as we could."

He glanced at her. "Why would she bother sending you a dream just to tell you the obvious?"

"I—don't know." She blinked, startled, for she hadn't thought to question that. "She dropped out so quickly from the battle. Maybe she was worried and wanted to check on us."

"Maybe." His voice was noncommittal. Mister Enigmatic was back. "Are you ready to drive now?"

She remembered that she was supposed to be annoyed. Her truculence returned. "Yes."

"Good."

He waited until she got out, then as she moved around the front of the car to the driver's side, he eased over the bench seat to the passenger side. She slid behind the wheel, adjusted the seat and mirrors for her shorter height, started the engine and pulled out. As she drove past the picnic tables she waved at Charlotte and her husband, who waved back. Michael's eyebrows rose at the exchange but she didn't volunteer an explanation and he didn't ask.

Mary had set his sunglasses on the dashboard earlier. She reached for them and slipped them on. They were too big for her and slid to the end of her nose, but they were better than nothing. The car leaped forward as she accelerated onto Highway 131. Taken aback at the engine's smooth surge of power, she eased off the gas pedal.

Michael opened another bottle of Gatorade and drank it

at a slower pace. After a minute, he said, "You stopped the bleeding and blocked the pain."

"I stopped *your* bleeding and I blocked *your* pain." Her tone was short. If he could be Mister Enigmatic, well then, she could be Miss Petulant.

He said slowly, "You're angry about something."

All she could hear in his voice was weariness and puzzlement. Her anger drained away and she felt ashamed of herself again.

She strove for a calmer, more conciliatory tone. "Sometimes you talk about things as though they are distant from you. I guess maybe you've had to do that. After the last couple of days, I think I can even understand it, but it still disturbs me. It was not a mistake for us to stop at the cabin for a rest."

"Maybe you're right." He didn't sound convinced.

She gave him a stern glance over the rim of the sunglasses. "We did the best we could with the information we had. It wasn't a mistake for me to help you just now either. You were suffering, and I couldn't stand the thought of doing nothing when I have the capacity to help. More than that, I need you to get better as fast as you can. I know I'm outmatched right now. If something else were to happen while you are incapacitated, I couldn't handle it by myself. I haven't recovered enough of my memories yet. I'm feeling stretched thin as it is."

He mulled over that while he drank his Gatorade and shifted the pillow to a more comfortable spot. When next he spoke, he seemed to be making a non sequitur. "I didn't care about anyone when I was a kid. Not my parents, not my so-called friends. Nothing seemed quite real."

She frowned. "How did you and Astra meet?"

"She found me when I was eight. Even at that early age, I had already started to do crazier things in an effort to feel something other than anger." He stretched his injured leg and winced. "Astra was the most amazing thing that had ever happened to me. She was real like nothing else had been. Of course now I understand why, and what that meant."

She drove with care as she listened. Her heart ached as he spoke with such matter-of-fact calm. "Do you have any idea how many lives you've lived since—over the last nine hundred years?"

Since you killed me, and I stopped reincarnating. Those had been the first words that came to mind, but she couldn't bear to say them. She might never be able to say them out loud. The memories were too raw. They lay between them like a shadow.

"A few. I connected with two others from our group, Ariel and Uriel, just before they were destroyed. Astra and I found each other in other lifetimes." He looked out his window. "I haven't bothered to try to recover much of those memories. They seemed pretty meaningless."

She gripped the steering wheel. She tried to imagine how he had lived, how he must have recovered his sense of identity time and again, only to realize after searching that she wasn't anywhere to be found, neither alive nor destroyed but lost somewhere in limbo. That all he could do was fight and wait—and wait—and wait. In all that time, the only person who had been anything like a kindred spirit, the only person he could rely on, had been Astra.

She took a deep breath. "Astra doesn't trust me."

"Probably not." He finished the second bottle of Gatorade.

"I don't blame her." She glanced at him sideways. "As damaged as I was—and by the Deceiver, no less—I wouldn't trust me either if I were her."

"Don't take it personally. Astra doesn't trust anybody, not even me," Michael said. He punched the pillow and eased his head onto it. "Maybe especially not me."

"Why especially not you?" Her anger was quick to flare again on his behalf.

One corner of his mouth quirked up. "She had her

reasons. Remember, she met and trained me when I was a young and budding criminal."

She asked, "Do you trust her?"

"I trust her to do anything and everything she can to destroy the Deceiver. So yes, in a way I do. For certain things."

She nodded although his eyes were closed. After a few minutes, she said in a soft voice, "I'm sorry I got mad."

She thought he might have fallen asleep until he replied, "You weren't really mad. You've just been scared and upset. You've had—"

"—a rough day," she finished with him. Although it wasn't really funny, they both chuckled and tension eased from the car. "Yeah, I guess I have."

He laid his arm along the back of the seat and settled his hand, large and warm and heavy, at the nape of her neck. She startled at his touch and forced herself to relax. A complex set of emotions surged in reaction. Primary among them was a deep sense of comfort.

"I was there. I know what the dragon did for you," he said. "You were injured, your spirit somehow bent, and now that's gone. I trust you."

She blinked. "I didn't know I needed to hear that, but I did. Thank you. I trust you too. Michael?"

"Yeah."

His voice was sleepy. She hated to say what she was going to say next, but it had been bothering her ever since she woke up.

"I think the Deceiver has to have ties to the police," she said. "Don't you? I can't think of any other way those two drones could have tracked me to South Bend to try to kidnap me. Nobody knew where I was going when I left my house. Hell, even I didn't know—most of what I did was on impulse. Maybe he could have found me through his abilities alone, but I don't think they could have. Could they?" She hesitated, then finished, "You see, I've been worrying about this car. He had to have gotten a good look at it, along with its license plate."

A pause. He released a heavy, exasperated sigh. "Where the fuck is my brain?"

She lifted a shoulder and gave him a wry look. "It's with the rest of your body, which is seriously injured and exhausted."

The glance he gave her said quite clearly that he didn't consider that an excuse. "I know for a fact he's got ties to the police, and to the FBI, and other organizations. And of course he would have noticed the make and model of this car, along with the license plates. I'll try to counteract that."

"By doing what?"

"I can project a kind of null space around us so that people will tend not to notice us."

She blinked. "A null space?"

"It's a kind of energy—a spell if you like—that encourages the mind to look elsewhere. But it doesn't really turn us invisible, so to be on the safe side, we still need to ditch this car and get a new one. Do you know how to get to Petoskey?"

She nodded. "I've been there before. The route I took was Highway 131 until it reaches 31, which follows the shoreline of Lake Michigan. Is that okay?"

He grunted. "That'll do. Wake me before we get there. We'll need to change vehicles before we go through town."

"Okay." She blew out a breath. "Can you at least try to rest while you do that null space thingy?"

He nodded and settled back into his seat. She listened as his breathing deepened, but his hand never moved from her neck and she could tell that he wasn't quite asleep.

Then she sensed something coming from him, a strange kind of subtle energy. She meant to focus on it, but then her thoughts slid away to something else and she forgot.

They continued to travel north in heavy traffic. People were getting a head start on Memorial Day weekend. She hoped it would make them even harder to spot.

The orderly procession along the highway produced an

illusion of normality, and the late afternoon sunshine made her sleepy. She sipped her black cherry Gatorade and chewed her lip as she thought through what she and Michael had discussed.

The Deceiver could have been in touch with his various police contacts by cell within minutes of leaving the cabin. It was logical to assume he had, so she had to believe they were now fugitives from the police. Did he have enough political clout to get the authorities to put an APB out on them?

He aspired to take the Presidency, so if she were a betting fool, she would bet yes, he did have that kind of clout. Their continued freedom might hinge on whether or not a police cruiser sighted their vehicle, which was why Michael couldn't let himself fully relax.

She gritted her teeth and put it out of her mind. There was nothing she could do about it. She had to concentrate on handling the challenges right in front of her. She just hoped that the null space that Michael was projecting . . . that strange energy coming from his lax body . . .

Her mind slid away again. What was she thinking? She just hoped the heavy traffic helped to camouflage them somewhat from their pursuers.

How had the Deceiver found Michael's cabin? What had given them away? Would they ever find out? If they didn't know how they had been discovered, how could they prevent it from happening again? How could they ever stop moving, even when they reached Astra?

Despair threatened to engulf her. They were already tired and wounded, and now they were fighting to meet up with an old woman who looked like she was at death's door. What if all three of them became fugitives?

She realized this was the first time she'd had to think in private since she had escaped from her would-be kidnappers a few days ago in northern Indiana. First she had been too shocked to absorb the enormity of what was happening.

Then Michael had found her, and events had hurtled forward at a breakneck pace.

A few days ago, she had been a different person, a person who questioned herself but did not think to question the reality she lived in. That Mary Byrne had suffered from disturbing dreams and the stress of knowing that in some fugitive, mysterious way she did not fit into her life.

That Mary had argued with her ex-husband and worried about losing her own sanity. She had bought a chocolate shake and had left town for an afternoon's outing. When her concept of reality had undertaken a radical, irreversible shift, so too had her sense of self, and that Mary Byrne had died.

As she had described once to Michael, she felt like she had lived in some kind of painting all her life. The painting had so much color and detail, it seemed as if it should have made sense, should have been real. But then somebody either smashed the frame or she had fallen out, and she couldn't go back to live there any longer. The painting was two-dimensional, and she didn't fit, but she barely understood this new reality either, or how to survive in it.

Or maybe she, like the painting, had been a two-dimensional creation, more illusion and memory and the reflection of other people's expectations than reality. Some aspects of her core nature lingered. She had an innate gentleness, her moral code, her artistic appreciation and healing abilities, but all her illusions had burned away. Michael had described her as being "bent." She thought of herself as crippled, not quite twisted into an aberrant existence, quietly subsisting as a shadow of her true self.

She thought of the shabby little house she had rented, her ivory tower, now burned to the ground by the Deceiver. All of the minutiae that had comprised her earlier human life, the mementoes and photographs from her family, her quilts and paintings and clothes, had been destroyed.

It would be a lie to say she didn't feel a twinge of loss, because she did, but she realized that the loss of her home would have hit her former self, the shadow Mary, much harder. She had lost a home but had regained her health and sense of identity, along with a strange heritage that might be terrible, but it was also powerful and real, and it was hers.

They could never go home again. (And she realized, even as she thought it, after all this time she still called the other alien place "home.") So gradually through the millennia they became more humanlike.

The times they forgot who they once were, they dreamed of human things, desires and ambitions, of satisfying work, a loving marriage, raising children and living peaceful lives. But even while they dreamed, they were troubled because they knew somewhere in their hearts that those dreams weren't real. Then they woke again and realized who they were. But they still remembered they had dreamed.

Then she thought, No.

In that line of thinking, she was inventing a community that did not exist. Perhaps it had at one point in the distant past. But of the original seven who had pursued the Deceiver to Earth, four of them were gone forever. Astra never forgot who she was, and the Deceiver stole human lives in order to remember his past.

And Michael had just admitted that nothing had seemed real before he met Astra. His sense of unreality had to stem in part from her long disappearance, but she couldn't have been the only reason. He must feel that way in part because he didn't feel human.

So she was talking only about herself.

She was the one who dreamed those human dreams. She kept going back in memory to her life nine hundred years ago, because she remembered living for too brief a time in a way that allowed her to celebrate and explore the two aspects of her identity, both the alien and the human, with people who loved and accepted her. Their lives had been gracious gifts imbued with hearth and magic and mystery. They had understood that about themselves, about each other and their world.

She realized how much she missed those people. They had been her family, and they had died so long ago she didn't even know where their graves were.

An ache settled deep under her ribs. She rubbed her face. Then she set the thought of them aside as gently as if she had been handling an old, fragile photo album and concentrated on moving toward her future.

Chapter Five

THE HIGHWAY UNFURLED in a long, winding ribbon that lay across a rolling wooded landscape, like an endless snake that encircled the world. The wooded landscape was interspersed with patches of sunlit farmland filled with fruit orchards and fields of golden grain dotted with giant bales of hay.

It wasn't long before Mary held on to the steering wheel and her concentration as she fought a combination of hunger and exhaustion. Every dip and curve in the road felt exaggerated. Dizziness was never far away. She kept her silence and kept driving.

Every mile she drove gave Michael a chance for more rest. She wanted to give him all the recovery time she could. She had no illusions about herself. She had gotten very lucky in her morning confrontation with the Deceiver. Michael was far more valuable in a fight.

Finally she came upon a stretch of landscape she recognized. The highway was dotted with intermittent clusters of neighborhoods, restaurants, various strip malls and antique stores. She guessed they were a half hour away from downtown Petoskey. She placed a reluctant hand on Michael's knee.

He straightened instantly. His large, warm hand, having never left the back of her neck, pressed against her skin. She sensed him scanning her, body and spirit, in a skillful, comprehensive sweep even as his light, sharp gaze took in the passing scenery.

"You know, you could just ask me how I'm doing," she said. She was glad she could talk to him again, glad to be doing anything different from driving in silence and getting sleepier.

He gave her a skeptical look. "How are you doing?"

She said strongly, "I'm fine."

His eyes narrowed. "Sure you are. You're also exhausted and faint from hunger. I think my scan gave me more accurate details, don't you?"

She scowled. "Like you couldn't deduce any of that anyway."

She felt his fingers curl around her short, thick braid. He gave it a gentle tug, then turned his attention to the road. "I like to see things for myself. I also want you to turn off the highway as soon as you can."

"All right." She eased off the gas pedal and started watching for intersections. "What road do you want me to take?"

"The next one." He pointed. "Turn right, into that neighborhood."

As she complied, she noted the painted wood sign at the corner of the road that read Lakeshore Estates. The road they turned onto was named Seahorse Drive.

It was cute. She wasn't in the mood for cute.

"Drive slow," he told her.

"Okay." She slowed the car to a crawl.

They passed by large homes with well-kept yards. Late afternoon was turning into early evening. Children played and rode their bikes, sprinkler systems flung water in wide sparkling arcs and people mowed their lawns. She rolled down her window. The smell of fresh-cut grass filled the car. Someone was barbecuing. The smell of roasting meat wafted into the car. Her empty stomach rumbled in miserable response.

She started talking to take her mind off her fatigue and hunger. "What are we doing here? If we had been getting close to Astra, you would have said something, wouldn't you? What am I saying, you don't speak unless you absolutely have to. Astra doesn't live in the suburbs, does she? Or maybe a middle-class lifestyle would be the perfect place for her to camouflage herself and hang out, but for some reason I expected something different. You know, this car doesn't look like much, but it handles like a dream. I thought you said we needed to change vehicles."

"Okay, chatterbox," he said, sounding amused. "You see where this road curves left and you can exit out of the development? Humor me, and follow that."

She turned and came to a stop sign at a three-way intersection. As she paused, both she and Michael looked in either direction.

They had come to a two-lane county road, appropriately named Orchard Road, as it bordered a large orchard filled with cherry trees. Turning left on Orchard Road would take them back to Highway 131. While she was mystified at Michael's directions, she wasn't surprised when he told her to turn left and continue slowly.

She glanced at the orchard, now on her right, while Michael stared at the houses lining the left-hand side of the road. "I like this better than inside the development," she said. "It's more quiet and secluded. It would be nice to look out your front window and see the orchard all year-round. I bet the scene is pretty in the wintertime. Why won't you answer any of my questions?"

"I'm busy," he said. "I can talk in a minute. Pull into the driveway here, two driveways up ahead."

Mister Enigmatic was busy? Doing what? She frowned at him.

She pulled into the driveway of a pleasant-looking, two-story house with a wide yard shaded by several mature maple trees. Relieved that they had left the busy highway and she could stop driving for a few minutes, she put the car in park and let the engine idle.

While Michael stared with a fixed gaze at the garage door in front of them, she let her head fall back on the rest and relaxed. Tiredness rose to blanket her in gray fuzz.

"Okay," he said. "The people who live here aren't home. They don't have dogs and there's an SUV in the garage. We're going to take fifteen minutes, use the bathroom and clean up, see if they have food and I'll hot-wire their SUV."

She swiveled to stare at him. He could scan buildings for people and pets—and vehicles? She looked at the garage door and saw the shadow of a large vehicle through a narrow shoulder-high row of windows. Well, okay, that part seemed obvious. Apparently he just scanned for people and pets.

"We can't steal from these people," she said.

He gave her a blank look. "Why not?"

Why not? She bit her lip, then spoke as though to a four-year-old. Or to an alien. "Because it's wrong."

"We have to." He still looked blank. He looked as if he might be the one talking to the four-year-old, and he wasn't sure how to do it. "I agree with what you said earlier. We have to assume that the police are hunting for us, and that they've got a description of this car and the license plates. We have to switch vehicles, but we can't rent one. Car rentals will be one of the first places they check. We need sustenance, yet we have to avoid public places. Our choices are limited."

"But. . . ." Her forehead wrinkled. She wanted to find fault in his logic, but she couldn't.

His grim expression gentled. "They're going to have a bad day. They'll feel violated. They'll have to deal with police statements and insurance companies, and if they haven't got one already, they'll probably decide to install an alarm system. They might miss a day or two of work, and they're going to tell their friends all about it, and suck up all the sympathy they can get. They might even start a Neighborhood Watch group. And we still have to do it."

"All right." She blew out a breath and rubbed the back of her neck. "I don't have to like it. And it's still wrong."

"Compared to what we're facing, it's not that big of a deal. They'll think it is, of course, but we know better. Besides, if everything goes well we won't have to borrow their car for long. We can leave it somewhere public for the police to find." His tone turned brisk. "We can't sit here all day. We're going to walk to the front door as though we have every right to be here. Ready?"

No. She scowled. "Yes."

She climbed out when he did, watching as he limped around the front of the car. He looked down at her set expression, sighed and gestured for her to walk ahead of him to the door. "If any of the neighbors come over, let me do the talking, okay?"

She nodded. She didn't trust herself to speak to anybody, not even to him. She understood everything he had said. She even agreed, which was why she was walking to the house with him.

Compared with the horrors she had faced over the last forty-eight hours, stealing someone's car and breaking into their house wasn't that big of a disaster. Michael was right. The people would have a bad time and they would get over it.

Her problem was that the pragmatic part of her head and the emotional part weren't speaking to each other.

She had gone from being Miss Petulant to Miss Criminal.

She growled under her breath as she hovered at Michael's side. He pulled a couple of thin tools from his wallet and picked the lock on the front door. Then he pushed the door open and stood back to let her walk in.

She looked down at the threshold. Lift up your foot,

dammit, she told herself. Step inside. She whispered, "You're sure nobody's home?"

"Positive." He put a hand to the small of her back and propelled her into the house. Then he shut the door behind him and locked it. He went to the front window and drew the curtains shut. "You take the bathroom first. Take a shower if you feel you need to, but be quick. You've got five minutes. I'll check out the kitchen."

She stood frozen inside the doorway. Her gaze swept around the living room. The house was clean, and the furniture looked comfortable and sturdy. She smelled a floral scent and also a hint of lemon, perhaps furniture polish. Her gaze snagged on a large photo collection on one wall.

Several antique photographs graced one section. The rest were more modern. She saw a smiling couple somewhere in their midfifties on a cruise ship, three wedding photos of younger couples, family portraits, candid snapshots of children and a formal photograph of a woman in uniform.

Those pictures told the story of their lives.

This house was the older couple's home. Their children grew up here. Their grandchildren loved to visit Nana's house. The family celebrated holidays here. Judging by the beams on everyone's faces, they were clearly overjoyed when the woman in the uniform came home for Christmas.

Mary's chest felt tight and hot. What was this? She pressed a hand to her breastbone. It took a couple heartbeats for her to realize she felt a crazy kind of love for this unknown family, a frustrated sense of protectiveness and deep regret.

They were so normal, she thought. And we don't belong here.

We never did.

"Mary." The intensity in Michael's voice broke through her reverie. She shook herself and looked at him. He was a troubling incongruity in the placid peacefulness of the living room, a tough, strongly built man with red-flecked bandages on his muscled chest and arms, his hard-angled face grim with shadows. "It will be far worse on these people if they come home before we get out of here. Hurry."

Her imagination galloped off with that idea and the results weren't pretty. She gave him an agonized nod and raced up the stairs.

She found four bedrooms and a hall bathroom. The master bedroom probably had an en suite bathroom, but she kept to the hall bath. She felt like enough of an intruder already.

She used the toilet and gave the bathtub and showerhead a longing glance. So much had happened since her bath at the cabin. She felt filthy. Her jeans had stains from dirt, grass and flecks of blood. But no matter how much she wanted to bathe, she couldn't make herself strip in this strange family's home.

There was no point in indulging in too much of a freak-out, or in overanalyzing things. She found a washcloth and scrubbed at her face, neck, arms and torso with cool water and a bar of scented soap. The wash was not as satisfying as a shower, but it was refreshing and helped her to wake up.

She rushed downstairs again.

Michael stood at the open refrigerator door. He was packing food into plastic grocery bags. He gave her a keen glance. "Couldn't stand to shower, huh?"

"Nope. I had a quick wash at the sink." She gestured at the fridge. "You'd better go. I can take over that."

"I'm done anyway," he told her. He handed her the two plastic bags. "This is quite enough to meet our needs. Take it to the garage and keep watch out the window. I'll be just a minute."

"Okay," she agreed, relieved to leave the house.

He disappeared. She located the door to the garage. The interior was shadowed, cluttered and smelled like engine oil and gasoline. The SUV was a late-model forest green Jeep. She stationed herself at the narrow windows and chewed her lip as she watched the street. A few minutes later, Michael stepped out of the house. He joined her at the window. His hair was wet and he smelled like the soap she had used.

She said, "I hate this."

"I know." He gripped her shoulder. "If it helps any, I left money on their kitchen counter to pay for the food."

It wouldn't take away the family's shock at their home being invaded, or lessen the sting from the theft of the Jeep, but it was something. It was very much something, especially since she was pretty sure that Michael didn't have a problem with anything they had done, and yet he had still thought to leave them money without her prompting him.

She leaned into his touch. "Thank you. Let's get out of here."

"I'll hot-wire the Jeep. Get in the car and drive back to the intersection where we turned out of the development. Wait for me there. I'll take the lead and you follow me until I stop, okay?"

"I guess," she said. "I can't believe we're going to get away with this. For God's sake, it's broad daylight."

"It's not that hard." His voice was calm and reassuring. He located the garage door switch and the door opened.

She sent him an accusing glance. "You've done this before, haven't you?"

His expression remained bland. "When I've had to. The critical times are isolated moments when a witness might realize something is wrong. One of those was when I picked the lock. But I'm good at it, and fast, and I stood so my body hid what I was doing. To anyone who might have glanced our way, it should have looked like I used a key. The other critical time will be when we drive away. Even then, the chances are that someone will see the Jeep passing but not the person driving it. Everything else looks normal."

As normal as the people who live here? She felt again that wild, unnamed surge of emotion. "Even your Ford sitting in the driveway?"

"It just looks like someone's visiting." He smiled at her. "Go on."

She hurried to the car, climbed in and put the two grocery bags on the passenger seat. Then she drove to the intersection and pulled as far as she could onto the shoulder of the road to wait for him.

Long moments trickled past. She clutched the steering wheel so tightly, the muscles in her arms, shoulders, back and neck were rigid with tension.

If she were a superheroine, she could do all this in tight leather pants and a bustier. She would have a coiled whip at one hip and a gun at the other, and a bored, sort of droopy-sexy pout on her lips. She would yawn as she kicked ass, sneer as she took any man she wanted, and she would boot him out of bed when she was done.

A superheroine, she was not. She was pretty sure she didn't achieve slightly cool. Maybe she managed somewhat capable. Sometimes. She sighed and pinched her nose with thumb and forefinger.

The green Jeep pulled alongside her at the stop.

Michael paused long enough to catch her eye and nod. Then he accelerated and she pulled into place behind him.

They drove for perhaps fifteen minutes. She had stopped trying to guess his intentions some time ago. The labyrinthine route he drove had her lost within a couple of turns. She worked at keeping the Jeep in sight, the rest of her mind a blank, so that she actually felt surprise when he signaled, turned down a gravel road and pulled to a stop.

Tangled overgrown forest crowded either side of the gravel road. They could almost have been where they had abandoned her Toyota. Wow, a lot of water had flowed under that bridge. She stopped behind him, put the Ford in park and rested her forehead against the steering wheel.

Tension spilled out of her body. Exhaustion roared back in. She felt limp as a rag doll. Michael opened her door and put a hand on her arm. "Come on, Mary. Climb out."

She tried. Her legs didn't cooperate very well. "We're fugitives in the age of information. Should we have worn gloves or something back at the house?"

He reached in the car, put his hands under her arms and hauled her bodily out of the car. She tried to get her rubbery legs to stiffen and support her weight. He pulled her into his arms and held her tight.

"We only used the bathroom and the kitchen. And I doubt the police will dust for fingerprints for a car theft and home invasion, but I still wiped everything down before I came out."

"The front doorknob," she said.

"I wiped that too, and the door to the garage, and the garage door switch." He ran his hands up and down her arms. "I've taken care of everything. Stop worrying."

She squinted up at him. "You've done this when you've had to, huh? How often was that?"

He grinned. "Often enough."

"Ooh-kay. Okay." She leaned against him. Words poured out of her. "Sometimes everything just hits me, you know? My house burned down a few days ago, and I called a dragon yesterday morning—*who answered me*—and I really think I would be okay if I could just take *a little time* and deal with it all."

"It has all hit you fast." He rested his cheek at the top of her head.

She slipped her arms around his waist and held on tight. "Only we can't take any time, can we? I want and need to help you and Astra in whatever way I can, but I'm really scared of what's coming next, and isn't it funny after all this? I'm scared to die. Or worse. There's much, much worse than dying."

"Yes," he said, very low. "There is."

She sucked air. "And if by some miracle we don't die, my job is gone, my life is gone and I don't know how to survive as a fugitive from the law. I feel—I feel like I've turned down this dead-end alley, and something terrible is blocking the mouth of it. It's coming for me, and there's nowhere to turn." She balled her hands into fists and said through her teeth, "And you don't have to say anything. I already know I'm babbling."

He steered her around the door to the hood of the Ford. "Sit here."

She climbed onto the hood and watched as he retrieved the bags of food. "I'm sorry."

"I know you're sorry. Shut up." He set the bags beside her. "Eat."

She wrapped her arms around herself. "What about you?"

"I will in a minute. I have things I need to do." He looked at her hard. "I mean it. Eat. Force yourself if you don't feel like it."

She nodded. The simple orders he gave her provided structure and purpose while she struggled with feeling overwhelmed. She recognized the technique. She had used it herself with trauma patients.

He opened the trunk of the Ford and the back of the Jeep, and he moved back and forth between the vehicles, transferring the contents from the car to the SUV. She couldn't identify what was in some of the bags but she thought she saw a tent go by, along with other camping supplies, and also a toolbox.

She asked, "I thought we were hoping we could ditch the Jeep soon."

He glanced at her. "I'm keeping our options open. You never know what may come at us."

She said, "You know, I'm not usually such a beta."

The sun fell into his eyes as he glanced at her, illuminating the pewter color to a pure keen light. "What do you mean?"

"Usually, I'm an alpha. Just wait until we get trapped sometime in a hospital." She pointed at him and winked. "I will rule. Then you'll see."

Laughter creased his face. "I can't wait."

She rummaged through the contents of the grocery bags. There were apples, grapes, a couple of containers of low-fat yogurt, chocolate and peanut butter–flavored breakfast bars, a package of sliced turkey, three Tupperware containers, a partial loaf of bread, cheese, a couple packages of tuna, a box of crackers and two cans of Coke.

He even remembered to pack two forks, which she discovered at the bottom of one bag. She inspected the Tupperware containers and found homemade potato salad, a garden salad and sliced ham—real sliced ham, not packaged and processed meat. The garden salad had fresh spinach, leafy romaine lettuce, radishes, carrots and green onions and was tossed with a creamy Italian dressing.

The sights and smells slammed into her. The food was wholesome, and her whole body wanted it. She wolfed down potato salad and bites of ham, chewing while she popped open one of the chilled cans of Coke. While she ate, she watched Michael.

She started on the garden salad as he emptied out the backseat of the Ford. The long, black weapons bag went into the rear seat of the Jeep. When he had shifted everything to his satisfaction, he opened up the toolbox, pulled out a license plate and a wrench, and he changed the license plate on the Jeep. Fascinated, she tried to see what else was in the toolbox. All she could see from where she was sitting were more license plates.

"How many license plates do you have?" she asked, her mouth full.

"I like to keep a dozen or so on hand." He tossed the wrench into the box, closed it and tucked the Jeep's legitimate license plate under the camping gear. "They provide more options."

Questions crowded her mind. Where had he gotten them? How many were stolen? All of them? He slammed the Jeep's rear door. Then the questions flew out of her head as he joined her. She noticed how pronounced his limp had become. She handed him containers of food and a fork. Then she opened a Coke for him while he bent his head and ate with quick economy.

She gave him the drink, opened a container of yogurt

and passed it to him when he was ready. She told him, "I packed the less perishable food into one bag to take with us."

"Good," he grunted.

He made an amazing amount of food disappear. At that moment he could have been any tired, hardworking man after a long day. Then he paused to strip off his flannel shirt in the heat of the early evening. She saw the bandages and bruises on his wide, taut torso, and the illusion vaporized.

She finished most of her own yogurt before she became too full to eat anymore. Taking a deep, replete breath, she sipped at her Coke as she looked around the scene.

The dense gathering of trees and underbrush shimmered with the Van Gogh effect that had started yesterday. She frowned. When had she last noticed it? She couldn't remember. She had become too depleted to notice, and then she became preoccupied with other things.

"Michael," she said. He looked up from finishing the ham. "Ever since I—what did you call it—ripped through the veil in the Grotto, something funny has happened to my eyesight. Everything has this transparent shimmer around the edges. Or it has whenever I've had the time to notice. I've been calling it the Van Gogh effect."

"The Van Gogh effect." He slanted an eyebrow at her.

"You know, because everything has rippling, wavy edges. It reminds me of his paintings. Do you know what it is?"

He studied the surrounding scene, then gave her a quizzical glance. "You've been coping with everything so well, I forget how new your memories are and how much you've yet to recover. What you're seeing is energy."

"Energy," she repeated. She cocked her head and squinted doubtfully at a tree.

"Everything has energy and movement," he replied. "Everything has a vibration, even things that most people think of as being stationary and immobile. Take a rock." He bent and picked up a piece of gravel. "Even this has vibration and movement. Think of the basic elements contained in an atom."

She squinted at him. "Do you mean electrons, neutrons, protons and a nucleus?"

"Yes. Do you know how the electrons and the protons rotate around the nucleus?"

"Sure."

He pressed the piece of gravel into her hand. "Movement is present in everything in the universe. It's our human senses that tell us that the rock is inert and stationary. The reality is quite different. The rock is in motion, just as the entire universe is in motion. The vibration of the rock's energy is simply at a much slower frequency than other things."

"Vibration," she echoed. She hefted the rock in her hand as she thought back to the moment when the Deceiver had taken Michael. She looked up at him. "Back at the cabin, when the Deceiver had you pinned to the ground, he made some kind of humming noise. It was a horrible sound. I wanted to stab things in my ears to keep from hearing it, but it wasn't actually a physical noise, was it? It was psychic, right?"

The angle of his mouth turned grim. "It was both psychic and physical. He was using vibration as a weapon. A vibration at a certain pitch and frequency can destroy us if it comes from both the physical and psychic realms at once, and if it is strong enough. Buddhist monks make use of physical vibration in their chants. Legend has it that with the right frequency they can cause a mountain to avalanche. When I'm fighting creatures in the psychic realm, I use the vibration of my energy to shape a weapon. A physical sword is useless in that kind of fight. It passes right through them."

She thought back to the tall, blazing figure that she had seen with her mind's eye. He had wielded what had looked like a spear of white light. "So you really were fighting psychically the same time that you were fighting physically?"

"Yes."

She looked down at the piece of gravel she held. In her last life, she'd had a teacher who had taught her about Eastern dragons and astral projection.

As you know, there are four realms, her teacher had said. *The inner realm, the physical realm, the psychic realm and the celestial or heavenly realm. Each realm is distinct, yet they are intricate in their entwinement.*

Michael, Astra and the Deceiver were all adept in more than one realm. Michael had entered her mind when she had been locked in the past. Both Astra and the Deceiver had the ability to enter her dreams. She realized all over again how much she had to recover of her true self and her abilities.

She muttered, "That's a whole lot more complicated than being ambidextrous."

The grim line to his mouth eased. "When we have time, I'll lend you my copy of *Zen Keys* so you can read more about it. To go back to your question, you're seeing what you call the Van Gogh effect because you're getting more attuned to the energies around you."

She stared at the rock. "That's also how I saw the golden stream you poured into me when you found me by my car. You were giving me energy."

"Of course." He smiled at the expression on her face. "You know all of this already. You just haven't remembered it yet. Like you said, you need more time to process and connect all your dots."

"I'm starting to realize how much work I have to do to catch up," she said. She was struck by another thought. "In the recurring dream I've had, when all of us who were in the original group drank the poison, I could see colors all around us but they were really emotions. When I woke up, I wondered if we'd had the ability to see pheromones."

"Maybe we did, or maybe we had an ability very like that. Are you feeling better?" She nodded. "We've had to push too hard. I knew eating good food would help. I have just two things to say."

She looked up when he paused. She wasn't the only one helped by the good food. He too looked better for having eaten, stronger and more vital. The marks of tension on his face had eased. "Yes?"

"First," he said into her upturned face. "You are a talking, walking miracle. Don't ever apologize to me again. I know how hard you're working on all levels and I'm doing my best to help. Okay?"

"Okay."

"Second thing," he said. He drew a light finger down her cheek. "You're not in a dead-end alley. That was your fatigue and fear speaking. You may not know how to survive as a fugitive in the age of information, but I do. You have to keep reminding yourself I've been training for this my whole life. It's what I do."

She nodded and gave him a small smile. "Okay."

He stroked her lower lip, his callused fingers gentle. "It is also a big mistake to discount Astra's abilities. I know from your perspective it must seem like things have gotten really outlandish, but have faith."

"I'll try." This was the first real chance they'd had to talk since the battle. She felt the tension ease from her neck and shoulders.

He checked his watch, and his mouth tightened. "First we had to stop at the house and now here. Well, it can't be helped. We needed to eat and change vehicles and we couldn't have done it any faster. Ready?"

"Not quite. Give me a few more minutes."

She put a hand on his leg, closed her eyes and sank her awareness into his body. Refreshed and bolstered by the food, she found it much easier than she had the first few times.

She journeyed through the vital pathways of his circulatory system with an almost lazy pleasure, exploring the strong, elegant lattice of his spinal column, checking the healing process on his various wounds and nudging them closer to completion.

She spent the longest time on the wound in his thigh.

Whatever had caused the puncture had narrowly missed his femoral artery, which was just another example of their incredible luck in that confrontation.

His wounds were physical and spiritual. That meant healing needed to be both physical and spiritual. If he could fight in both realms at once, maybe she could heal in both realms at once as well.

She had already physically healed herself, and she had given him energy. Now she just had to combine them.

Be healed, she told his wounded flesh.

Energy in the form of argent radiance poured from her hand. His thigh grew hot to the touch. She lingered over the blissful sensation and then, because he had suffered and because she could, she spilled that bright cascade over his psychic wounds, the long clawlike marks along with a faint, shadowy web of fracture lines that lingered from the Deceiver's abuse.

His spirit and body resonated in instant, magnificent response, not with the strained keening she remembered from earlier, but with a healthy harmonious vibrancy.

Then the radiance she poured into him doubled back on her in a tremendous gush. She too began to resonate in a deep, melodious thrumming that was as old as their existence.

She had intended to be as sensible and sparing with him as she had been with healing herself. She had meant to focus her energy on his worst injuries and let the rest heal as they would, but she quickly lost control of the connection.

Helpless to stop, surprised by joy, her energy poured into him, and his came back into her, doubling and redoubling. As he healed, so did she, completely. All of the aches, pains and bruises she had collected over the last couple of days smoothed over, until together they reverberated throughout the realms with a pure belling power like Roland's horn and a sweetness like children singing.

Gradually, she became aware of their bodies. They had come together, wrapping around each other. Michael bowed over her, his head resting on top of hers. She had one hand splayed at the back of his neck, the other arm locked tight around his waist.

He lifted his head, and her eyes slit open. He glowed with such a fierce, arcane light she could hardly look at him with her human eyes. He laid his cheek against hers. Either his face was wet or hers was, or perhaps both.

"Holy cow, Batman," she whispered. She touched his face, ran her fingers over the planes and angles, reading him like Braille. "Talk about having so much to relearn. I had forgotten this. I had forgotten that I'd forgotten. How could I do that? How stupid, how wrong of me."

"You were bent." His voice was gruff. His presence felt steady again, and as powerful as ever. He kissed her fingers as they passed over his lips.

"You're being charitable," she told him. "I'll never get cocky about what I think I know again. I don't deserve it."

"You deserve to have the world laid at your feet." He hooked his arm around her neck. Her head fell back against his forearm as his head came down, and he kissed her. His hard mouth moved over hers with a gentle reverence that brought fresh tears to her eyes. She murmured and touched his lean cheek as she kissed him back.

He lifted his head, looking blinded. She gave him a tentative smile. Gradually the blind look left his eyes. Together they had banished Mister Enigmatic again. He looked like a different man from the hard-bitten, expressionless stranger she had first met.

He said vividly, "Well, that's got to have pissed him off."

"I beg your pardon?"

He grinned, a rakish, wicked sight on that dark, unshaven face. "Sweetheart, we were making about as much noise just now in the psychic realm as a couple having sex in a cheap motel."

"Ooh-kay," she said, her cheeks burning with heat. She laughed. "That's certainly an image I didn't have in my head before."

He looked unrepentant. "I like it, but what we did was

definitely an attention grabber, and the Deceiver will have heard it loud and clear. Now we've really got to haul ass."

"I know." She wiped at her face and saw that her hands were still emitting a silvery glow. She spread her fingers and turned them over, staring at them. She gave her hand an experimental shake. It still glowed.

He had started to tear off his bandages. He paused to look at her. "What on earth are you doing?"

"I can't get it to stop," she told him. She shook the other hand.

He started to laugh. "That isn't going to help."

She gave him a fierce frown, delighted with him, his laughter, the forest around them and the whole universe. "It might."

He was still laughing. "You need to stop it the way you started it."

"Right, but what did I do?" She thought back.

Michael tore off the rest of his bandages, tossed them on the floor of his old car, shrugged on his shirt and grabbed the bags of food. He gestured to her. She ran to collect the pillow and blanket and her purse from the Ford before clambering into the Jeep's passenger seat.

He dug into his weapons bag and pulled out the nine-millimeter, which he set in the driver's door pocket. When they had both snapped on their seat belts he turned the SUV around and inched past the Ford toward the main road.

Then she remembered. She had to will it to start. She flung out her hands and commanded, "Stop!"

Michael slammed on the brakes. He scanned the surrounding scene. "What?"

She waved her hands at him in triumph. "I did it!"

He looked at her from under lowered brows. "Try doing it silently next time."

It was a look of such ordinary exasperation she grinned. "I will," she told him. "Come on, lighten up. I just remembered how to do something else. This is a good thing."

A corner of his well-made mouth lifted. Really, he was sexier than any man had a right to be.

"Yes," he said, as he accelerated the Jeep again. "This is a very good thing."

Chapter Six

AFTER ASTRA LEFT the dream with Mary, she cast her awareness through her house, checking on her uninvited guests.

Jerry lay in the bed of one of her guest rooms. He had been a big, strong man in his youth. Astra remembered his childhood well. Now his body looked shrunken under the covers, and his copper skin had an unhealthy pallor. His grandson Jamie had pulled his long, dark gray hair out of the ponytail, and it rippled over the pillow. She sighed. Jerry was a good man. It was hard to watch him die.

Jamie had dragged a chair in from the living room. He sat in it, slumped sideways in a dejected heap, resting his head on the crook of one arm on the bed beside Jerry's right hand. Like his grandfather, he wore his hair long and pulled back in a ponytail. Leather and silver bracelets adorned his lean wrists.

He was a good-looking boy, Astra thought, as she studied him. He was tall and rangy, around twenty-two or twenty-three. His body had yet to finish filling out the promise of power in those wide shoulders. His hair gleamed black like a raven's wing, and he had his grandfather's strong, proud features, only Jamie's were molded with more sensuality, with large, dark eyes and full, sensual lips.

There was a third person in the room, a ghost of a tall man.

He was a faint shimmer in the quiet bedroom, a strong, steady presence. Jerry wasn't awake, and apparently Jamie didn't have the capacity to see or sense him, because the boy never reacted when the ghost laid a hand on Jamie's shoulder.

Astra, however, could see the ghost very well. He had short black hair, distinguished aquiline features and the same copper skin as his father and nephew.

Nicholas Crow had indeed come, and just as she had expected, he had gone straight to his father's sickbed.

She couldn't do anything for any of them. She had no platitudes to speak. Nicholas was already dead. Jerry was going to die. And she didn't have a clue what she was going to do about Jamie.

Thanks to Jerry, now Jamie knew where she lived. And soon Jerry would no longer be around to teach the boy. Left alone, Jamie would mature without either Nicholas or his grandfather's discipline or steadying influence.

In Astra's mind, that turned him into a loose cannon. She might very well end up having to kill the boy just to ensure his silence, and wouldn't that be a pretty turn of events. Then the deaths of all three males in the Crow family could be laid at her feet.

She turned away and put the sadness in that room out of her mind. She had work to do, and being maudlin wasn't going to get any of it done.

As she regained energy, she worked while her old body rested.

She sent out psychic calls and waited for responses. When they came, she issued orders. Her creatures flew off to do her bidding. The Deceiver might have his spies, but so did she.

She still couldn't discover how the Deceiver had traced Michael and Mary to Michael's cabin. She knew he hadn't found them through conventional means. As far as legal documentation went, the cabin didn't exist. Finding the discrepancy in the county records would take a land surveyor with a significant amount of extra time on his hands.

Besides, nothing Michael carried or used could be traced back to his original identity in this life. Michael's name and his Social Security number were pristine. From the time he had been a young boy, Astra had constructed several different aliases for him, complete with work, family and credit histories, mailing addresses and medical records. She created an elaborate web of smoke and mirrors that Michael had taken over when he had become an adult, and through which he now walked as easily as he breathed.

Perhaps it mattered how the Deceiver had found them. Perhaps it didn't. Spies were everywhere. Michael had already admitted to being exhausted and overstretched. Either the issue would become relevant or it wouldn't. She decided to concentrate her efforts on more productive tasks.

Then she heard something in the psychic realm, a sound so faint at first it was a mere tickle at the distant edges of her consciousness.

It grew rapidly in strength and harmony. She hadn't heard anything like it for so very long, at first she almost didn't recognize it.

Then memory settled over her like a warm blanket. Once her life had been filled with so many harmonic vibrations of such similar caliber that they had resounded to the heavens in a vast, ebullient symphony. Their crystal-shot planet had resonated with the thrum of their existence.

Though she had grown to enjoy Earth's own unique complexity of vibrations, its interconnected psychic web that made up its own web of life, this world would never be the same for her. A part of her would forever remember her home. That part had listened, yearning through eons of silence.

Now her consciousness strained toward the gorgeous unearthly sound.

She laughed, a ghostly exhalation comprised of incredulity, pain and genuine amusement. Mary and Michael. What were those idiots doing now?

While the harmony lasted, she scanned for the direction from which it came, knowing all the while that the Deceiver was doing the same. Mary and Michael were traveling to northern Michigan and getting closer to her. That was both good news and bad, for she saw with her wider vision how much of the Deceiver's attention and resources had been focused in that direction.

Meanwhile her spies began to fly in. They whispered of human activities, roadblocks erected along major highways and intensive police searches in port cities and towns. So much of Michigan's borders were coastline that she knew the Deceiver had to be stretched to the utmost of even his massive capacity.

That passing realization gave her a grim smile. He couldn't police the entire Michigan coast, but he was giving it his best shot, which would make life extremely challenging for her two idiots.

She had to get in touch with them, but she couldn't do it with another dream sending because it was quite obvious they were wide awake. A spirit messenger would be prey to all of the Deceiver's creatures in that realm, but a physical messenger would take too long and be just as vulnerable. She thought hard, but she didn't have any other real choice.

She sighed. Either way, she had to wake up and get out of bed. She shifted levels in her consciousness, settled her psyche back into its fragile human body and surfaced to full wakefulness.

The body that housed her spirit groaned. She yawned and struggled to a sitting position, reacquainting herself with all the various aches and pains that attended her extreme old age. She sucked a tooth. Actually she didn't feel too bad, all things considered. She heaved out of bed, drew on her bathrobe and slippers and shuffled out of the bedroom.

Jerry's grandson had left his bedside. Jamie sat at the dining table, with his head in his hands. An empty coffee cup sat in front of him.

"I guess Jerry's asleep," she said, even though she already knew the answer.

The boy's head jerked up. His eyes swam with misery. "Yes. Can you check on him now?"

"I will in a minute," she said, stifling a sigh.

The boy whispered, "I think he should go to the hospital. The thing is, I'm not sure he's well enough to be moved. Grandmother, I'm scared."

The boy was beginning to realize that Jerry wouldn't be getting any better. Astra's mouth tightened. Jerry should be in his own bed, surrounded by the love and respect of his family and friends as he passed, not lingering here like some unpleasant household chore.

She nodded. "I'll be right back."

She walked outside. The early evening air felt fresh and peaceful. The freshness was always welcome, the peace always illusory. She paused by her favorite tree, a massive four-hundred-year-old oak, and braced a hand on its trunk. As always when she touched it, the tree responded by generously giving her energy from its deep, green strength.

She patted it, braced her back and sent out a call. Moments later, Nicholas walked to her. Sunlight shone through his tall, transparent figure.

She remembered the generous, kind boy he had been, and the strong, young warrior who became a Green Beret. In maturity he had been a powerful, quiet man. He had only been in his early forties when he'd been killed. Sudden moisture dampened her eyes, surprising her, and she gritted her teeth against the unwelcome emotion.

Some would say that Nicholas had already given the

ultimate sacrifice and that he deserved peace. Both of those things might be true, but she couldn't afford pretty sentiment. She needed to use every tool she could in order to defeat the Deceiver.

Jamie is right, Nicholas said. *My father is dying.*

As a spirit, Nicholas would be able to see how Jerry was beginning to disconnect from his physical body.

She didn't try to prevaricate. Instead she said simply, *yes.*

In the pale, shimmery figure, a hint of dark, intelligent eyes regarded her. *Is there nothing you can do for him?*

I'm sorry, no, there isn't, she said. Now she was lying to a ghost. *But I need to ask you to do something for me.*

He said nothing, but just watched her. It was so reminiscent of Nicholas's impassive expression when he had been alive that it goaded her into talking.

I know you would rather stay with your father right now, she said. *I'm sorry, but this is important, or I wouldn't ask. I need you to find Michael and Mary for me. I need to get a message to them.*

You have creatures that serve you, he said. *Why not ask them? Why me?*

She nodded. *You're right, I could ask one of them to do it, but you are so . . .* Valuable. Lucid. Reliable. *Because of your skills and your intelligence, you have the best chance of getting to them and delivering the message safely. And that's what matters right now, getting the mission done.* She searched his expression for any sign that her words had resonated with him. *Will you do that for me? For them?*

He still didn't answer right away, and his face was too blurred and indistinct for her to read. Instead he appeared to be scrutinizing her.

Astra felt an uncharacteristic uncertainty. Had he sensed that she had been lying about Jerry? She was a damn good liar, but often ghosts and spirits could sense things that embodied creatures couldn't, and as a young man, Nicholas had witnessed her helping some of his people with healing from time to time.

It goaded her into saying, *Nicholas, please. I will work to see that your father doesn't pass until you return and can be by his side.*

That would be good of you, he said.

His guarded, measured tone stung, and her mouth tightened. Damn it, she would not feel chastened by him. After his years in the army, he should understand better than anybody the concepts of utilizing limited resources and necessary loss. Jerry would, if he were conscious.

Her voice was curt as she asked, *So will you do it?*

Yes, he said. *What do you need me to tell them?*

She gave him the message, and he nodded and turned away. Her eyes stung as she watched his figure fade. She wondered if he would succeed or fail in finding Michael or Mary, or if the Deceiver's minions would find him and tear him to shreds

She added the fate of Nicholas's spirit to her own crushing list of burdens as she turned back to the cabin. Maybe she could indulge in the luxury of maudlin emotions at a later time. For now she had to keep her end of the bargain and bolster her dying friend's strength. Then she had a lot more work to do and more favors to ask.

Chapter Seven

THIS HAD BEEN a bitch of a day, he thought, but things were looking up.

After his scalding shower, he tried to dress in the clothes he'd already had in the motel room. Of course none of them fit. They were sleek and streamlined, and had been much more suited to his last two human hosts.

One had been a handsome, young computer salesman who had been a fitness fanatic. The other had been Mary's clever, charming ex-husband Justin, who had also been handsome.

He had enjoyed Mary's ex. Justin had dealt with his kidnapping with a remarkable composure, and even a certain wry humor, and he had been smart enough to recognize a predator when he saw one.

He had enjoyed taking over Justin's body even more, but he had only inhabited the body for a day before Mary had killed it. What a waste of a good host.

The monkey suit he currently inhabited was much bulkier

than the bodies of the previous two men. When he tried to slip on a clean pair of slacks, the monkey's thigh muscles strained at the expensive material, and he couldn't fasten them at the waist. He tore off the pants, kicked them across the room and sneered at the pile of clothes he had tossed in the corner earlier. He refused to put on the monkey's filthy clothes again. Instead he tied a towel around his waist and got to work making more phone calls.

He had dozens of drones, the careful harvest of several years' work, scattered across Indiana, Illinois, Michigan and Wisconsin. They had been actively involved in the hunt for Mary and Michael. It would take some of the drones longer than others to drive to Grand Rapids, but by the time Martin and his colleagues from DC arrived later that evening, he would have assembled another team.

In a half an hour, one of the nearest drones would bring him clean, serviceable clothes that would fit the monkey. He didn't bother ordering anything too fancy. He had no plans to stay in this body a moment longer than necessary.

Once he finished the phone calls, he ordered a couple of pizzas and paid for the food with the monkey's credit card. After all, like Warren Buffett, he believed that one of the best traits of the very wealthy was maintaining frugal financial habits. Then he was ready to sit down with his laptop.

The first thing he saw when he opened his in-box was an e-mail from Martin, with an attachment. Martin's note was short and to the point.

> Here's the info on Crow. I have one of my staff digging around for more information, but in the meantime, here is the FBI file on our subject.

Smiling with satisfaction, he clicked on the encrypted attachment, punched in a pass code and opened the digital copy of a dossier on Nicholas. He began to read the contents.

Naturally Crow had excelled at everything from an early

age. As a teenager, he'd had his choice of career paths. Several universities had courted him with football scholarships, but instead he chose to go the Ivy League route. He took a scholarship to study public policy and public administration at the John F. Kennedy School of Government at Harvard. When he graduated, Crow joined the army, where he distinguished himself again.

Boring.

He stopped reading and started to scan. He already knew that Crow had been an exceptional man. Crow had to have been in order to have occupied the position he'd had.

No, he was looking for something else on Crow, something meaty that he could sink his teeth into, and hopefully shake something useful out of it.

Crow's mother and father had been divorced from the time that he was six years old. He had lived in Chicago with his mother, who had been a nurse, and he had spent summers and Christmas vacations with his father, Jerry Crow, now retired. Crow's father had owned a couple of antique stores, which he sold several years ago, and he was reputed to be a First Nation elder and active in his tribal community.

And the elder Crow lived in northern Michigan.

There we go.

There was the first little nugget of something to nibble on.

His mother had died in a car accident in the nineties when Crow had been serving overseas. His father, Jerry Crow, was still alive. The dossier even had a digitized photo of him, although it appeared to be at least ten years old. The man in the photo was around sixty or so.

He had terrible dress sense. He wore a flannel shirt and Levi's, and he held a lit cigarette between the fingers of one hand. His gray-streaked black hair was pulled back into a ponytail, and his strong face was creased with laughter as he looked off camera.

"I think I need to pay you a visit, Jerry," he said to the photo. He tapped the laptop screen with a blunt fingernail. "Offer my condolences on the loss of your son. I feel optimistic that you and I will have an interesting conversation."

A knock sounded on his motel door. He strolled over to look through the peephole. The first of his drones had arrived, carrying packages of clothes. As he dressed, other drones arrived until within a couple of hours, he felt replenished with both energy and resources.

The state patrol had not yet reported any sign of the car Michael and Mary had been driving, but that had been a long shot anyway. It was more to keep pressure on the pair and make sure they kept moving than anything else.

In the meantime, he was clean, well fed, dressed and he had manpower, weapons and equipment. Plus he had a man in northern Michigan that he was very much interested in talking to. He set his drones to various tasks, then he settled on top of the bedcovers, folded his hairy monkey hands together and closed his eyes to focus on marshaling his forces in the psychic realm.

First he had to cast the net out. He needed to have a presence in every port town. Then he had to tighten the perimeters. Then they could concentrate on sweeping the countryside. He would tear this state apart with his bare hands, if that was what it took to find them.

Another knock sounded on his door. One of his drones answered it. He did not let the interruption disrupt his work until he heard Martin's voice. Then he sat up in bed to watch Martin usher two other people into the room, a man and a woman. They both wore dark suits and were sharp looking, intelligent and fit. These would be Martin's colleagues from DC.

As intelligent and as capable as they no doubt were, they had trusted Martin. They never stood a chance. The moment the door closed, several of his drones, including Martin himself, faced the two FBI agents with guns drawn.

Slowly they put their hands up. Martin stepped forward to divest them of their weapons, while their wary gazes darted from drone to drone, until finally they looked at him, as well they should.

He rolled off the bed and onto his feet.

"Hello, hello," he said cheerfully. "It's about time you showed up."

Martin said, "We've been in dialogue with the director of the Michigan State Police about how best to direct the manhunt. I have set up a personal meeting with him in an hour, at the District Six headquarters in Rockford, and I told him that I would be bringing a consultant with me."

"Excellent," he said. "That should give us plenty of time to finish up things here. After I meet the director, we're going to travel north to visit Nicholas's father. You'll need to arrange for air transportation. We have a lot to do and a lot of ground to cover before it gets dark."

"Certainly."

While drones might have their limitations, the more intelligent people were, the better-functioning drones they made, and really, Martin was the best example of what a drone could be.

"Martin," the female said, "I don't know what the fuck is going on here, but so far, you haven't done anything that you can't back out of."

She kept her voice low and controlled. Her hard, composed expression said that she was ready for the slightest opportunity they might give her, and she would turn it to her advantage.

Oh, he liked her. He wanted to take her first.

He strode forward, one of the monkey's paws outstretched.

"Please, allow me to introduce myself," he said, smiling. "Although, there really isn't any need for an exchange of names. I've had so many over the years, and you're never going to remember what I tell you, anyway."

Chapter Eight

MARY HAD LEARNED to count her life in small segments, and at the moment she was vastly contented with life. She didn't have to drive anymore, her belly was stretched full with good food, her body no longer ached from bruises or any deeper injuries and she had a pillow. And a blanket. Sufficient unto the day.

She intended to pay attention to the passing scenery as Michael located a route back to Highway 131. But she did have that pillow, and somehow it found its way between her ear and the car door. She rested her eyes for a minute.

Nasty things whispered in the dark. She surfaced back to consciousness fast.

"That's the fourth time I've woken up bad in the last couple of days. It's starting to piss me off," she muttered, before she opened her eyes. She sat up and sent a bleary gaze around, reaching out to touch Michael's arm for comfort. "What's happened? How did they find us?"

"It's not how they found us," he said. "It's what we're driving into."

The dichotomy between how things felt in the psychic realm and how things looked in the physical realm was disorienting. Visually everything appeared normal, even scenic. She hadn't slept more than ten minutes. The architectural landscape had condensed and the early evening traffic had worsened. Michael's arm felt warm and bulky with muscle.

She noticed his face had gone wary and still. His gaze held an alert expression she was beginning to recognize. The expression did peculiar things to his eyes, turning their gray color polished and impenetrable, like the hard, reflective surface of a drawn sword.

How many dead bodies had they left behind in the cabin's clearing? Twenty? Thirty? They had been trained hardened soldiers, probably mercenaries. How many had looked into Michael's executioner gaze as they died? A convulsive shudder ran through her.

He nudged her hand. "You wanted a vacation on the beach," he said. "Tell me about it."

She shook her head slowly as she watched the people in nearby cars. "At first I was shooting for a month, but after the last couple of days, I think I was lowballing it. I'm gonna go for a full summer."

"During your summer off, you can sleep as much as you like," he said. A slight smile softened the hard line of his mouth.

"There are no alarm clocks on that beach," she told him. "Nobody hurries anywhere, because nothing urgent is happening. The most pressing thing I have to decide is whether I want a margarita or a mai tai. And all is right with the world." She sighed. "It doesn't matter where it is. The Bahamas, Mexico, Hawaii—I'm ready to go. Right now."

"I am too."

In an abrupt movement that startled her, he signaled and

pulled into the parking lot of a liquor store at one end of a strip mall. Then he put the Jeep into park. With the engine idling, he crossed his arms over the top of the steering wheel and leaned forward to rest his chin on them. His light eyes moved over the scene.

She waited, her gaze moving from Michael to the nearby shops and the traffic that sped past them. Finally, she asked, "What now, Mister Enigmatic?"

"You keep calling me that," he murmured. Thoughts shifted behind those steely eyes.

"I don't mean it in a bad way," she told him. She grinned. "Not anymore. I'm getting used to you turning all silent and mysterious. I think more caffeine might be a good idea. Do you mind if I buy more Coke while you use your spidey sense or inner periscope, or whatever it is that you've got?"

She gestured to the vending machines located outside the liquor store.

He swept the parking lot and the immediate area again with that sharp, assessing gaze. "Okay."

"Want one?"

"Sure."

She dug in her purse for change, climbed out of the Jeep and walked the short distance to the vending machines. Gray clouds mottled the sky. The temperature had turned sharp and chilly, while a brisk breeze blew off the nearby Lake and tugged at loose tendrils of her hair. She had been uncomfortable earlier in the heat of the day, but now she was grateful she was wearing the flannel shirt.

Her nerves jangled from the turmoil she sensed in the psychic realm. She felt exposed standing outside, even though she knew Michael was not more than thirty feet away and aware of her every move. Getting the Coke had been as much an act of bravado as practicality, but the small sanctuary of the Jeep suddenly seemed too far away. She grabbed the two cans and jogged back.

Once she'd climbed back inside, Michael said, "I'm sensing psychic movement in the direction of all the northern towns and cities, especially the closest ones—Petoskey, Charlevoix, Norwood and Traverse City. He's concentrating on the ports. I'll bet that all the local airports and landing strips are being watched too. There's also a concentration of some kind of energy mass on I-75, in the direction of the Mackinac Bridge. He will have set up a roadblock on the bridge."

Her stomach muscles tightened as a now-familiar sense of dread washed over her. The five-mile-long Mackinac Bridge spanned the Straits of Mackinac. It was the only route they could travel by car to the Upper Peninsula of Michigan. A roadblock on I-75 meant they had been correct. The Deceiver did have powerful contacts in the police force. They had already been acting as if he had, but somehow it seemed worse to have their deductions confirmed.

"He's done all of that already?" she asked in dismay. "It's barely been twelve hours since we left the cabin."

Michael shook his head. "I'll bet a lot of this is something he set in motion earlier. It's what I would have done if I were chasing someone who appeared to be traveling north on 131. It's a logical strategy. Work to cut off the exit points, then quarter the area and search section by section."

They fell silent for a few moments. She asked, "What about that thing you can do—the null space?"

"That will get us farther than we could get without it," he replied. "But it won't get us past any roadblocks."

She stuffed his can of Coke into a drink holder. "I guess this might be the worse-before-it-gets-better part."

"Something like that." He rubbed his eyes. He looked as tired as she felt.

"Where are we trying to go, anyway?" she asked. "I keep meaning to ask, but then something happens."

Michael pointed in a northwestern direction. "Right about there. You know where Beaver Island is?"

"I have a rough idea," she said. Beaver Island was located almost directly north from Grand Traverse Bay and south of Michigan's Upper Peninsula. If she remembered right, it was barely more than a one-town island. She'd always thought the remote location sounded like the perfect place for a quiet vacation.

"There's a cluster of smaller islands around it. Astra lives on one of them. We need a boat or a seaplane to get to her. I keep a boat docked at Charlevoix, which is about sixteen or seventeen miles west of Petoskey. I was hoping we could hook up to Highway 31, which follows the coast, and shoot over to Charlevoix to use the boat." He grimaced. "It might be too risky for us to get to it."

She rubbed at her temple where a tension headache had begun to throb. "We could always go to Cancun," she muttered. "You know, try back in a decade or two."

She knew that the Deceiver would never leave them alone for an entire decade. He would keep hunting until he found and destroyed them. She also knew Michael would never consent to hide while his enemy was loose in the world committing atrocities. And she knew her own conscience wouldn't allow her to hide for that long either.

She was being truculent and illogical and unrealistic, and she didn't care. She popped open her can of Coke and glared at it.

He glanced at her. "I was actually thinking about traveling south again. Not as far south as Mexico, of course. But there are smaller towns dotting the entire Michigan coastline, and almost all of them have marinas. Unless he has a good portion of the U.S. Army invade Michigan, there's no way he can watch all of those ports. All he can do is patrol the water and the coastal highways."

"Why can't Astra come to us?" The image of that frail, elderly body stretched on a narrow bed came back to her. She gritted her teeth. "Never mind. She can't."

"No, she can't," he agreed. "So, south it is."

He put the Jeep in reverse, backed out of the parking space and shifted into drive. Then he accelerated—directly into a transparent, blurred figure that appeared in front of the Jeep.

Mary cried out sharply, even as Michael slammed on the brakes. He was too late, and the car passed through Nicholas's ghost.

Mary had accidentally passed through Nicholas's ghost once before, and she felt it again, that sensation of warmness, of a strong male presence.

And just as she had before, she flashed on a knife rising on the periphery of his/her vision. He/she turned to combat the threat. The knife snaked out, and fiery pain flared at his/her throat. Wetness gushed down his/her front. He/she fell to his/her knees. . . .

Just as quickly as the vision hit her, it disappeared again. She was fully back in her own body, in the parking lot with Michael.

"Jesus," she said. Belatedly, she realized that she had spilled Coke over her flannel shirt and jeans. She set the can in her drink holder, fingers shaking.

"It's all right," Michael said. "It was just Nicholas."

She stared at him. He looked calm and unaffected. Either he hadn't passed through any part of Nicholas, or he hadn't gotten any vision when he had. He pulled into another parking space, unbuckled his seat belt and stepped outside.

She followed him out, walking around the hood of the Jeep to where Michael stood. As she reached Michael's side, Nicholas reappeared in front of them.

The ghost was easier to see than he had been early this morning. In full sunshine, he was barely a glimmer. Now the strong, powerful lines of his body were distinct in the gray, cloudy evening.

He looked at Mary and seemed to hesitate. Had he felt something when she'd seen his death? She shuddered, hoping he would never ask, and Michael put a bracing arm around her shoulders.

"What is it?" Michael asked. "What's happened?"

Michael and Nicholas had been, if not friends, at least colleagues. She might have frowned at Michael's abrupt attitude, except that she saw how his gaze traveled over the scene again. He was as wary as she was of staying in one spot for too long.

Astra sent me with a message for you, Nicholas said. *She said she knows of the traps the enemy has set for you. Don't turn away from your course. Don't turn south. Push through their barriers, and move quickly, because she is calling in all of her favors and sending help.*

Mary waited expectantly for more, but instead of saying anything further, Nicholas fell silent.

She muttered, "Was that meant to be cryptic, or is it just me?"

The ghost said to Michael, *She said that you would understand.*

Michael's arm tightened on her shoulders. He glanced down at her, and he looked grimmer than ever. He said, "I do." He looked north. "We don't have time to try to play it safe and go south. We need to go into Petoskey and get a boat. We'd better hurry. There's a hell of a storm coming our way."

"And getting on a boat right now is supposed to be a good thing?" She looked between Michael and Nicholas doubtfully. "I'm pretty sure I'm missing something important here, because usually people like to get off the water when there's a hell of a storm coming their way."

Michael said, "If we go south we won't be able to get on the water in time to take advantage of the cover she's offering. When it hits, the storm will be the dominant image on any radar systems, and it will help to disguise our presence from pursuers. It will also drive police patrols to dock until it has passed."

"It still sounds awfully risky," she said.

Michael nodded. "It is. So is going south."

"But if we go south, you can do the null space thing while we're on the boat, right?"

"Yes, but I can't project the effect onto long-distance radar equipment," he said. He lifted one broad shoulder. "Going north or going south—there's going to be dangers and risks either way. What do you want to do? Whatever we decide, we'd better do it quickly. We shouldn't keep standing here. If we don't move north fast enough, we may not be able to get out on the water in time."

A sharp gust of wind hit them. She shivered as she said, "I don't know. . . ."

Nicholas interrupted her. *My father is dying.*

Her mouth snapped shut. She and Michael stared at the ghost. She said softly, "Oh, damn. I'm so sorry."

Michael asked, "What happened?"

The ghost seemed to shake his head. *I don't know. He was already unconscious when I reached him. All I know is that he is on the island, and Astra has said that she can't do anything for him.* His glimmering, dark eyes fixed on Mary. *But perhaps you could, if you reached him in time.*

Nicholas had come to help her, unasked, when she had been running alone and terrified in the forest. She didn't even have to think about it. "Of course," she said, instinctively reaching a hand out toward him even though he was insubstantial. "We'll be there as soon as we can."

Nicholas raised his own hand, as if he would clasp hers.

But he couldn't, of course, because he was dead.

Unless she could do something about that too.

That morning, she had examined two men whose souls were dead, although their bodies were still active and dangerous. Drones, Michael called them. Their spirits were gone, and there was no way to recall them. She could even see how the Deceiver had killed the spirits but left the bodies animate and functional. The long, slashing psychic scar on both drones had been clearly visible to her mind's eye.

While here she looked at a ghost of a courageous and extraordinary man who had not deserved to die.

She bit her lip. What she was considering did not seem as chilling as it had the first time it had occurred to her. She wasn't sure what that said about her. In the next breath, she decided she didn't care.

Because on the one hand, there was one man who did not

deserve to be dead. While on the other hand, the Deceiver had created so many drones that no longer deserved to live.

"I have something I want to discuss with you," she said to Nicholas.

"That's going to have to wait," Michael said. He turned her around and propelled her toward the front of the Jeep. "Either that or we'll have to talk about it on the road, because we've got to get moving."

I must return to my father while I can, said Nicholas. *I will see you on the island, and we can talk there. Safe journey.*

"And to you," Michael said.

Nicholas vanished.

They were right, of course. She loped around to the passenger side of the Jeep and climbed in.

Michael slid into the driver's seat and started the engine. As he pulled out of the parking lot, he said, "What did you want to discuss with Nicholas?"

"He's very present and remarkably lucid for a ghost, isn't he?" She chewed on a thumbnail as she thought.

"Yes, he is." Michael accelerated into a gap of traffic. "Some ghosts are fragments of personality, or traumatized by what happened to them, and most don't stay long after their death. Nicholas is different. He is whole and present, at least for now. Maybe after he loses his sense of mission or responsibility, he will pass on too."

"But what if he doesn't pass on?" There, she said it.

He frowned. "What do you mean?"

She took a deep breath. "If the Deceiver can take over another person's body, why can't someone else do it too?"

He stared at her. "What are you talking about? None of us have done that, ever."

She rushed on, the words tumbling over one another. "Of course, I'm not talking about taking over a person who is alive and aware. That would be murder. I'm talking about people who are already dead—the drones. Their bodies are functional, but the spirit is gone. This morning when I examined those two men, I got to thinking, if the Deceiver can take over a drone, why can't someone else do it too? It would be like—like organ harvesting. Sort of. Wouldn't it?"

After his initial reaction, he looked quite alert and fascinated, without any sign of the revulsion she had feared. "You're thinking of trying something like that for Nicholas."

She lifted a shoulder. "I haven't had a chance to think any of this through, and there's a lot to consider. Many of those drones must have some kind of family. Either they are pretending to live their normal lives, or they've left their families behind. Or maybe they have criminal records. After all, they're doing things at the Deceiver's bidding. And who knows how Nicholas would feel about any of this? Even if he agreed, I think he would have to live in hiding for the rest of his life . . . or for the rest of the life span of the drone he inhabited."

He gave her a keen glance. "But you still want to offer him the chance."

"Yes."

"And you could help him enter the body and take it over?"

She blew out a breath. "I don't know, but I think I would like to try, if he would let me."

"If you could resurrect him, then Nicholas would really be back in the game."

"Or not," she said strongly. "He's sacrificed enough. If I could do it, he might want to retire, and he deserves that chance."

"You don't know Nicholas. He wouldn't be able to stay uninvolved. For one thing, his murderer hasn't been caught." Michael grinned. "It's never dull, is it?"

"No, it never is," she said. She made a wry face. "Even if we manage to destroy the Deceiver, we'll never live any kind of normal life. Or at least what other people consider normal."

"We'll have to achieve our own kind of normal." His big hand covered hers. She turned her hand over and clasped his.

“That’s a deal,” she told him. “In the meantime, honey, would you mind picking up a drone for me whenever you can?”

He laughed softly. “Just as soon as an opportunity presents itself.”

Chapter Nine

MICHAEL TURNED OFF the main highway and drove through Petoskey's side streets. Mary looked out her window. She didn't know much about the city other than it was small, attractive and full of large Victorian houses. Petoskey's old downtown Gaslight District, an area of about six blocks, had been restored and was populated with cafés, pubs, galleries, antique shops and boutiques.

She had once driven through Petoskey. She had stopped to have a late lunch in a small restaurant and had fallen into a conversation with her waitress, who was a student at North Central Michigan College.

Apparently, her waitress had told her, Ernest Hemingway had referred to many local landmarks in his novel *The Torrents of Spring*. Mary had resolved to read the novel and had gone so far as to buy a copy, but she disliked Hemingway's writing, so she had never followed through with her original intention.

She tried to think back. What had happened to that book?

Had she ever unpacked it, or was it still in the boxes in the garage?

Then she remembered. The book no longer existed. It had been destroyed along with the rest of her house.

Following hard on the heels of that realization, in a one-two knockout punch, an image surfaced of Justin's face surrounded by the sparkling black corona of the Deceiver's aura. Dread shot adrenaline through her veins and left her feeling sick. The Deceiver's smile had been an alien unwholesome travesty on Justin's clever face.

Her life and her sense of identity had transformed almost beyond recognition, but her feelings for the people she knew and loved were still the same.

Justin's partner, Tony, had to be so worried, not just about Justin but about her as well. He needed to hear that Justin had died. He deserved the right to mourn instead of enduring an endless agony of not knowing. When would she find time to call him? Was it safe to contact him? Was she reaching a point when she never would?

Her mouth tightened. She wouldn't accept that. If they managed to live through this hellish mess, she would figure out how to live with both halves of herself. She would call Tony as soon as she knew that it wouldn't put him in danger. She would tell him about Justin and tell him something about herself that didn't sound too crazy. She had to call him, if for no other reason than to give him closure and to say good-bye.

An array of colorful Victorian houses with tall, wide porches passed by outside her window. The town twinkled with charm and serenity in the deepening twilight. It epitomized the small-town American myth, like Cabot Cove from the television detective series *Murder, She Wrote.*

Only people were murdered every week in Cabot Cove. Or maybe, she thought, it was more like the location in a Stephen King novel, where wholesome-looking restaurants had red-and-white-checkered tablecloths, but evil rotted underneath the quaint scenery.

The route Michael was driving clicked into a pattern. She realized he was working to get them as close to Lake Michigan as he could without drawing attention to them. Every time she turned her senses toward the shoreline, she sensed an oily dark whispering at the edge of her mind. Her stomach tightened.

They had to pass through that malevolent barrier. Somehow they had to get on a boat and sail to an island before an impending storm hit. The task sounded worse than impossible. It sounded like lighting oneself on fire and jumping off a cliff.

She chewed her lip as doubts attacked. She asked carefully, "It's hard to wrap my brain around the fact that Astra has the capacity to create a storm so big it can block our presence on radar."

"She's not actually creating the storm," he said. "She's working with natural forces to create the storm."

Mary paused as she thought about that. She didn't see the difference. "What does it mean that Astra's calling in all her favors?"

He shot her a quick glance. "You remember the small wind spirit that helped you in South Bend?"

"Of course. And you sent it away." She remembered how bitter she felt at the time.

"There are wind spirits in the world that are much larger and more powerful."

Gretchen, the psychic Mary had visited in South Bend, had talked about wind spirits. "Do you mean like the First Nation thunder beings, the Wakean?"

"Exactly like that."

She blinked. "How did Astra grow acquainted enough with the Wakean that they would owe her favors?"

"We don't have time to talk about it anymore right now," he said. "Just trust me, if she said a storm is coming, it's coming."

He pulled parallel to a car parked on the side of the street, then signaled and reversed into the parking space behind it.

Mary looked at the nearby building. It was a huge old house that had been converted into a law office, already closed for the night.

"I trust you," she said. She kept her voice steady and patient. "I'm asking all these questions, because maybe I do sometimes still have a bit of a problem with Mister Enigmatic, and I need to understand what is going on."

He rubbed the back of his head. "I promise that Mister Enigmatic will take more time to explain things when we're not in so much danger."

She felt her mouth quirk into a reluctant smile. "Is that ever going to happen?"

His eyebrows rose. He smiled back. "If we can pull this off, it should happen soon. As far as the Deceiver and his drones are concerned, it should seem like we've disappeared off the face of the earth."

"Okay," she said. That sounded a lot better than lighting themselves on fire and jumping off a cliff. "I've got more questions, but they can wait. Thank you."

"I'm sorry about Mister Enigmatic." He unbuckled his seat belt, twisted and dug into his black bag. "I expect he's a pretty maddening character."

"I like him when I'm not scared," she told him. "He's a man of mystery."

He snorted and pulled a dark cap out of the bag. He handed it to her. "He's a social misfit who's not used to talking to people or explaining himself. Tuck your hair up in this. It's too distinctive."

She took the cap and jammed it down on her head, her attention snagged by the trees across the street. Branches were beginning to whip in the rising wind that blew off the Lake. She glanced at the heavy clouds amassing in the darkened sky. If Astra could instigate something of this magnitude, no wonder Michael believed it was to their advantage to unite with her.

Mary fought to keep from sounding as awestruck as she felt. "It looks like our help is arriving."

He glanced at the sky. "It's going to be an interesting boat ride. I want you to take the nine-millimeter with you."

"Yeah, I don't think so." He just gave her a steady look. She growled, "Fine, although I don't know where I'm going to put it."

She looked down at herself. Her jacket was in a different part of the state. In their stress and preoccupation, they had left it back at the cabin. All she had was her borrowed flannel shirt, and the temperature was plummeting fast. She suspected she was going to be sorry about losing that jacket soon.

He paused, glancing around to make sure there weren't any close pedestrians. "Tuck it into your jeans under the shirt."

"Wait, I forgot. I've still got my purse." Gingerly, she took the nine-millimeter and an extra clip from him. She tucked both into her purse, grumbling, "Just my luck I'll drop the purse in front of a cop and everything will spill out."

"You'll be fine. Keep watch for me." She watched the street while he stuffed things into a backpack and wiped down surfaces. "Got it," he said after a few moments. He straightened in his seat, resting the backpack on his thighs, those sword gray eyes assessing the scene in front of them.

Her heartbeat sped up. The palms of her hands turned clammy.

She thought, here we go.

He said, "Come on."

Mary slung her purse onto her shoulder and climbed out of the Jeep when he did. She gasped as the wind, icy and wet with the storm's sullen promise, sliced through her baggy flannel shirt, flattening it against her torso.

"My hotel on the beach is so hot I won't need clothes," she said through gritted teeth. She started to shiver. "I'll have just three red triangles of cloth with strings to hold them in place. And that's my dress-up-for-dinner outfit."

"Oh, man," said Michael. "I'm so there." He grinned at her, teeth white against his dark, unshaven face.

He put his backpack on one shoulder, rounded the end of the Jeep and put an arm across her shoulders. She slid hers around his waist and huddled close to his warmth. Then he took off at a pace that was so brisk she had to trot to keep up. She bent her head and watched their legs. For every step he took she had to take three.

They walked a block, crossed the street and turned toward the Lake. The air was thick with wicked shadows. She started to breathe hard and not just from the pace Michael set.

"Keep telling me about the beach," he said. His quiet voice was unhurried.

She shook her head, unable to reply. Trepidation locked her throat, and her leg muscles quivered. Bad things waited for them up ahead, men like the ones who had tried to kidnap her. In the psychic realm something black, glistening and hungry lurked near the shore.

She could see it in her mind's eye, lazily testing the air with long, shadowy tendrils like tentacles. It was all she could do to force her quaking body to keep pace with Michael, to keep taking one step after another.

"All right," Michael said. He pulled her into a short, shadowed alley. They walked the length of it. "I'll tell you about the beach. We'll be finished with all of this, of course."

"Of course," she echoed.

"We'll go snorkeling any time we want," he told her. "And because the afternoons are long and lazy and full of sunshine, we'll be able to explore the nearby coral reefs for hours. Every color imaginable is in that coral reef, framed by clear, cobalt blue water." They reached the mouth of the alley and paused. "You're going to get sick of swimming."

"That's hard to imagine." Wretched with cold and fear, she sniffled and swiped at her nose with the back of one hand. "Healer and warrior. Balancing energies. Bleh. Try warrior and coward—there's a balance for you."

"You're not a coward," he said. He cupped her cheek with

one big, warm hand. "Cowards don't do things that scare them, and you do."

"Don't try to tell me what a coward is," she growled. "I know exactly what I am. I am a coward. I wouldn't be here if you weren't. I'd be hiding in somebody's basement in Tennessee."

He laughed. "Is that cowardice or common sense?" He pushed her against one wall, while he peered around the corner of the building. After a moment, he pulled back. The streetlights had come on in the darkening night. Illumination from a nearby street lamp sliced across his cheekbone and jaw. "Besides, I don't believe you." He looked down at her and ran callused fingers down the side of her upturned face. "You complain when you're scared. You don't run. Are you ready?"

She gave him a jerky nod. His dark head swooped down and he gave her a quick, hard kiss. She felt his warm, firm lips, the scrape of his short whiskers against her cheek, and her mouth moved against his in startled response.

He lifted his head too soon. "There's a mile-long waterfront park, with a small municipal marina located at the western end. I've docked there before. The marina's our best chance for quick access to a boat. When we exit the alley, it will be about a quarter of a mile west, to our left. We've got to cross the highway to get to it. There are two obvious places to cross the highway. One is at a stoplight at Lake Street or there's a lighted tunnel that runs under the highway. Both are being watched, I think by humans."

"There's something else out there," she said. "Something in the psychic realm. I don't know what it is, but it's big. It feels malevolent."

"I know," he said. "I sense it too. It's watching the shoreline. We could wait for a break in the traffic and dash across the highway to the park. That would avoid the two crossings, but there's not a lot of cover in the park, and that's where the creature is lurking."

She watched his face as she said, "We're not going to get to a boat without a fight, are we?"

"No. The question is do we pick a human fight, or a psychic one? And either fight might draw attention from the other realm." He cocked his head, which brought his gray eyes into the light. "How do you want to play this?"

She licked dry lips and twisted her hands together. "You're the fighter," she said. "Use your best judgment. I'll back you up. Just tell me what you want to do, and I'll do it."

He said, "I'm tired of skulking. We'll cross at the stoplight on Lake Street, and humans be damned."

She tilted her face up and looked into the light-filled eyes of the tiger. With sudden surety, she knew he wasn't afraid. He stood poised and balanced on the balls of his feet, an archetypical warrior wearing only the lightest of human facades. A realization occurred to her that felt as though it echoed back through time.

"You're a madman," she muttered. "I've always known it, haven't I? And I'm mad too for following you."

"I gave you a choice," he said. His gaze sparkled with brilliance.

She glanced in the direction of the Lake, toward the black thing that waited to wrap them tight in its tentacles and suck the life out of them. She said again, "We'll do it your way."

He smiled.

They stepped out of the alley. They walked west toward the Lake Street intersection and Petoskey's municipal marina. The sidewalks were deserted. Once again, Mary had to trot to keep up with him.

The wind had increased to a ferocious velocity. Across the vehicle-lit highway she could see the wide stretch of lawn that was the park. Beyond that curved the vast shadowed bowl of Little Traverse Bay. The water foamed with high, white-capped waves.

They approached a tree that creaked audibly as the wind whipped its upper limbs back and forth. Mary eyed it with wariness as she walked past. Ahead she could see the stoplight where they would have to cross the street. She caught a glimpse of the white arm of the dock as it protruded into the bay.

As the first heavy drops of rain lashed down, she thought perhaps the storm was already beginning to help them. People had moved inside to shelter.

Hopefully any guards watching for them would have wanted to get out of the storm too, and would be less vigilant. Wouldn't they?

All too soon she and Michael reached the intersection. They had to wait for the light to change to create a break in the constant flow of traffic. Michael squeezed her shoulders one last time before his arm slid away.

Feeling anchorless, Mary shifted from one skittish foot to the other as her nervous gaze darted over the brilliantly lit, moving traffic. A parking lot dotted with cars lay on the other side of the highway along with a building attached to the marina.

The light changed. Traffic rolled to a stop. Michael moved across the highway with the smooth, purring grace of a Porsche. She followed humbly, clutching her purse.

They reached the other side of the crossing. She noticed what she had forgotten to look for before. A railing and sidewalk led downward to the entrance to the lighted tunnel. She looked sideways at it as she caught the faintest echo of chittering. Humans weren't the only creatures that guarded the tunnel that night.

"Mary," Michael said in a conversational tone.

Her attention snapped to him. "Yes?"

"When the fighting starts, I want you to move to the slips. Pick out a boat and wait for me there."

"All right, but I've got to warn you, I don't know anything about boats."

"Just pick one that seems big and fast," he said casually over his shoulder. "If it looks racy, it probably is."

She nodded, although he was already four feet ahead of her and picking up speed.

Heavy clouds lit with lightning. Moments later, the rumble of thunder reached her ears. The rain started to fall more heavily. In the glow of the street lamps, the air was filled with streaks of silver.

Michael reached into his backpack, pulled out a bulky ammunition belt and slung it over his neck and one shoulder. Then he drew out his knife sheath and belt and buckled it to his waist, all while he walked in a fast, ground-eating stride toward the parking lot and building.

Last he pulled out his semiautomatic. He held it in one strong, muscle-corded hand, nose pointed to the ground. He let the backpack fall to the ground and broke into a run.

Four men appeared around the end of a nondescript van. The increasing rain obscured visibility, but she thought they were uniformed policemen. They started to pull their guns.

Michael whirled. He threw a black missile with such force it shattered one of the van's windows. Then in the same seamless, balletic movement, he spun until he faced the building adjacent to the parking lot. He sprinted headlong for the nearest wall.

Mary watched as he *ran up the side of the building* and disappeared onto the roof.

She blinked, feeling slow and stupid with surprise.

Did she just see what she thought she saw?

Her footsteps brought her beside the backpack Michael had dropped where she came to a stop.

The men by the van finished pulling their weapons. They shouted to one another and began to run. They were all much slower and clumsier than Michael.

Her astonished gaze traveled from them back to the roof of the building. She felt like she had just been transported into a John Woo movie.

The van exploded.

A fireball enveloped two neighboring cars. The concussion knocked the men off their feet.

A scant fraction of a second later, a fast-dissipating blast of hot air slammed into her. She staggered, more from shock than anything else.

Michael said in her head, *Mary. Get to the boat slips NOW.*

She nodded. As if he could see her. Idiot. She bent to pick up the backpack he had dropped.

A fresh burst of chittering broke out behind her, sounding like nothing so much as a flock of disturbed bats bursting from a cave. She looked back at the tunnel. A man, dressed in black, raced toward her.

Whoops. She bolted.

Someone shouted. In the parking lot, the frames of three cars boiled with heat and light. The men struggled to their knees. A short, staccato burst of gunfire sounded from the roof, then another. The men in the parking lot fell again and didn't move. She threw a glance over her shoulder. The man chasing her had fallen to the ground as well.

With her psychic sense she could see a cloud of dark things, like ragged scraps of black lace, hovering outside the tunnel, but she didn't dare look any longer. She ducked her head and raced in a wide circle around the burning chaos in the parking lot. Then she cut across the lawn to the water.

Almost there. The parking lot lay behind her and the long dock filled with boat slips lay just ahead. She heard more shouting from the direction of the building, more shots. Michael was drawing all the gunfire. Sirens wailed in the distance. The sound grew closer rapidly.

Her gaze bounced from shadowed boat to boat as she ran toward the slip. She tried to decide which one was the best to pick. Not that it mattered. She was sure Michael only meant to get her out of the way until he could join her.

Two dark-dressed men rose up from the nearest boat. They leveled guns on her.

"Well, shit," she said.

There was nowhere to hide on the wide, open lawn. She had no time to do anything except get braced. Everything slowed down as her awareness heightened to a sparkling clarity. They fired on her even as she slipped and skidded, awkward on the wet, short grass.

She had the briefest of moments in which to feel a foolish sense of betrayal. They hadn't shouted for her to halt. They didn't identify themselves as police officers.

They fired on her when she carried no visible weapon.

The first bullet entered her torso just under her left breast. Her sparkling awareness centered on it. It burst through the fragile barrier of her skin.

She was already at the point of entrance saying, *No. No. HEAL.*

Her skin closed behind the bullet. The cells knitted together in an instant from the force of her command.

The bullet continued its destructive path. It passed between two ribs and tore through powerful tendons and muscle. It entered her chest cavity.

HEAL, she demanded.

The tendons and muscle obeyed her command, and healed.

The bullet pierced her lung and passed through, and left pink scar tissue behind.

Meanwhile the second bullet entered her abdominal cavity. It began to tear through her pancreas. The third struck her right clavicle, broke it and ricocheted off the bone to pass through the muscle of her shoulder. The fourth pierced her throat by the Adam's apple.

No, she said.

No, and *No*, and *No*.

Her body continued to heal each time she demanded it, but each time a wound closed over, it cost her. Each time she weakened.

Her consciousness centered in the bloodred, lightning-quick battlefield her body had become.

In another, much slower reality, an unimaginable distance away, as the bullets struck her, someone else roared as if he was the one being shot. Someone else strained every ounce of mind and body to race toward her. He was impossibly, inhumanly fast, but he would still not reach the battlefield in time.

No matter how fiercely she demanded, she couldn't heal all the wounds if enough bullets kept striking her. Her body would fail. She had to do something to stop the men from shooting.

She opened her purse and pulled out the nine-millimeter. As the men on the boat straightened, she pushed off the safety latch. She pointed the gun and emptied the clip at them, just like Michael had taught her.

Some of the shots went wild. She had forgotten what he had told her, that the gun would have a kick.

She sank to one knee. The world wobbled. She put a hand to the ground to steady herself on it.

"Now look what you made me do," she said to the men, who had disappeared. She looked in disgust at the gun and dropped it.

She heard her name spoken in a voice gone hoarse from extremity. She turned her face up as Michael skidded to his knees beside her. His expression was unrecognizable, his chest heaved in sobbing breaths and the rain poured down his face like tears.

"Oh, God," he said.

She reached out to grip the front of his shirt. Her hand slipped on the wet cloth. His shaking hands descended on her shoulders. She pulled his face down to hers and growled, "I don't want to get shot ANYMORE TODAY."

He knelt, gathered her into his arms and held her with his whole body. "You won't be. I swear it."

Lightning seared the sky overhead, thunder shook the air and the black glistening creature from the psychic realm attacked.

She was in such a weakened state she couldn't struggle against the dark tentacle that wrapped around her right leg. The touch of it was so cold it seemed to burn into her bones. It started to draw the living warmth out of her.

Michael's arms loosened, and he let go of her. She writhed

in helpless agony as he surged to his feet. Then he erupted into a silver-hot rage that burned against her mind. His presence towered over her prone body, and a flaming sword appeared in his hand. The creature's black tentacle fell away.

The storm flashed and thundered. Sheets of bitterly cold rain spewed down. His flaming sword arcing like lightning, Michael danced and struck with savage grace at the large, sinuous black creature. It undulated and hissed like a feral cat as it lashed back. Mary pulled her body into a small compact ball, squeezed her eyes shut and curled an arm over her head. But she couldn't close off her psychic senses.

A complicated flurry of movements followed. Michael spun. The white-hot flame of his energy sliced deep into the creature's midnight form. An eerie shrieking filled her head, almost like the whistle of a teakettle. The creature recoiled from Michael's shining figure and dragged itself away.

She jerked as two large hands gripped her.

Michael said in a hoarse voice, "It's just me."

She uncurled and tried to push herself up on one trembling arm. Rain poured into her face. She scrubbed at her eyes. Michael slid his arms under her knees and shoulders and picked her up.

Vehicles crowned with the screaming flash of sirens pulled into the far side of the parking lot. Michael sprinted down the long, slippery pier. Black water boiled and foamed around the planks. Her head bounced as he ran. She hooked an arm around his neck.

"Jesus Christ, how bad is it?" he demanded. "Are you bleeding?"

"No," she stuttered, quaking from cold and shock. "I'm just shaky."

He stopped running and tipped her carefully over a rail, onto the deck of a boat.

"Try to get below," he shouted in her ear. He unsheathed his knife, slashed at the moorings, then vaulted onto the deck. He lunged to a small, enclosed cabin. There was a sound of splintering glass. Moments later he disappeared inside.

Disoriented, bewildered, she forced her chilled muscles to work. She didn't trust her shaky balance on the streaming wet deck. She crawled past the cabin Michael had entered until she reached some kind of flattened door.

Think nautical. Maybe that was the hatch. She tried the latch. It was locked. She stumbled toward the cabin again as the boat's powerful engine growled to life.

She managed to grab hold of the edge of the narrow doorway as Michael slammed the boat into reverse and gunned the engine. It roared out of the slip. The water was so rough the boat bucked violently as they pulled out. It slammed against the neighboring boat and dragged along the side with a long, earsplitting screech.

"Is the hatch locked?" Michael asked without looking at her. As soon as the boat was clear of the slip, he spun the wheel hard and changed gears, and the boat's engine labored to comply.

"Yes," she gasped. She looked through the rain-smeared glass back toward shore. Fire trucks ringed the bombed vehicles, which were still blazing in spite of the storm's deluge. Silhouettes of armed men raced toward the dock.

"Get down," he told her.

She got down.

More gunfire. Some of the bullets may have struck their boat. She wasn't sure. With her head so close to the deck, the roar of the engine filled her ears. The boat creaked in complaint as Michael threw the throttle wide open. He returned fire in short, sharp bursts. Then the gunfire ceased.

She couldn't see anything so she closed her eyes and waited. It felt like a long time. Nothing was stable, nothing. They rose and fell, shuddering with each wave they hit. With the small cabin door broken, they were exposed to the storm. Frigid, filthy water swirled around her.

She thought of sliding out the open doorway with the next toss of the waves, and she groped until she found something that was bolted to the deck. She wrapped an arm around it, anchoring herself in place.

At last, Michael said, "Okay. We're out of gunshot range. Mary. You can get up now."

She nodded in the dark. It sounded good in theory.

A hand connected with her shoulder, groped down her arm and tightened in a grip just above her elbow. "Come on," he coaxed.

With his help, she forced her cramped and trembling body upright. He pulled her back against him with one arm and held her tight, while he maintained a strong grip on the steering wheel with the other. The control dials provided a slight illumination. Beyond the tiny cabin she could see the Lake swelling into waves that had to be as high as fifteen feet.

Michael put his mouth by her ear. "How bad off are you?"

She said through numb lips, "I'm pretty depleted."

"I want you to do one last thing if you can," he told her. "We need to try to get farther out into the bay. Take the wheel and hold us on our course while I break into the galley. It'll be just for a few minutes. Can you do that?"

She nodded. He pulled her in front of the steering wheel. Her cold hands and feet were about as wieldy as blocks of wood, and she had lost most of the strength in her grip, so she wedged her forearms in between the spokes of the wheel. She felt the power of the storm vibrating through the tension in the structure.

Michael disappeared. She kept her hold on the wheel by leaning her body against it. She held on through a dark, swirling space of time, while the engine strained and the boat rose and plummeted again and again.

Then he was back, shouldering through the narrow doorway. He came up behind her and enveloped her in a dry blanket.

"Waste of a g-good blanket," she stuttered. Her clothes were as sodden as if she'd tripped and fallen in the water.

"There's more down below."

He reached over to turn off the engine and pulled her away from the wheel.

"What are you doing?" she gasped.

It was terrifying to hear the sound of the engine die away, to be replaced by the wild sounds of wind and rain and the interminable roar of the Lake.

"There's nothing more we can do," he said. "The boat's engine is too small—we're not making any headway against the storm. We have to trust Astra now, and the entities that are allied with her. Come on."

He clamped an arm tight around her and supported her drunken progress along the treacherous slippery deck. Then he transferred his grip to around her waist. He half-carried her down the narrow steps to the galley, twisting to slam the hatch shut behind them.

A battery-powered emergency light was fastened high against one wall. By its faint glow she could see a tiny kitchenette and a small table bolted to the floor, surrounded by booth seats. Against the far wall of the kitchenette was a narrow doorway that led to darkness.

The boat rolled, and Michael staggered. He pushed her into the nearest seat. "Can you strip off your wet clothes and shoes?"

"S-sure." She fumbled with the buttons of the flannel shirt but she couldn't feel her fingers, so she dragged it over her head and dropped the sodden material on the floor.

The boat creaked and groaned. It sounded like it was alive and in pain. Michael made his way to the shadowed doorway beyond the kitchenette.

She struggled to remove her wet shoes as he dragged two narrow mattresses onto the floor from bunks on either side of the doorway. He stacked them on top of each other. Then he opened a cabinet, pulled out a pile of blankets and pillows and threw them on the mattresses.

He walked back to her, maintaining his balance with bracing handholds on nearby cabinets. She managed to get her jeans unbuttoned and unzipped as he knelt in front of her. He took one of her narrow feet in his hands and stripped off her sock.

"Jesus," he said. He took her other foot and peeled the sock off. "Your feet are like ice. Lie back."

She complied, flopping back in the booth and lifting her hips when he told her to. He dragged her heavy wet jeans over her slim legs. She sighed in relief as the freezing denim left her skin.

Michael pulled her back to a sitting position. The blanket she'd kept draped across her shoulders fell away. She was naked except for her panties. He stared for a long silent moment at the high, gentle curve of her breasts, her narrow rib cage and the slight swell of her abdomen.

Her blue-tinged skin was raised with goose bumps and mottled with several small purplish marks. He gently touched the purple mark on her rib cage under her left breast, then the one at her collarbone.

"Jesus," he said again. "How many times did you get shot?"

"F-four or five," she replied. "I l-lost count."

His eyes were stark and black in the dim light. They shimmered with sudden wetness. "I'm so sorry," he said from the back of his throat. He pulled the blanket tight around her with hands that shook. "I didn't sense them hiding there. I never would have told you to run to the dock if I had. I didn't sense anything but that creature guarding the shoreline—"

"Shut up, Michael," she said wearily. A convulsive shudder rippled through her aching body. "It's not your f-fault. God, I feel like I'm never going to be warm again."

He reacted immediately, standing and drawing her to her feet. With one arm around her waist and the other protecting their progress against the roll of the boat, he helped her to the mattresses on the floor.

She crawled on them and, wracked with violent shivers, she fell face-first onto one of the pillows. She felt weight on her body increase as he piled more blankets on top of her. They smelled like mothballs.

The small room was in near total darkness, like a cave,

shot intermittently with white flashes of lightning that showed through two small, round portholes set high near the ceiling. Michael tucked cushions from the booth on either side of the makeshift bed. Then he lifted one corner of the blankets and slid the length of his naked body next to hers.

Compared with the hazardous chill of her body temperature, his skin felt furnace-hot. He pulled her against the wide bulk of his chest, wrapping his arms tight around her, and he hooked one heavily muscled leg over hers. She put her arms around him, rested her head on his chest and groaned as spasms racked her body.

"Shh," he murmured. He rubbed at her back, her arms and her legs. "It'll get better in a minute."

"I know," she gritted.

Soon the combined warmth from their bodies soaked in deep. Bit by bit the clench of her muscles loosened. She rubbed her cheek against the sprinkle of crisp hair on his chest, savoring his warmth and the simple animal comfort of being held. That was when she realized he was shaking almost as badly as she had been.

She tried to lift her head but his hold on her was too tight. She stroked the broad, taut muscles of his back. "Michael?"

In a voice so low and raw, she could barely hear it over the creak of the boat and the lash of the wind, he whispered, "I can't lose you. Not so soon after finding you again. Not after so long."

She was glad she had warmed enough so her reply could be steady and gentle. "You won't lose me. I'm not going anywhere. My memories are returning, and I've got my sense of identity back. I'm not about to let go when I've just started to really live. Did you see? I even shot your damn gun."

With one hand at the back of her head, he pressed her face into his neck. A smile threaded through the other emotions in his voice. "I know, I saw."

She stroked his hair. "Do you think I hit anything?"

"Probably not. But you made them duck for cover, which is the most important thing."

Was it? She relaxed further. "That's all right then."

"Yes." He pressed his lips to her forehead and kept his mouth there. "That's all right then."

The boat pitched and tossed, the movement unpredictable. Michael rolled onto his back and held her tight against him, one arm wrapped around her waist and his legs spread wide as he braced them both from the worst of the rolling.

She curled into his side, her head on his bare shoulder, one leg hooked over his. The beat of his heart was steady and calm under her ear. Soon she trusted his support so totally her body fell lax. She had used up too many of her resources to continue being afraid.

For a short while, seasickness tried to take hold. She couldn't decide if she would vomit or fall asleep.

With a cranky mutter, she focused and shifted something inside and the nausea vanished. Then her own exhausted body took her away from the whirling dark cabin into a darkness that went much deeper.

Chapter Ten

THE ENTITY WAS one of the great behemoths of Earth.

Born several thousand years ago, its body was carved from a massive sheet of ice that had once covered the northern hemisphere. It was three hundred and seven miles long, a hundred and eighteen miles wide, and nearly a thousand feet deep.

Humans ascribed a feminine gender to it, but the truth was that it had neither a male nor female spirit. Generally, it paid no more attention to the humans that relied upon it for sustenance, skimmed across its surface or played along its edges than a dog paid attention to its fleas.

It was also one of the oldest entities on Earth, and now it was dying. Parts of it already rotted with such cancers as decay and pollution and radiation poisoning, from the Cook Nuclear Power Plant in the southwestern part of Michigan, or the greater Chicago area, or the coastline along the city of Milwaukee in Wisconsin. Careless industrialization was slowly but surely bringing its temperature up to the equivalent of a long-lasting fever that would kill off all its marine life.

Because it was so immense, its death would take several decades or even as long as a century. For now, it lay in its rocky bed under an infinite sky, endlessly shifting throughout the interchanging seasons. It was most asleep during the winter, most awake during the summer, most restless during the greening season.

When it was asked if it would dance with the folk of the air, those stern towering thunder spirits, it accepted with easy pleasure. All creatures danced and mated in the spring. But then it was asked to do something more.

Lake Michigan chuckled to itself at the absurdity of the request. Searching for two tiny humanlike creatures along its vast surface was like looking for a pair of needles in a haystack.

Still, it bore some affection for the person that asked, who, while as tiny as a human creature, was after all at least as old as itself.

They had been friends for a long time.

So it would try.

Chapter Eleven

MARY DREAMED OF a darkness that creaked and shifted, of strong, bare, warm limbs that tangled with hers, and of a queasy stomach that never quite needed to empty, nor did it quite allow her to sink into complete unconsciousness.

At some point, her dream shifted outside, to the wild lash of rain and the tempestuous writhing of the Lake. There seemed something sexual in the commingling of energies, the gushing wetness of the roaring wind and the airy, champagne-like bubbling of the foamy waves.

Thunder rumbled like guttural laughter that echoed across the heavens. The sound intrigued her and drew her out of her body. She left Michael dozing, and traveled through the kitchenette and up the steps to the hatch.

Then she passed through the hatch, for it was only a physical barrier, and she stood on the pitching deck. The corporeal sting of the cold and rain could not touch her, but the storm's energy was exhilarating, and she raised a hand to it in gleeful salute.

Something vast chuckled overhead. Unafraid, she climbed to the top of the boat's cabin. Once there she crossed her legs and sat, perching on the roof as light as a thought, while the glow from her energy shone like a beacon in the darkness.

Something was happening. Something was coming. She had roused in response to it. She cocked her head and waited.

It came out of the deep so gently, at first she hadn't realized it had arrived.

Gradually she grew aware that the boat was cupped like a tiny toy held in colossal hands. A black, archetypical eye, huge as the mouth of a volcano, peered at her from below, and all the foaming water was the creature's streaming hair.

If she had been awake and in her physical body, she might have lost her battle with nausea. But she was dreaming and quite calm. She stood and moved to the edge of the boat so that she could better study the fabulous creature.

With a careful finger that could have crushed an ocean-faring ship, it tilted the boat to a more upright position.

You aren't human, it said. It had a pensive, siren's voice.

No, Mary said. *I guess I'm not.*

You look like one. That tremendous eye came closer to the water's surface and regarded her with grave curiosity. The creature said, *You are like the other one, my friend. You are older than I am.*

I don't feel very old, Mary told it. She perched on the rail and swung a foot. *I think it's because I've forgotten a lot of things.*

The entity hummed, the savage euphoria of the storm lingering in its words, *I could kill you and your companion.*

She shook her head. She still was not afraid, although she probably should have been. *You can't kill us. You could only destroy the bodies we inhabit. Eventually we would come back again.*

Why would you come back? The creature sang, its song yearning and mournful. *How would you come back?*

We have to come back, because our people owe a debt

to this world. She leaned forward, caught by the absolute loneliness in that massive black eye. Now that the storm's dance had been suspended the entity seemed forlorn, eternally sad. She held out a hand to it. *We owe a debt to you.*

And when you have paid it? it murmured.

She confessed in a whisper, *We must still come back because we can't go home. We have nowhere else to go.*

The primeval fathomless eye seemed to smile. *Sacred child,* it crooned. *Be at peace now and sleep.*

Released, she yawned and nodded, and turned to walk back into the galley. There she climbed back into her body with the matter-of-factness of a toddler climbing into bed. She fell into a profound, deep sleep.

She had no more dreams.

Chapter Twelve

SHE WAS NEVER sure what woke her the second time.

It couldn't have been the storm's end. As she surfaced to wakefulness, she sensed that they had been stationary for some time. She might have been disturbed by the scratchiness of the wool blankets piled around her shoulders, or the lumpiness of the bed, or perhaps by Michael's absence.

Whatever the cause, she yawned, rolled over and stared at the ceiling as she registered the changes in her environment.

A pale, thin light fell into the tiny wood-paneled room from the two portholes set high into the walls. The second change she noticed was the relative quiet. The roar of the storm and groans from the overstressed boat no longer assaulted her ears. Instead she could hear the quiet lap of water. The boat rocked gently as if it rested at dock, instead of pitching and tossing in high waves.

The air outside her nest felt damp and chilly on her exposed face and neck. She stretched and slipped one foot out from under the pile of blankets. Her questing toes told her the same tale.

Her body throbbed with phantom aches from wounds it hadn't had the time to fully assimilate. She pushed down the covers and stared at herself, her pink nipples crinkling in the cold. Silver scars dotted her torso. She touched one in wonder. It looked as if it were already months old.

Something insubstantial brushed into the room. The tiny hairs on the back of her arms rose. She yanked the covers up to her neck as she sat.

Nicholas's transparent, shimmery form appeared, and he knelt in front of her. She received an impression of black military-short hair, hawkish features and the glitter of his intelligent eyes.

Relaxing, she anchored the blanket more securely around her torso. "Nicholas," she said. "It's good to see you. How is your father?"

He has not yet passed, Nicholas said. *Perhaps there is still something that you can do for him.*

Exhaustion pulled at her bones. Healing herself from so many gunshot wounds yesterday had sorely strained her body's already taxed resources, but she tried not to let her weariness show on her face.

Just like any other family member of patients she had treated, Nicholas didn't need to see her own struggle. She had survived more than one brutal shift in the ER. She would survive this too. "I'll have to find some clothes," she said. "I need to eat something too. Do you think he will be all right for that long?"

He seems to be resting comfortably enough at the moment, the ghost said. He regarded her for a moment. *It cost you a great deal to come here so quickly. Thank you.*

She had the impulse to deflect what he said, but the gravity in his indistinct gaze wouldn't let her. Instead, she gave him a small smile. *You're very welcome.*

He rose to his feet and turned away. She had seen him do that before when he prepared to leave. It was as if the ghost needed to go through the same kind of gesture that he would have done if he had been alive.

Impulsively, she said, "Nicholas."

He paused to look over his shoulder at her.

No doubt this was not the time to talk about things. But she was afraid that there would never be a time to talk about things, unless she just made the talk happen.

She asked, "If you were offered a chance at resurrection, would you want to take it?"

That got his attention. He turned and kneeled in front of her, and his gaze turned piercing. *There is no chance at resurrection*, he said gently. *My body has been cremated.*

She shook her head. "I didn't mean resurrection with your original body, and I'm not promising that I can make it happen."

Nicholas lifted a wide shoulder in a shrug. *What are you talking about?*

While she knew she needed to move soon, right at the moment, sitting up straight seemed like too much effort. She leaned back against the nearby wall. It felt frigid against her bare shoulders.

At any other time, she would have taken a great deal of time to think about how to tactfully approach a difficult, delicate subject with a patient.

Now she said baldly, "Yesterday morning when I examined those injured drones, the only thing wrong with them was that their spirit was gone. Their bodies were strong and healthy. If they had been really alive, they would have recovered from their injuries just fine. I see that as a damn waste, don't you?"

He was smart. He was really smart, and he was familiar with the Deceiver's attributes and habits. She couldn't see the details of his face very well, but when he rose to pace the length of the small cabin, she could see that she didn't have to spell everything out for him.

Energy poured off of him. He said, his tone rapid and

bitter, *The Dark One has the ability to take over human bodies, but he isn't human. I am.*

She raised her eyebrows. "I'm not human either."

Listen to her, sounding all confident and accepting of who she was. She almost convinced herself.

He whirled to go down on one knee in front of her. Tension vibrated off of him in waves that were so tangible it felt nearly physical. She leaned forward, searching for any hint of what he was feeling in the blurred lines of his face.

"I really think it's possible," she said again, softly. "When I was looking at the two men, I could sense how the body and spirit were supposed to fuse together. But I can't promise you anything. All I can do is ask if you want to try. Even if we did succeed, taking over a drone's body would be a strange life for you, and I think in a lot of ways it would be a difficult one. What do you think? Are you willing at least to consider it?"

The hand he rested on his upraised knee tightened into a fist.

He said, *Yes.*

NICHOLAS LEFT TO go back to his father's side, taking his powerful, whirlwind emotions with him.

Left alone, she slumped back against the cold wall again until she started to shiver. The end of her braid had unraveled. She searched through the blankets and cushions until she found the rubber band. She snapped it back on the end of her tangled hair.

Then, starving, thirsty and curious, she climbed to her feet, shook out the top blanket and wrapped the bulky material sarong-like around her torso. With one hand, she held the blanket so she wouldn't trip over the edges. With the other, she held it anchored across her breasts. It was an awkward way to try to keep covered.

The bare floorboards were so cold they made the bones

of her feet ache, but that couldn't be helped. Her sodden socks and shoes were unfit to wear.

She stepped gingerly into the kitchenette and glanced around.

Not a kitchenette. Remember, think nautical. This would be a galley. Whatever, the galley was a kitchenette. A small refrigerator was built into the wall. She unlatched the door and peered inside, unsurprised but disappointed to find it empty.

When she saw Michael's knife resting in its battered leather sheath on the table, she took the blanket, folded it in half and used the long blade to saw a slit through the middle of the fold. Then she poked her head through the slit to wear it like a poncho. The corners still dragged on the ground, but it covered better than before.

She looked for her clothes and shoes. Neither her nor Michael's things were anywhere to be found. That seemed to be her cue to exit.

She ascended the stairs to the deck.

The first thing she saw was the placid surface of the Lake, glimmering in the silvery early morning light. The sun had yet to appear on the horizon. A thin layer of clouds draped across the pale sky like the last people to leave an all-night party. Land curved to either side of her, rising into a sharp incline from a rocky shore where gentle waves lapped at a jumble of rocks. The incline was covered with a thick cluster of pine trees and a tangle of underbrush.

The boat had been moored alongside a weathered pier, the nose pointed toward land, opposite a smaller, battered motorboat. As she gained the surface of the deck, she realized the pier was located in the relative shelter of a small, shallow bay.

Her socks and dingy jeans, the bullet-torn flannel shirt and her shoes were arranged on the deck to dry in the open air. Michael's clothes had been spread out beside hers.

She heard quiet voices. As she turned the corner of the cabin, a steady breeze ruffled the edges of her makeshift poncho and brought with it the acrid scent of wood smoke. She shivered and pulled the wool closer around her torso.

At the land end of the pier there was a space of beach more or less level and cleared of rock. A path with rough staggered steps led from the beach up the incline into the woods. Michael and a tiny old woman were on the beach, sitting on two large, sawed-off logs in front of a small campfire.

Her gaze lingered on Michael. He wore rumpled black cotton pants with a drawstring waist and a flannel-lined anorak. His chest and feet were bare. Looking weary but relatively peaceful, he leaned forward to feed sticks to the bright, flickering flame. He was relaxed. Seeing that, she relaxed too.

Her attention left him and centered on the old woman, who leaned her elbows on knees almost as thin as the sticks that Michael fed to the fire. The ground around the woman was littered with bags, two thermos flasks and food containers. Her short white hair stood around her head in wild, fluffy wisps. She wore canvas mules without socks, baggy sweatpants, an overlarge knit sweater and a denim jacket that was at least a couple of decades old.

It was such a small frail body to house such a strong will. Mary swallowed in an effort to ease her dry throat and hesitated. For the first time, she realized she was jealous of the old woman, and afraid.

She hadn't made any noise discernable over the Lake's constant murmuring, but the pair on the shore looked in her direction at the same time.

Michael stood. "Good morning," he said. His quiet voice carried over the water. "How are you feeling? Do you need help?"

Now she was on her feet and had been moving around, she wasn't feeling as steady as she would have liked. Still, she shook her head. Under the combined weight of their gazes, she found a space in the boat's railing where a hinged bar had been propped open. She stepped onto the pier.

A sharp gust of wind lifted a flap of the blanket and exposed the long line of one slender, honey-colored leg up to her waist. Though her thin nylon panties didn't offer much cover, she was grateful she wasn't totally nude under the poncho. She gripped the edges of the recalcitrant blanket to hold it in place as she walked toward the waiting pair.

The old woman watched her progress with a neutral expression. Her wrinkled face was classic. Mary could see in it the ghost of the beautiful woman who had appeared in her vision and the dream. With a pronounced bone structure and high cheeks, she could have been at home on an American Indian reservation, or a Greek island, or the streets of Moscow.

Michael said, "After the trip we had, I thought you would sleep longer. If I'd known you would wake this early, I would have brought you the dry clothes Astra brought. At least you've managed to find a solution for yourself."

"It'll do for now, but I could wish for a little less breeze," she said wryly. "And my feet are freezing." She shook her head at the seat Michael offered. Instead she held herself erect as she turned to meet the shrewd black gaze that watched her with an inscrutable patience. Feeling at a complete loss, she said, "Hello, Astra."

Chapter Thirteen

ASTRA'S DARK, UPTURNED eyes filled with a sudden glitter of tears, and her delicate, papery expression reformed. "Thank you, Creator," Astra breathed. "It's been so long."

Without warning, a huge, tangled wave of emotion welled inside of Mary, like the creature from her dream that had risen from an immeasurable depth.

Deep gladness, grief, anger and pain, and a baffled kind of love. To her intense shock and embarrassment, a sob broke out of her. The sound cracked through the quiet.

Astra lifted both hands to her. She sank to her knees and took them. Then she leaned forward to put her face in the old woman's lap. Her shoulders clenched as she tried to rein in her emotion. Astra leaned over and held her tight.

"I'm so sorry," Mary said when she could speak. Her breathing had turned ragged as she struggled for control. "Sometimes I don't understand myself."

"Don't hover, Michael," Astra snapped over her head. "This is mine to deal with. Go away."

"Mary, would you like me to stay?" Michael asked. She felt his large, warm hand press against her back.

"It's okay," she said, swiping at her eyes and nose with the corner of her blanket. Regardless of whether or not Astra could hear her, she added telepathically, *I need to talk with her, but I would appreciate it if you didn't go far.*

I won't. Call if you need me.

Thank you.

She felt his fingers brush her tangled hair. His departure was noiseless, but she knew without looking when his presence had moved away. She lifted her head from Astra's lap and sat back on her heels, rubbing her scratchy eyes.

After a keen, searching glance, Astra turned brisk.

"I brought down hot tea and water, biscuits and bacon," she said, taking one of the two thermos bottles and pouring a measure of hot brown liquid into its lid. "There are more amenities up at the cabin, of course, but I also have a couple of visitors. I thought it would be better if we could have a little privacy before we head up."

Mary said, "When Nicholas brought your message, he told us that his father is here."

"Yes. Nicholas's young nephew Jamie is here as well." Astra's gaze stayed focused on the hot drink she held. "Michael and I also didn't want to leave or disturb you, so I fixed a snack to bring down here for when you woke. Here, drink up. It's sweet."

"Thank you," Mary said.

She sipped with care at the steaming cup. She wanted the tea badly but her thirst was too strong to be assuaged by delicate sips. Before she could ask, Astra handed her the second opened flask. She set the tea aside to gulp at the cool fresh-tasting water until the flask was empty.

In silence, Astra offered her other things. Unable to face solid food just yet, she shook her head at the plastic container filled with biscuits and bacon. When the older woman dug into nearby canvas bags and held out a pair of thermal socks, she gladly accepted them and tugged them over her chilled feet.

Then she edged as close to the campfire as she could without sitting in the middle of the coals and setting herself on fire. After she had tucked the blanket around her cross-legged form and picked up her tea again, Astra spoke.

"What is it that you don't understand about yourself?" the old woman asked as she picked up a long stick and poked at the fire. "Why you bawled, or why you're so angry with me?"

Shocked by the directness, she took a deep breath. Unsure of how to respond, she hid her face in her cup. The steam from the liquid warmed the cold end of her nose. "I didn't know I was so obvious."

"You know," Astra said after a moment. "You probably don't remember this, at least not yet, but the decision to come after the Deceiver wasn't just a group one. Each of you had to make the decision for yourself. The understanding was that if either one in a mated pair chose not to come on this journey, that one's partner would abide by that choice and stay home."

"No, I don't remember that," she muttered, keeping her head bent.

"All of you chose to go after the Deceiver with me, and you followed me here. None of us could have known how long this fight would take." The seams around her mouth deepened. They seemed to cut as deep into her face as fractured granite cut into the earth. "Is that why you're angry?"

Mary listened intently, picking through the information Astra offered in an effort to see if any of it matched with her emotions. When the other woman finished speaking, she shook her head.

"That's not it," she said. The thermos lid of tea had cooled enough for her to drain it. "I could say that seeing you felt like coming home, but it doesn't. Other than one recurring dream where we all drank the poison, I don't even remember what our home was like. Seeing you feels more like seeing some long-lost member of the family."

"Do you even know why you're angry?"

She grimaced. "This doesn't make any sense. It isn't rational, and I know it's not fair, but I'm mad at you because you've been with Michael for so long when I wasn't able to."

Astra's face went blank. Then she barked out a laugh. "That explains it too," she said. They fell silent again. Astra sighed and looked over the water. Her expression turned dreamy. "I don't know if it's a good thing or not that you don't remember home," she said. "We could see colors that humans can't even imagine. When we heard the vibration of each other's energy, it was like listening to the most beautiful singing imaginable. I remember everything, and it hasn't made it any easier to be here."

On impulse, Mary reached out and touched Astra's knee. Astra covered her fingers with a gnarled, blue-veined hand. She felt a subtle, delicate probing through their joined hands, quite unlike the straightforward vigor and assured authority in Michael's presence.

In a deliberate act of trust she forced herself to maintain physical contact. She thought she caught a glimmer of approval in those bird-bright eyes before Astra's manner changed.

"Come on, fool," the old woman scolded, leaning forward to reopen the plastic container of food and shove it under her nose. "Eat a biscuit. Michael told me everything that happened yesterday. You've accomplished some undeniable miracles, but that body of yours has taken some harsh punishment. There's a limit to what you can demand of it. Be nice to it and feed it something."

"I'm pretty tired," Mary admitted. Obediently she chose a biscuit, broke it in half and took a bite. To her intense pleasure, it was light and flaky and rich with a buttery taste. It melted in her mouth. She bolted the rest of it down and, having rediscovered her appetite, she reached for a slice of bacon.

Astra poured her another cup of tea. "I'm glad the Lake likes you and decided to bring you two here."

Mary stared, the half-eaten piece of bacon held suspended in front of her open mouth. She lowered her hand, swallowed hard and looked over her shoulder. The sun had crested the horizon with a glorious blaze of color. The serene water winked with a reflected array of light.

"I had a dream about the Lake last night," she said. "But I thought it was just a dream." Feeling like the fool Astra had called her, she hurried on to say, "I mean, I dreamt that I had a strange conversation with this entity that—it didn't seem to make any sense, so I thought I made it up."

Astra chuckled. "Since when did you get to decide that all creatures have to make sense? You don't make sense all the time. You just said so. What does 'make sense' mean anyway, operate on human logic?"

Her cheeks washed with color. She muttered, "I'm newly reawakened to all this, remember?"

"I know, I know." Still grinning, Astra shook her head. "Don't mind me laughing at you. You managed not to jump in after it when it sang to you, like a lot of humans do when they hear the water spirits. They're beautiful but eerily seductive. Half the time you can't trust a word they say. Whatever the Lake coaxed out of you made it happy, so you did just fine."

Mary stared at her, appalled. "You trusted it with our rescue?"

"I trusted it as much as you can trust any wild creature, to do what is in its own nature," Astra said. She looked out over the water with a flash of calculation in her black eyes. "I figured you and Michael would end up either safely dead or back here. Turns out I was right."

Mary threw her half-eaten piece of bacon in the fire. She snapped, "It creeps me out how you and Michael talk so casually of killing and dying. I like being alive, thank you very much. It's taken me a lot of hard damn work to get here.

I would appreciate it if you would treat my life with more respect."

Astra looked at her, all amusement gone. "I do, you know," she said. "In all the ways that really matter."

She covered her face with her hands, breathing hard.

She forced herself to think of the difference between physical death and total dissolution. If they died, they could be reborn. If they were destroyed, they were gone forever. She remembered the keening noise that had come from Michael's trapped spirit, a sound so unbearable she would do anything to avoid hearing it again.

"Okay," she muttered. "Like I said, I'm still getting used to this. I'm sorry."

"No, I'm sorry," Astra told her. "I'm too old and jaded. I've had this single goal in front of me, leading me around like some damned pillar of fire for so long I sometimes forget about other things that are also important. You're right to remind me. All life is sacred."

"Speaking of which," Mary said. Astra's attention sharpened on her, her black gaze hardening. "I promised Nicholas that I would see if there was anything I could do for his father as soon as I could."

Astra hunched her thin shoulders in the shabby denim jacket. "Jerry is very sick." She gave Mary a keen look. "Maybe you can do something to help him. It would be a blessing if you could. He's an old friend and a good ally. But you also almost died a couple of times yesterday, and I know you're running on empty. There's no shame in admitting that it would be asking too much from you."

Mary looked at the path. She said, "If he wants my help, I'll have a look at him and do what I can. I can rest afterward."

Astra threw the rest of the tea on the campfire, gathered up the various scattered items and stuffed them into the canvas bags at her feet, pushed against her knees and stood. "Come on then."

Mary stood as well. Even though she was not a tall

woman, Astra was still several inches shorter. She paused, looking at the fire that sputtered fitfully. "Shouldn't we finish putting it out?" she asked.

Astra picked up the bags and grunted, "Michael will see to it. He'll get the wet clothes and shoes too, and bring them up."

He's not your servant, Mary thought. Immediately she felt ashamed of herself. With an effort, she managed to keep her surge of resentment from showing in her expression.

Instead she said with care, "He's tired too."

A sly blackbird gaze slid sideways toward her. "Yes, but unlike you, who's sensibly exhausted and no doubt quite happy to think of a hot bath and a real bed in your near future, he's itching to do something manly and useful. Hovering is not useful. Cleaning up our mess down here is."

Mary struggled with her unruly temper. Astra was her elder and held valuable information. She should show respect.

She asked, "Can I carry those bags for you?"

Astra chuckled and handed to her the heavier one filled with the food and thermoses. "So polite. You were brought up well in this life, I can see. Michael was a gifted, horrible little boy whom his parents spoiled dreadfully. I couldn't stand him for years. I don't think he liked me much either, but I was useful to him. We've made our peace, though." She tilted her head back, white hair waving in the languid breeze. "Just wait and see. You and I will too."

Mary struggled with mortification as she followed Astra's slight figure up the path. She gritted, "I didn't realize I was that obvious."

"To me you are," Astra said over her shoulder. "And I could go down on my knees and thank the Creator for it. I'm a paranoid old bitch, and I have fretted so over you, for such a long time. But you, bless your heart, are as clear and as transparent as that silly Lake can be on a sunny day. There isn't a deceitful, corrupt atom in your spirit. Michael tried to tell me, but I had a hard time listening to him. Sometimes I just need to see things for myself."

"You and he have some things in common," Mary said.

A sharp twig jabbed her foot through the sole of her sock. She watched the path with more care.

An old green awareness canopied them. The forest they moved through felt similar to the one where Michael's cabin was located, only more intense and alive. The rustling of the wind in the trees sounded like whispers. Greedily she took breath after breath of the rich fresh air. A tightness that had settled in her chest, one that she hadn't even realized she carried, eased away.

"He and I have discussed this," Astra said. "We share some of our least attractive traits. I acquired mine over the centuries in order to survive. Unfortunately, I think Michael was just born with his. You have my deepest sympathies." She stopped moving, and her voice changed, acquiring a lighthearted malice. "Oh, hello. Eavesdroppers never hear anything good about themselves, you know. It's axiomatic."

Mary raised her head. They had reached the end of the incline and the trees. Beyond Astra's shabby little figure, she glimpsed a large, sunlit clearing with a cabin at one end.

Michael lounged on a large cedar swing suspended in a sturdy frame located at the edge of the forest, not fifteen feet away. His big body looked relaxed, but the tiger was roused and close underneath his skin.

The swing was positioned so an occupant could look at the small bay below through a break in the trees. He tilted back his black-haired head. His smiling gray gaze met Astra's in a connection that was like the metallic clash of two slender rapiers.

Then he looked at Mary. His eyes and face warmed. "You'll soon catch on that one of Astra's favorite games is to bait someone until she gets a reaction. She considers it amusing." He switched to telepathy. *How are you holding up?*

About how you would expect when reuniting with

someone after lifetimes, she said. *Complicated. Tired. Emotional. Okay, I think.*

"It's considered bad manners to listen in on other people's telepathic conversations." Astra said, and switched back to her chatty voice. "But I gave up worrying about my manners long ago. I do it all the time now." She said to Michael, "She's going to have a look at Jerry and see what she can do for him. After that, I'm going to dunk her in a hot bath, throw a nightgown on her and stuff her in bed. Would you make sure the campfire is out and bring up your things? We'll put your shoes by the stove. With any luck, they'll be dry by lunchtime."

"Of course," he said. He rolled off the swing and rose to his feet with an easy grace.

The movement acted like a trigger. Mary flashed back to the previous night, and the startling destructive beauty of Michael's balletic movements, the chill of the freezing rain and the two black muzzles that had turned on her, filled with hot, metallic death.

A spasmodic shudder rippled through her body. Her blood pressure took a sharp, quick drop, and she pressed both hands to her shaking mouth.

In two swift strides he was in front of her, gripping her upper arms. "What is it?" he asked, his voice sharp. "What's wrong?"

She shook her head and covered her eyes, unable to speak. Then she felt Astra interpose her calm energy between them.

"She's been traveling at the speed of light over some rough terrain over the last few days," the old woman said to Michael, as she put a gnarled hand on his chest and pushed him back. "Give her some space and let her react."

He resisted her feeble push. "Mary?"

It was too much. She felt too many complicated nuances with too many people. Too many subterranean, half-understood emotions.

She pointed the gun and emptied the clip at them.

Just like Michael had taught her.

The physician in her noted with clinical detachment her clammy skin, shaking hands, her sick sense of nausea and racing heart rate, and diagnosed post-trauma stress. Instinctively she made the decisions that would slow her heart rate down and ease her other symptoms.

She said hoarsely, "I can't talk right now."

"Why not?" His gaze was sword sharp.

"I need some time to process what's happened."

He stepped around Astra and moved in close to her. He moved in too close, and she knew he did it deliberately. He was crowding her, trying to get her to look up at him. "Mary, look at me."

It was too much. She dropped her hand and looked up. "Michael, I shot a gun at two people," she said between her teeth. "I swore once that I would never shoot a gun. Sometimes I don't know who I am, so I need you to give me a little bit of space."

His expression went cold and still. His fingers loosened and slid away from her arms. "I understand," he said. "I'll be down at the boat if either of you need me." He stepped around them and disappeared down the path.

She stared down the path where he had disappeared. "I didn't mean it that way."

"Of course you did," Astra said in exasperation. "What you didn't mean to do was hurt him. Well, his feelings are hurt and that's his choice. He didn't have to take it that way."

She said, "I need to go after him."

"No, you don't. Both of you are stressed, overtired and overwrought, which magnifies everything. Just leave things be for a while." Astra paused, then snapped, "Goddammit, listen to me. I don't have time to mother-hen you two. While you're busy playing soap opera, we have real problems."

Mary remembered the sick man in the cabin, and she turned back to Astra. "I'm sorry," she said. "You're right."

"Of course I'm right." The other woman snorted as if any other possibility were inconceivable.

Mary took several deep breaths until she felt steadier. "I've been talking to you for under an hour, and I've already lost count of how many times I've apologized."

"Some people might take that as a sign that they need to shut up for a while," Astra said as she stomped off toward the cabin.

Mary started to laugh. The sound seemed somewhat lost and forlorn. It earned her a glare, so she struggled to contain herself.

As she followed Astra, she looked over the well-tended scene that spanned several acres. Fruit trees dotted the clipped lawn. An extensive herb bed curved around the cabin. A large vegetable garden covered the south end of the clearing. On the far side of the building she saw a corner of a greenhouse, and beyond that a tangle of what appeared to be black raspberry bushes. A couple of other small buildings dotted the sunlit space.

It was an idyllic place. She imagined what it would be like to winter here in profound isolation, with the thunderous grays and gorgeous icy whites of the Lake, and the sound of the wind as it sliced through the trees while snow blanketed the clearing. She couldn't know for sure without experiencing it, but she thought she might love it.

The cabin was more spacious and well appointed than she expected, with a large communal space that contained the kitchen, dining and living room area. Several doorways led off from the main area. A thin staircase, so steep it was almost a ladder, led to an overhead loft.

Later, she would find out the doorways led to a couple of bedrooms, a bathroom, a mud and laundry room and a locked room that held an office with the latest electronics and a compact lethal armory.

As she and Astra stepped inside, a tall, dark-haired teenage boy appeared in one of the doorways. He was large and gangly like a colt, with a hint of more growth in the width of his shoulders. The utter misery in his reddened eyes made Mary wince with sympathy.

He's a good boy, but watch what you say around him, Astra said to her. *Unlike his grandfather and his uncle, he doesn't have a clue about what is really going on.*

Mary nodded.

Astra said aloud, "Jamie, Mary's a doctor. She's going to take a look at your grandpa."

Sudden hope flared to life in his young, dark eyes. "Good." His mouth trembled. "He's not doing so well."

Mary set aside everything else to deal with later. She smiled at Jamie as she walked over. "It's nice to meet you. Why don't you take a break right now? Eat something if you can, go outside and get a breath of fresh air, while I talk to your grandpa."

"You'll come get me if you need me?" the boy asked, his gaze clinging to hers. "If—if anything happens?"

"Of course I will." She touched his shoulder and walked into the bedroom, and closed the door firmly in the boy's anxious face.

THE MAN ASLEEP on the bed had been handsome once. The remnant of it lingered in his strong, haggard features, and in the gray and black hair that fell to the pillow. She thought she saw a shadow of what his son had looked like, and a hint of what his grandson might achieve one day.

She could sense Nicholas's presence in the room, but he didn't take visible form. Then she put all thought of him aside. It was time to focus on the reason why she was here.

She sat in the chair that had been pulled close to the bed. It was still warm from Jamie's body. She leaned forward, took one of the sick man's big weathered hands and cradled it between both of hers.

It was a strange, quiet examination. Not only was Jerry a complete stranger, but she realized that he was also the first human—not counting the drones—that she might use her newly recovered skills on.

She sent her awareness over the surface of his cool skin,

then sank deep into his body. She explored his rangy, musculoskeletal frame and ran along pathways of his circulatory system with a reflexive pleasure even as she observed his symptoms, noted the lung damage from years of smoking and diagnosed severe pulmonary heart disease.

She sent small pulses of energy in targeted bursts to clear out the worst of the blockage she found in his pulmonary artery, and worked to strengthen the right ventricle even as she discovered answers to questions she had not thought to ask.

She sensed the difference between this man, who was purely human, and the forcefulness of spirit radiated by Michael, Astra and the Deceiver. The difference was like stepping out of a well-lit room into a sunny day. Both were powered with light, but the sun's illumination was so much stronger.

Twenty minutes later, she finished what would have taken several hours of risky open-heart surgery. When she pulled her awareness out of his body, she discovered a shimmering, transparent presence kneeling at her side.

He needs to take things easy and eat a careful diet, but he is going to be fine now, she said to Nicholas. She smiled at him. *And if he doesn't stop smoking, I'm going to kick his ass.*

The ghost turned to her. *If there is anything I can ever do for you, call me and I will come.*

She shook her head. *You already came once without asking. And that's not why I did this.*

The blur of his strong, hawkish features seemed to flash with a smile. *That is why I will come.*

She felt enveloped in warm male energy and felt something against her skin, as if lips brushed across her cheek. She caught her breath and held it, raising a hand in wonder.

The presence melted away.

Smiling and tearful, she stood. She held on to the back of the chair as the room whirled. The psychic surgery had been relatively brief and controlled, but it had taken concentrated effort to manipulate the energy in such a way that it would promote healing without damaging an already faltering, delicate system.

After the fact, she felt distant from everything, as if she were surrounded by bullet-riddled glass. She was lightheaded from too many powerful, unresolved emotions. All she wanted to do was to lay her head down on something dry and stationary.

Astra was wiping off the kitchen counters when she walked out of the bedroom. The old woman's face was grim, her wrinkled mouth pursed tight. "How'd it go?"

She said, "I am a goddess without compare. Nubile young men should lay flowers and chocolates and large monetary contributions at my feet."

A startled smile broke over Astra's face. "Really?"

"He was dying, but I'm sure you already knew that. He needs more rest and a careful diet. I want to examine him again to see if he needs more work, but for now he'll do." She staggered, and Astra hurried over to put an arm around her waist. Her breath hitched. "Okay, I need to lie down now."

"Come on, you'll rest more comfortably if we get you clean first."

Her mind shut down and she let herself be bullied by Astra, who ran her a hot, deep bath, sprinkled with rose-scented bubble bath, and made her strip off the poncho and her underwear and climb into the tub.

Then Astra knelt by the tub, unraveled her tangled braid and helped wash her hair. Afterward Astra brushed out the unruly tangles while Mary rested in the liquid warmth.

Tears prickled at the back of her eyes at the old woman's gentle touch. The kindness touched all the raw places in her soul. She was so bone weary. She had been beyond terrified too many times over the last couple of days, and she had seen good people die, and she mourned Justin, and she wished Nicholas hadn't been murdered, and she had hurt Michael's feelings.

She said, "I need to talk to Michael."

"Not until after you've both had a chance to rest."

She opened her eyes and looked at Astra, who sighed. "I will tell him that you wanted to talk, but I put my foot down. How's that?"

"Okay," she whispered.

When Astra was through with her hair, she wrapped it in a towel and left the bathroom so Mary could finish washing in privacy, returning a few minutes later with a simple cotton nightgown, a new toothbrush still in its wrapper and a clean pair of cotton socks.

"I used to get visitors like Jerry and Jamie from all over," Astra said when Mary asked about the toothbrush. "I've had friends among the Potawatomi, the Shawnee and the Ojibwa nations. I don't have your spectacular gift for healing, but I do have some small talent. Those visitors have fallen off in this generation, but sometimes Jerry will still bring someone by who needs help, so I've learned to keep a few things handy."

"Whatever the reason, I'm grateful," she said when her teeth were clean.

"I'm going to tuck you in the loft, I think," Astra told her.

They made their way up the narrow stairs to a bedroom simply furnished with a double bed, a dresser, a battered armchair and a bookcase half-filled with paperbacks.

Astra drew back the covers and Mary fell onto the bed. She didn't move as the covers were tucked around her.

She realized another truth. She whispered, "I have missed you."

Astra echoed softly, "I have missed you."

With a great effort, she managed to ask another question. "Is it safe?"

"It is safe, and you can rest," the old woman told her, then added a warning. "But you need to count this safe time in days, not weeks."

She couldn't think ahead. She turned her face away. She

had the impulse to say something else, but a small frail hand came down on her forehead. Something quick and deft and slippery happened. She lost what she was going to say. As she tried to pay attention to that slippery something, she fell asleep.

Chapter Fourteen

THERE WERE TWO ways to react to what had happened the previous evening. Was the glass half empty, or was it half full?

The half-empty glass held rage and frustration. Yes, he went there, but after a few hours, he calmed down and started to think.

The half-full glass was absolutely frothing with sharp interest. Why did Mary and Michael push so hard to get to water? They could have changed direction. They could have avoided all the major highways and gone to ground, so to speak. Instead they chose a risky, difficult path that had, by all accounts, cost them a great deal, and they did it just as a major storm broke.

What did these new puzzle pieces tell him?

He didn't know yet. They could have gotten on the boat to go anywhere. They could even have used it as a convoluted feint. Maybe they doubled back to shore at another location on the Lower Peninsula, although that didn't feel right. Not when his people told him that they had sustained multiple injuries and risked death to do it.

No, he thought they were heading somewhere else. The problem was, if they survived their injuries, and the storm didn't sink them, there were so many choices open to them once they got on that boat—the Upper Peninsula, Wisconsin, even Illinois.

He needed to scare up a few more puzzle pieces and see how they all fit together. And by damn, he hoped they hadn't yet met up with Astra.

As he mulled over the different possible reasons for Michael and Mary's actions, he gazed out the window of a black SUV and Martin drove them to their destination.

Jerry Crow lived within walking distance of the Lake, in an older rural neighborhood with smallish ranch houses and acre-large yards. Newer housing developments with large, expensive homes bordered the neighborhood. Dawn had broken. Gold arced across the sky, and rosy pink topped the green trees in the distance.

He studied the elder Crow's property with a critical eye as Martin drove up the gravel drive. The house was well kept but modest, with light blue aluminum siding and white shutters. The land itself was probably worth twice as much as the house, if the surrounding developments were anything to go by. A 2005 Ford truck sat in the driveway, along with a 1994 Chevrolet Impala. Both vehicles looked well maintained too.

Despite the early hour, he could tell that nobody was home before they even reached the end of the drive.

He murmured, "Where have you gone this early in the morning, Jerry? And why did you go there?"

A second black SUV followed theirs. It parked when they parked, and his two new FBI drones, Ryan and Alison, climbed out of the car to meet him and Martin.

"Canvass the neighbors," he told the pair. "See if anybody knows where Crow has gone, or when he'll be back." He paused. "If anyone asks, tell them you're investigating his son's death and have a few questions to ask him. We want the right story to get back to him, in case any of his neighbors think to give him a call."

They nodded and took off. He walked up the path to the front door, while Martin followed.

How did he want to play this? Stealthy or straightforward?

Sometimes he wished he had Michael's aptitude for stealth. Someone might see him if he broke a pane of glass to get in the house. If they contacted Jerry, he might be scared off from coming home. This was the kind of neighborhood where folks looked out for one another.

He didn't even know why he tried the knob.

The door was unlocked.

He chuckled. Guess it was that kind of neighborhood too.

"Keep watch," he said to Martin after they stepped inside. Martin stayed obediently by the front door, looking out.

He strolled through the quiet, empty house. It was modestly decorated with older furniture, and neat without being fussy. The faint odor of cigarette smoke tinged the air, but he did not find it unpleasant. American Indian artwork hung on the walls. Good pieces too, not flea market cast-off stuff. Out the back, a round sweat lodge was tucked into a corner of the yard, covered with tarps.

There were three bedrooms, which was more than he would have guessed. One bedroom had been turned into an office. Clothes were strewn all over another bedroom.

He eyed that room with interest. They were clothes that a young male might wear, mostly jeans and T-shirts. The third bedroom was simple and tidy, with a double bed that was neatly made, two nightstands and a dresser.

An opened letter rested on top of the dresser. He recognized the official seal. It was Nicholas's death notification.

This was Jerry's bedroom.

He sat at the foot of the bed and contemplated the dresser.

For all that he worked to avoid it, he was intimately acquainted with death. He had killed so many people. Still, the aftermath of death was not something that he usually concerned himself with.

Nicholas had been killed just a few days ago. Because he had been murdered, there would have been an autopsy before the body was released for burial. He wondered where Nicholas's body was, or if he had been cremated. Perhaps Jerry had requested that his son be brought home, or Nicholas might be buried in a soldier's grave in Arlington National Cemetery.

If that was the case, Jerry might be traveling to the funeral.

He checked under the bed and around the room. Suitcases lay tucked in the corner of the closet.

The old Crow hadn't gone far then. Perhaps he had taken an outing with the young male who stayed in the second bedroom.

An opened pack of Marlboro Reds lay on one of the nightstands, along with an old-fashioned metal lighter and an ashtray.

He helped himself to a cigarette, lit up and took a deep drag. Smoke filled his lungs. He could tell right away that his host body was no stranger to smoking. The nicotine hit his system. He settled back against the headboard of Jerry's bed and relaxed with a sigh.

What to do.

Should he focus on this and let his forces churn through the process of the larger hunt? Or should he leave this to his FBI drones and focus on some other angle of the hunt?

Jerry Crow wasn't so much a long shot as he was a wild card. He had no way of knowing if questioning Crow would lead anywhere until after he had done it. He turned the monkey's head from side to side to stretch tight neck muscles.

The front door of the house opened and closed. Footsteps sounded in the hall. Alison appeared in the doorway. "One of Crow's neighbors told us that he kept a motorboat down at the dock at the end of the road. She said she saw Jerry and his grandson head out early a few days ago, and she hasn't seen them since. We checked the dock, and the space where he keeps his boat is empty."

He finished his cigarette leisurely and tapped out the stub.

A few days ago Nicholas had died, and a notifying officer, along with a chaplain, had come to deliver the news. Jerry left the house soon afterward, and he hadn't been seen since.

And he went out on the Lake.

They were such slender puzzle pieces to fit together. But they did fit.

He smiled at Alison. "I like this house, don't you?"

Obediently, she said, "Yes."

Of course, he knew she would say yes.

"We're going to use this place as our search headquarters while we wait to see if Jerry returns anytime soon. One of you get on the computer in the office to see if there's anything useful on it." He scooped up the pack of cigarettes, the lighter and ashtray and got to his feet. "And do something less obvious with our SUVs, will you? Right now they stand out like sore thumbs."

The drones got to work. Life was so peaceful when everybody did exactly what he said.

He wandered into the kitchen to see what Jerry had to eat in his refrigerator.

Chapter Fifteen

ASTRA WASHED DISHES with an excess of energy. As she flung items around, her mind operated on several different levels.

She had one overwrought healer tucked in the loft. One overwrought human boy asleep on the couch. One warrior sulking on the beach. One old man taking a nap. One anxious ghost.

Look at all of that drama, and none of it was relevant. May God protect her from a passel of fools. Worse, she was a fool to put up with all of it.

She looked out the window over the sink at the grove of fruit trees. She had planted those trees by seed so long ago. Now they were mature, and each year, they produced more bounty than she was able to use.

A long time ago, she had foreseen that she might need a sanctuary separate from the growing human population. She had searched until she found this small rocky island and made it her home.

The island was located north of Beaver Island and west of Garden Island. Only three-quarters of a mile long and little over a half a mile wide, it was absent from all but the oldest and most crudely drawn explorers' maps.

At first, she had needed to expend energy to hide the island from other eyes. Then, as the spirit of the island grew more aware, it turned eccentric and secretive. It became a participant in the process and learned to cloak itself.

Over the years, ships and pleasure boats passed by with increasing frequency. While their occupants might register the island long enough to navigate around the dangerous, broken shoreline, they soon forgot about it as they moved on to other, more pressing matters in their lives.

Now, aside from Michael and Mary, only a dwindling handful of people remembered the island's existence, or her existence either, for that matter. They were people who knew how to keep a secret—traditionally raised First Nation elders who sometimes went to their graves with a thousand years of knowledge locked in the treasure vaults of their minds because they hadn't found pupils trustworthy enough to teach.

As she had told Mary, those elders used to bring creatures of all species to her, creatures so injured or broken in body or spirit Astra was their last chance for recovery. She did what she could for them.

Sometimes the healing worked and sometimes it didn't. But the elders were always grateful she tried. They had kept her supplied with offerings of food, seeds for her garden, firewood and candles, clothing and other essentials.

PtesanWi, they called her.

Over the centuries she had acquired other names. Dream Weaver, for the protections she could offer against dark spirits that preyed upon the helpless in nightmares. Star Woman, for she came from another world. Grandmother Spider, for she could spin webs that could heal, but her bite could also poison.

As those elders grew old and died, her visitors dwindled

until only Jerry, his son Nicholas and now Jamie knew of her home. Jerry continued to bring her creatures that needed healing, and some of the birds and animals stayed, such as her shy little fox friend and a young golden eagle that nested at the top of the four-hundred-year-old oak. They were both under stern orders to leave her chickens alone, and they meekly obeyed.

She finished cleaning the kitchen, wiped the area by the sink and leaned her hands on the counter with a frustrated sigh. Then having made a decision, she shrugged into her battered jacket again and stomped down to the pier.

The campfire had been doused, and Michael had piled wet clothes and shoes at the end of the pier. She couldn't see him anywhere but she heard a slight metallic clanking that came from somewhere on the boat.

She cast a scowling glance around as she climbed aboard. She didn't like modern boats. She found Michael with his head buried in the bowels of the engine.

Manly and useful. Hrmph.

She snapped, "Hello, idiot."

"Go away." His voice echoed in the confined space.

"I will not." She kicked one of his feet. "Get out here."

"Fuck off."

She kicked him again because it felt good. "I came down here to tell you that you are an idiot."

He pulled out of the engine with the swiftness of a coiling snake. "The *hell*."

She grinned, in a fine, fun rage. She had grown to adore this tall, deadly man. "What's the matter with you?" she said. "You should be in bed resting." She pointed in the direction of the mainland. "He's on the hunt. We have no idea how long this haven will hold."

His hard, white teeth shaped words with biting precision. "Which is why I am making sure there's been no permanent damage done to our only fucking boat. Then I will check my store of weapons and check the fucking news. Then I will take a fucking nap. Got it?"

"All right." She gave him a sweet smile and almost laughed out loud at his expression of baffled wrath. She hadn't managed to get him this riled in years. "That's not why you're an idiot, you know."

He had a wrench gripped in one muscled fist. He threw it, and it bounced off a wall. "You evil, old elf," he said in a conversational tone. "I could always strangle you. That would shut you up."

She wagged a finger. "But only for a while." Her gleeful energy faded. She grew tired again and abandoned her adversarial stance. "You're an idiot because we could all be gone in a matter of hours. You're choosing to spend what precious time you have left closed off in that fortress of yours. That's not who the Creator intended you to be, Michael."

"Don't tell me who I'm supposed to be," he snapped.

His anger was a palpable force that beat at her skin, but she had withstood it before. "That's my *job*. To help you remember who you are."

"You've already done that," he growled. "I know very well who and what I am."

She blew a frustrated breath out between her teeth. "Mary told me off earlier, and she was right to do so," she said. "Life isn't some kind of pale, distant thing you hold at arm's length. Maybe I have treated our lifetimes as though they are disposable. I watch human lives go by so fast anymore they're gone in an eyeblink. And I always keep in mind the ultimate price we must be prepared to pay. None of that means we aren't supposed to live."

He sighed and rubbed at his forehead, leaving behind a dark smudge. "Are you through?"

She hesitated at his clipped tone, but then pushed on. "No. Like I said to Mary earlier, I don't have time to mother-hen you two, so I won't talk about this again. But I'm warning you now. Make peace. Make peace with her, with me, with the Creator, with yourself. Make it now while you can."

"Old crone." That too was one of her names. "You've

made your point." His expression was bitter but she noticed his voice had lost its edge. He rubbed his forehead with the back of one hand and left a black smear of grease behind. He looked as tired as she felt, tired to the bone and beyond. "How's Mary?"

"Let me see," Astra replied in a thoughtful tone. "In the last couple of days, she has lost her sense of her own humanity, her career and her home. She has suffered multiple gunshot wounds, been terrorized by monsters and survived a kidnapping attempt. She went up against the Deceiver and lived to tell about it. She lived through a killer storm, and she just saved a dying man's life. I think she's bloody fabulous."

"That's not what I meant." His voice was low.

"Right now, her only friends are two reclusive lunatics on a mission. She leaked a few tears when she took a bath, but she'll be all right. There's nothing wrong with her that good sleep, good food and a little time won't cure. I wove some protections around her and gave her a healing dream when I tucked her in bed."

He frowned, a quiet, pained expression. "Good."

Astra sucked a tooth and glanced at the wrench. She wanted to beat on him. She wanted to yell at him some more.

She wanted to say, *Idiot. Blockhead. Are you getting my point? Don't you think you overreacted a bit? All Mary said was she didn't want to shoot a gun again. Make your damned peace. What happened was not that big of a deal.*

But for Michael, for some reason it was, and she feared she knew why.

She feared he had gone and fallen in love, that somewhere in that maddening fortress of his, he had been nursing irrelevant and treacherously distracting fantasies. That he was sulking because his feelings were hurt.

Oh God, why did her tools and companions have to be so young and at the mercy of their human hormones, right when they most needed their focus and commitment? Would she really have to kill them after all, despite her impassioned lecture to Michael about rediscovering the sacredness of life? Distasteful as it was, she had to consider it.

On their home world, twinned pairs of soul mates were born at the same moment. Here on Earth, they were born and reborn in lifetimes that were compatible to each other's. At least, they had been born at compatible times when their spirits hadn't been damaged, as Mary's had been.

During gestation, their human parents grew sensitive to the unique vibration of their energies. With a few notable exceptions, they tended to bear the same, or similar, names throughout history.

Now that Mary was whole again, if Michael and Mary died, they would be reborn, and Astra had every reason to hope for a new, more amenable start to their lives than what they had suffered in this one. With two new, healthy young children, she would have a far greater chance to control and shape their attitudes and destinies.

Gabriel and Raphael had managed a near seamless partnership. She had never seen a pair so closely connected as those two rapscallions, and it had all come about quite naturally. Time and again, they had been born as brothers, until their last sad, short life when they had been born as princes. The Deceiver had them imprisoned in the White Tower of London "for their own safety" until he could destroy them in secret and shove their bodies under a staircase where animals gnawed on their bones.

Tragic though it was, that was the only lifetime the Deceiver had successfully taken any of their group as children. Locating Mary and Michael again after their rebirth would be a dangerous scramble, but Astra had more talent than the Deceiver for hearing the vibrations of recurring dreams that their kind experienced during childhood.

Starting over would be a calculated risk. She could find Michael and Mary, snatch them from their birth parents, and raise them together like siblings.

Of course, nothing would destroy their spiritual connection. She wouldn't think of attempting such a sacrilegious act. But they would be pair-bonded from an early age.

By the time they would be old enough to be effective in a fight, she could have them trained until they were a seamless partnership, as Gabriel and Raphael had been. That would bypass any maudlin irrelevancies like sex or romantic feelings that might get them all destroyed.

Her shoulders sagged. If she took that path, it would involve more decades of waiting and patient effort. She would have to watch as the Deceiver took control of the Presidency. He already stood at the brink, ready to shape this world again to fit his vision of conquest. Once he gained control, it would become easier for him to take it again and again as each new President took office.

How exhausting.

Also, the thought of raising two young, energetic children at her age made her want to crawl back into bed and pull the covers over her head.

Just staying alive took all of her enormous, sustained will and continual work at rejuvenation. It also took the generous, daily offering of energy from the living entities that surrounded her. The trees, bushes, the island and Lake, the spirits of air and water, the rich, life-sustaining dirt and the ancient rocks that were the bones of this planet, all sustained her in her purpose.

She had committed herself to remembering so much, not only for her people but also for this adopted world, but she had forgotten how to die. Somewhere deep inside, though, her body knew better and longed to return to the earth. She was so tired that drawing each breath was a conscious choice. Only Creator knew how long she might have to wait for all four of them to be in one area again, awake and aware and able to do battle.

Besides, taking Michael's and Mary's lives didn't feel right, no matter what kind of brutal sense it made or how she was tempted.

They were flawed and inconvenient tools, but wasn't she

just as flawed and just as inconvenient? Who could say that they would become any better in their next life or the lifetime after that?

How twisted had her reality become if she had to kill them to keep them safe?

Over the centuries, she had watched Michael's spirit grow more edged and feral without Mary's presence to balance and temper him. Astra had been poised to kill him as a child because of his potential danger to society. She had also been relieved he had responded to her so that she never had to make that choice.

She would wait and hope he still responded to her. Maybe she had pushed him hard enough already. She sucked on her withered cheeks and said nothing more.

Besides, she had warned him enough over the years. Now she had to sit back and trust him to remember.

Soul mates did not always equate with romantic love.

Balanced energies did not always equate with compatibility. Opposites not only attracted. They also repelled. Completion did not guarantee hearts and flowers, or even friendship.

Yin did not necessarily see eye to eye with yang. Sometimes the twinned pairs struggled through terrible conflicts.

Then there was nothing pretty about life. It became a fight for survival, a bone-breaking bitch-slap of a brawl.

She should know.

Just look at how sick to death she and the Deceiver were of each other.

Chapter Sixteen

IT TOOK MICHAEL another forty-five minutes before he was confident the stolen boat's engine would not only start on the first attempt, but also take more punishment on the water. He kept barrels of gas stored in a shed at one side of the small bay, and after he finished tinkering, he topped off the tank.

He wished he had his own boat at hand. His was a sleek cigarette boat, a drug runner's wet dream. Like a good thoroughbred, it was a little flashy and, at roughly one-point-five mil, worth the price for its speed. Now that boat sat useless, moored at Charlevoix.

This boat was an older model, built in the late seventies with a clunky hull design and lots of dated wood paneling, but its owner had lavished a lot of care on it.

Now hopefully he and the others would reap the benefits of that devotion. After a rough night, it was battered and the worse for wear, but the hull was not taking on water and the engine was still good to go. None of them were as young or as resilient as they used to be, boats included.

Most important, very much most important, the cruiser was here and useable.

Of course if Astra had her way, she would take to the Lake in her little bark canoe and hand-carved paddle. She would never set foot on one of these newfangled, motored contraptions if she had a choice.

He shook his head with a snort. She must have experienced some powerful motivation to step onto the boat's deck, let alone to pick a fight with him right after she had put Mary to bed.

He closed up the engine, and stretched. His tired joints popped.

He could run five miles in ten minutes, twenty-six miles in under fifty and swim almost a mile underwater with a single breath. By the time he had turned seventeen, he had reached expert levels in half a dozen forms of martial arts and adapted them to his peculiar abilities, among them karate, tae kwon do and the different forms of jujitsu, including judo and the aikido "way of harmony" with its Zen principles.

He had mastery over a variety of weapons, a two-handed broadsword, a *katana*, a bamboo pole and a rapier. He had yet to find a motor he couldn't hot-wire, could slip past the most sophisticated electronic firewalls and knew to a fine point the relative merits of a Glock versus a Mauser or a Walther. He could sever the stem of a maple leaf at a hundred yards with a crossbow bolt, and could either construct or dismantle explosive devices within seconds.

It's what he did.

He didn't figure out women. He especially didn't figure out shriveled-up, mischievous, horrible, cranky, old, contrary women. That's not what he did.

Astra was dangerous as only an entity thousands of years old could be. She was one of the most dangerous entities on Earth. He had known it since he was a child. He had come to understand it more as he had grown older, or at least he had come to understand it as much as he was able.

Creatures that were so old simply thought a different way. They had different priorities that arose from different perspectives. As Astra said, human lifetimes seemed to go by in an eyeblink. It was very easy to look at such fleeting lifetimes as disposable commodities.

Both Astra and the Deceiver had retained something or had aged into something—he wasn't sure which—that aped humanlike behavior but could commit a shattering act on an instant, for reasons that no other creature could comprehend. He compared it to a family dog that might behave in a loving, predictable manner for years, but then one day without warning, it might savage a baby in its crib.

For example, Astra had charged onto the boat and provoked him into a recreational spat. Then she had lectured him to make peace with the world, kumbaya, yadda yadda yadda. All of that was decent enough advice as far as it went.

Then, like a cloud passing over the sun, her energy underwent a subtle change.

His instinct for danger was one of the few things in the universe that he trusted implicitly. That instinct was honed finer than the most delicate butterfly's antenna. When Astra's energy changed, he knew that he was closer to death by her hand than he had been in over twenty-five years.

A few moments later, just as inexplicably, the cloud passed. She reverted back to the harmless, careworn and eccentric old biddy she enjoyed pretending she was.

He and Mary had their shards of ancient memories and subterranean motivations, yet they were entirely different creatures than either Astra or the Deceiver. He and Mary had become far more humanlike. They might do something bewildering, to both themselves and to others, but he didn't think it would be on such a dramatic scale.

He grunted and rubbed the back of his stiff neck with a callused hand.

Here was some irony:

As he had grown to adulthood, the only person who had felt real to him had held his life in iron jaws poised to snap shut and send him into oblivion.

Astra railed at him for locking himself inside his fortress and holding the world at a distance, but she bore the responsibility for having the most influence on him in recent lifetimes.

She valued his warrior energy as a useful weapon. She squandered a fortune of time and money on his training. Then she became alarmed when that weapon turned razor sharp and dangerous.

Not that he was complaining. Growing up with Astra as an adversary and teacher had brought him to the peak of his abilities. Learning how to survive in the teeth of those iron jaws had heightened his instinct for danger to an exquisite sensitivity.

But they shaped each other in ways that even the oldest and wisest of them didn't fully understand. Then they rampaged across this vulnerable earth wielding their rage, hatred and power.

Sometimes when he fell into this bitter mood, he thought their very existence was an unforgivable sin.

He climbed the hill to the cabin. Astra had disappeared somewhere. He could have found her with his psychic sense if he had been so inclined, but a little of her company went a long way with him. He would be happy if he didn't see her again for another month, or even a year.

A pity that wasn't possible.

Perhaps they were, in spite of everything, like a lot of normal human families. They might love each other but they didn't often like each other much. At least life was never dull when they got together.

His biological family was another story. He had been unable to respond to his human parents in any meaningful way. To him their existence was relentlessly banal, and he had gradually lost touch with them. He hadn't seen them in years. Feeling a rare sympathy for them, he was glad that they had other children. He hoped it lessened their disappointment in losing him.

He entered the cabin on quiet cat feet and cast around for the other occupants. Jerry rested in one of the guest bedrooms, and Jamie was sprawled facedown on the couch. He didn't sense Nicholas in the immediate vicinity.

Mary sprawled asleep in the loft. His attention lingered on her sleeping presence. He marveled at her light energy that was, nevertheless, most distinctly not pastel. Her delicate, tensile strength held resilience and purpose. She was stronger, and so much better than he. In the midst of their group's worst battles, their most malicious creations, she retained a wealth of compassion and caring for others, which was a fineness of being he would never achieve.

He moved to the room that was a combined office-armory and keyed in the combination on the electronic lock. Almost all of Astra's visitors had slowed to a trickle, then stopped, and Michael had known Jerry and Nicholas from the time he was a child. Still, the contents of the room were dangerous enough that he didn't take chances by leaving it open and available when he wasn't present.

Astra was the only other person who knew the combination. She rarely bothered to enter the room anymore. She preferred to use her more esoteric, less technical tools. When he pushed the door open to the windowless room, everything was as he had last left it.

He accessed the Internet by satellite and used a uniquely designed search engine to gather news. Highly placed individuals from various government agencies, banks, private businesses, risk assessment companies and a few international nonprofits would have had fits if they knew of the ghost that glided past their sophisticated, expensive firewalls to make use of their databases.

He also scanned public news networks. His grim mood darkened further as he read the various headlines and data that had accumulated over the last week.

The body of a young male had been found in the ruins

of Mary's burned-out house. The police claimed the body was as yet unidentified. In reality, they had identified the man from dental records. The victim was twenty-nine-year-old Steven Ellis, a computer salesman from Joliet, Illinois, reported as missing by his wife, Vicki, over a month ago.

In Mishawaka, Indiana, the site of the kidnapping attempt on Mary, two gunmen killed a family of four in front of a T.G.I. Friday's restaurant. The victims were James Atkins and his wife, Christine, their eleven-year-old son, Robert, and Christine's mother, Gina Barclay. Gina Barclay's husband, Ray Barclay, a retired bank manager who had gone to a baseball game with friends, had suffered a heart attack when he had received the news.

After murdering the family, the gunmen had also been killed. Different sources said several eyewitnesses saw an unnatural flocking of birds in the area, but no official statement had yet been made. Police reports stated that the two gunmen had been plainclothes undercover cops, supposedly investigating a series of arsons that spanned four states. Police had not established a known motive for any of the killings.

From St. Joseph, Michigan, on the evening of Mary's house fire, Justin Byrne had been reported missing by his partner, Dr. Anthony Sheffield. Earlier that same evening, St. Joseph police had acknowledged that Justin's car, a late-model Lexus, had been parked at Mary's house. They were investigating possible connections between Justin's and Mary's disappearances, the house fire and the dead victim, Steven Ellis.

Michael's eyes narrowed as he read through other reports.

The police had also connected Mary to something else. News of that crime had exploded onto national networks early yesterday evening and had been picked up in syndicated newspapers and online news services.

Eight people had been massacred in a small country diner in midstate Michigan yesterday. A state trooper who had stopped for coffee discovered the multiple homicides. Those killed were: Ruth Tandy, Jackie Parsons, Emilio Gonzales, Greg and Jeffrey Macomb, Beau Chambers, Dickey Boxleitner, Bobby Jackson, Cherry Tandy and Sue Evans. Three of the victims had been local high school students. Several of them had attended the same church.

The authorities had already made several public statements indicating they knew of some connection between Mary Byrne, an unidentified dark-haired man and the massacre. Various news service websites speculated whether Mary, who initial investigations revealed to have lived a quiet, law-abiding life, was the victim of a kidnapping. Some wondered if Justin was her kidnapper and also the killer.

Then there was the car bombing and shoot-out at the Petoskey municipal marina, in which several people, including some members of the local police force, were killed. Survivors described how a small blond woman fitting Mary's description drew a weapon and fired on two police officers down by the dock.

Mary's purse, along with her identification, had been found on the scene. The FBI had instigated a nationwide manhunt for her, along with her male companion. Very accurate sketches of both him and Mary had been shared with the public.

He sighed. That damn purse. He had to rub his eyes before he could resume reading.

No official database or news agency carried any information on the battle at Wolf Lake, or the twenty bodies left strewn throughout the clearing and surrounding forest. That carnage might not have been discovered yet. The cabin was, after all, in a remote location.

More likely, Michael thought, the Deceiver had sent in a crew to clean up the mess, not because he was in the habit of cleaning up his own messes but because something might have been left behind at the scene that could inconvenience him later. The Deceiver might also have hoped to discover that Michael had screwed up and left evidence behind of where he and Mary were headed.

Dream on, he thought, picturing the last face he had seen his opponent wear. Dream the fuck on.

At last he leaned back and rocked in his leather chair, his sightless gaze fixed on the wall behind his computer screen. Close to sixty people had been slaughtered in the last few days. Some of their names and their smiling faces, from published photos, lingered in his mind.

Sixty people.

Collateral damage, modern war professionals called it.

Chump change, considering the panoramic glut of WWII, when the Deceiver had run amok with a pack of human-born monsters.

Sixty people were a drop in a bucket, compared with the World Trade Center, the desecration of Afghanistan, Iraq or any of the monstrosities that had mowed down millions of people in Germany, Russia, Cambodia, China, Tibet and Africa.

The last century had been the century of mass murder. It was the Deceiver's century. This world had become riddled with people who had looked into the Deceiver's eyes and lost their souls, puppets that sat in powerful places and committed his atrocities while they pretended to their families and the rest of the world that they still lived.

Sixty people didn't sound like much, stacked up against that kind of past, the entire unimaginable, crushing weight of the Deceiver's dead.

It might take someone with the sensitivity of a butterfly's antenna to hear in the stories of those sixty people the soft-building crescendo of six thousand years of hatred.

But he heard it.

He rubbed at his tired eyes. His thoughts switched to Mary.

I don't ever want to shoot a gun again, she had said, her eyes dark with remembered horror. After craving to find her for such a crushing long time, he had suddenly become wild to get away from her.

Not because he didn't understand, but because he did.

Each bullet took a life, and each life was a world, and Mary was a healer. She flung everything she had at each world in an attempt to save it. He knew that. He remembered that much.

But the Deceiver sat upon a mountain of bodies so high it reached the sky. If each life was a world, he was the destroyer of a cosmos. Now he was poised to slide onto the modern-day international stage in yet another grab for power. He was an addict who would do anything to get his fix. Unchecked, he would turn the earth into a charnel house.

Once long ago, Michael had been a military general in a society far removed from modern Western thought. That society had understood the essential energy of action and existence, that which flowed behind the physical realm. To bring the understanding of the Tao onto the battlefield had been to raise warfare to an art.

He had written, *If you only know yourself, but not your opponent, you may win or may lose. If you know neither yourself nor your enemy, you will always endanger yourself.*

It was essential to recognize the truth of what lay behind the mask of a face, the truth of the forces that moved behind nature. Know your enemy, he had warned that long-ago people. The one who wages this war will never tire. He will always deceive.

Michael's reason for being, his entire ageless passion, had forged into a singular purpose, and that was to bring that destroyer down.

So he fought to save innocent worlds from dying, just as Mary did in her own way. But his skill was in violence, which bore its own cost.

He needed to know Mary existed. He hungered for her healing energy, for both the wounds he created and the wounds he sustained.

But he would either win this battle by violence or die by violence. He wouldn't stop. Not ever. Not even for the horror in her eyes as she looked at what he was, and all because each life was a world.

Irony:

Make peace, Astra said, when she of all people should have remembered.

That's not what he did.

Chapter Seventeen

FOR A WHILE, Mary floated in a soft darkness without dreaming.

Then she remembered that something slippery had happened, something subtle and lightning quick, and a thin, silver thread formed in front of her. In some deeply recessed part of herself, she knew the silver thread was part of a much larger tapestry than she could comprehend. It was a single shining piece in a measureless web.

Everything is connected, she realized. Everything touches something else.

When she discovered the thread, she also rediscovered curiosity. The thread widened to become a silver path, and she stepped onto it. She walked where it led her. The path was cool, quiet and filled with moonlight.

As she walked, she became aware of shadowed hedges that grew on either side of the path. The ragged tops of the hedges were higher than her head. The leaves rustled in a quiet breeze, lifting strands of her loose hair and pulling them across her face in a veil.

She ran her fingers through her hair and lifted the veil from her eyes. She wore a simple cotton shift. The night was balmy and punctuated with a gentle symphony of crickets, so she was quite comfortable to have her arms and legs bare. The worn dirt path was easy on the soles of her feet.

She came to an old, battered door in the hedge. It was locked. She pounded on the door and yanked at the latch. Something heavy swung from a chain around her neck. Surprised, she looked down to discover an antique gold key swinging on a necklace between her breasts.

She fingered the key, studying it by the moon's pale smile, then fit it into the lock and turned it.

The door opened. She pushed it wide to discover an immense meadow filled with wildflowers. Dawn had begun to illuminate the meadow on the other side of the hedge. The rosy gold morning sun picked up lavender, red, yellow, white and blue blossoms dotting the thick green grass. Honeybees, bumblebees and hummingbirds flew from flower to flower.

Mary closed the door behind her before she began to explore the meadow.

She wasn't sure if she should pick the flowers, so she contented herself with bending over the blossoms to discover which ones gave off the rich perfume that permeated the air. Soon her cheeks were dusted with pollen.

A golden eagle plummeted from the sky. She watched it reach into a rosebush, grasp a stem in its talons and rise into the air again. As it glided overhead it dropped the rose, which landed at her feet.

This place was giving itself to her. She picked up the rose, careful of its thorns, and walked through the meadow until she saw the edge of a dark green forest. Still curious, she walked to the far side of the meadow. As the forest came closer into view, she came upon the most enormous tree she had ever seen.

The tree was so tall it reached higher than a mountain. The top disappeared into clouds. She had never seen anything alive that was so colossal. The Eastern dragon she had called for healing would have fit in its branches. The Lake that had sung such a strange, sweet song to her could have nestled between two of its roots. She walked and walked until at last she could lean against the smallest of its roots and rest.

The tree lived, and died, and was born anew with green, growing promise. As she leaned against its root, she knew it held a secret in its strength. It was the same as the secret of the silver thread. Mary picked up one of the fallen leaves and tucked it behind one ear so that the leaf could whisper the secret to her.

A brook ribboned through the land beside the tree. She had walked for so long she had grown hot and thirsty, so she went straight to the water. It rushed in a silvery tumble over a bed of slippery rocks. She let the rose fall and watched as it floated away over the rocks. Then she scooped her hair away from her face so she could drink.

Now that she had reached the brook, she realized it tumbled down to the sea. A wide tan beach stretched just ahead, and more old, tangled forest, and a glimpse of an ancient gray wall of ivy-covered stone. It looked like the corner of a wall or a building.

She searched for a place where she could ford the tumbling water. Nearby, a wide area was shallow enough she could pick her way across.

Running water for protection, she thought.

Or perhaps she didn't think. Perhaps the brook whispered it to her as the cold water swirled around her calves. Or the leaf that she had tucked behind her ear told her, as it murmured of the sacred green places of Earth.

On the other side of the brook, she walked along the beach and looked over the white-capped waves. She would have liked to swim and explore the water's edges, but first she needed to discover what story the old stone building would tell her.

She picked her way through the lush, tangled growth surrounding the ruins. At last, under the shadow of a white oak, she reached an open place where she could see the building.

It was the ruins of an ancient chapel. The door and windows were long gone but their arching frames, outlined in stone, still stood. The roof had long since caved in and decayed. She could see through the open arch of doorway that gold sunlight dappled the grassy green floor.

A bird flew by in the forest, trilling madly. Inside the chapel, the air was old, silent and still. The power that filled the place sank into her bones. The place might stand in ruins but it was still holy.

Bracing herself with a slim hand on a granite arch, she took a tentative step over the debris in the doorway. As she stepped inside, intense recognition flooded her.

"I know this place," she breathed, eyes wide.

She was familiar with every moss-covered rock in this place. In wonder, she walked along one wall and saw that underneath the tangle of ivy, each stone bore a carved inscription. Careful to avoid breaking the vines, she pulled the curtain of ivy aside and read the word on the first stone.

Marah.

The stone beside it bore the word, *Mearr.* The one underneath that read *Muire.*

Then onto the next. *Moire*, *Maryse*, *Miryam*, and on the oldest stone closest to the ground was inscribed the word *Myrrh.*

All were variations of her name.

She backed away from the chapel wall and stumbled against a waist-high black stone that was an altar. She put both hands on its pitted surface as she leaned against it for stability.

Power welled from the black stone, pouring through the fragile flesh of her hands. She felt it like the roar of an oncoming tornado as the noonday sun spilled down on her head and blinded her.

The light and dark energies connected inside of her and detonated. The power of the resulting blast knocked her . . . someplace.

She floated, light as thistledown, and collided with a handkerchief of bright orange energy, which startled a giggle out of it. It was a little wind spirit, like the lavender spirit that had helped her escape from the drones who had tried to kidnap her.

It darted out an open window, flapping and soaring in fits and spurts like a drunken butterfly. Looking around, Mary discovered that she stood at the top of the stairs that led to the loft.

She could see Astra cooking on the ground floor. She jumped, floated down the stairs and over to the counter, where Astra rolled out a thick layer of dough.

"What are you doing out of your body, miss?" Astra grunted without looking up. She took a knife and sliced the dough into thick strips. "I know you think you've learned a clever trick or two, but now is not the time to be wandering through the realms, not even here."

I didn't mean to do it, she protested. *It was my dream.* As Astra paused to look at her speculatively, realization dawned. She demanded, *You gave me that dream, didn't you? What did all those images mean?*

Astra cackled, her black eyes bright. "I don't have a clue. It wasn't my dream, it was yours. I don't know what images you saw." She added in a casual tone of voice, "Want to tell me what they were?"

Mary didn't take time to analyze her instinctive reaction. All she knew was that she didn't want Astra near her chapel.

She said quickly, *No, thanks.*

"Suit yourself. Then you've got to be the one to figure out what it means."

She hesitated. *How could you give me the dream if you don't know what it was?*

"All I did was to nudge you in the right direction," the old woman said. "You said that sometimes you don't know yourself. You had somewhere inside of you that you needed to go, and some things that you needed to realize and remember. You would have gotten there on your own eventually—you were halfway there already. I just saved you some grief and time so that we could move on to other things."

Oh. Thank you. The large steaming pot on the stove distracted Mary. She peered inside at the bubbling liquid, trying to determine the contents.

"It's going to be chicken and dumplings," Astra told her. "And you can have some when you get up." She slapped a floury hand on the counter. "Now go back to bed!"

As Astra said the words, Mary felt a shove that sent her tumbling head over heels up the stairs. When she connected with her body, she fell again into darkness.

A FORMLESS TIME later, Mary opened her eyes.

She looked around, cataloguing the details of her environment. Pleasant cool air moved through the loft, carrying with it the rich, enticing smell of chicken stew. She rolled over and looked at the open window. As she remembered her collision with the bright orange handkerchief in her dream, she smiled.

There was no part of her body that ached, or was cold, cramped, overtired, bloody, dirty, wet, beaten or bruised. It was a miracle.

Her unruly hair still felt damp but not uncomfortably so. She had a whole wide double bed to roll around in. It would take a good week of regular sleep and nutrition for her to feel fully rested, but this new reality was miles better than what she had just experienced. She wiggled her toes and rotated her ankles, and luxuriated in the simple wonder of being physically comfortable, content to rest and think.

After a while, hunger and a resurgence of curiosity drove her out of bed. Someone had left a pile of clothing just outside her door. As she sorted through the items, she found her cleaned and dried nylon panties, a baggy purple T-shirt and a gray sweat suit.

She had lost her bra back at Michael's cabin, but she was small enough that she could get away without wearing one. Grateful for the clean clothing, she shrugged into the T-shirt, sweatpants and underwear, slipped on her socks from early that morning and left her nightgown folded on her pillow. Then she went down the stairs.

No one else was in sight. She found a pot on the stove on low simmer, a small stack of spoons and bowls beside it and a note on the kitchen counter. Astra was outside doing chores, the stew was ready, iced tea and a salad waited in the refrigerator and fools were welcome to eat whenever they awakened.

Mary felt a small pang when she read the note. Her fingers smoothed the edges of the paper. She wondered where Michael was sleeping. Had he been tempted to crawl into bed with her, or was he glad for the chance to put some distance between them after that morning?

Earlier she had been too exhausted to care about anything but getting her body horizontal as fast as she could, so she hadn't missed him when she'd collapsed in the loft.

She missed him now, though. They had fast learned to rely on each other during the trip north. Or at least she had learned to rely on him. Already it felt strange to be apart from the visceral comfort of his big, warm body.

She helped herself to a generous meal of chicken and dumplings, salad and tea. The stew was well seasoned, starchy and delicious, perfect comfort food for people who had suffered from stress and recent injury. She couldn't resist a second bowlful. When she finally finished, she washed her dirty dishes.

Then, driven by motives she preferred not to dissect, she explored the ground floor.

The cabin was filled with a treasure trove of carved statues and masks, stone bowls, pottery, handwoven wall hangings, dried herbs and a variety of tools.

A central fieldstone fireplace dominated the living room area. Both her and Michael's shoes had been set on the hearth, along with the blanket that she had cut to make a makeshift poncho.

She paused to study an eighteen-inch artifact on the mantel. It was a doll constructed of sticks, scraps of cloth and a painted black-and-white face. It was an odd, compelling figure that somehow embodied both gaiety and menace. She stood on tiptoe to get a closer look.

A man said behind her, "What do you think of the Haokah?"

She turned around.

Jerry stood taller than she thought he would. He was every bit as tall as Nicholas and his grandson. She ran a professional gaze down his body. His face was still haggard but he seemed steady on his feet, and his color was good. He had pulled his gray-streaked hair back in a ponytail, and he was dressed and wearing a jacket.

Jamie stood at his grandfather's shoulder, his youthful, handsome face lively with curiosity.

Jerry looked at Jamie and jerked his chin toward the door. With a flash of disappointment in his eyes, Jamie gave her a sullen smile that was startlingly sexy and left the cabin.

"Hello," she said to Jerry. She held out a hand, and Jerry took it in both of his. He squeezed her fingers. "I was just wondering what this doll was. What did you call it?"

"It is the figure of a Haokah, or a sacred clown. A Haokah teaches us through adversity. Sometimes the lessons are funny, like slapstick. You might slip on a banana peel and laugh, but you know you've learned to watch your step." Jerry regarded the figure on the mantel with a complex, unreadable expression. "Sometimes the lessons are darker and harder, like how to live with the death of your son."

"I'm so sorry for your loss," she murmured, even as Nicholas took form beside them.

The ghost put his hand on his father's shoulder. She held her breath, waiting to see if Jerry would sense it.

He did not appear to notice, and her gaze moistened, for

both father and son. She cleared her throat and turned away to focus on the doll on the mantel.

"A Haokah teaching is a big gift," Jerry said. "It makes the soul grow. We honor our Haokah teachers but we are wary of them too, because those lessons can hurt like a son of a bitch." He paused. "I dreamed of Nicholas. He said I owe you my life. He also said that you would kick my ass if I didn't stop smoking."

She glanced sidelong at Nicholas, who nodded, and she felt somewhat better for the both of them. She told Jerry, "He was right."

Jerry's dark eyes studied her as he grumbled, "I make no promises."

"Then I make no promises about not kicking your ass," she told him with a small grin. "You shouldn't be out of bed yet."

Jerry grunted. "I see you're one of those doctors."

"Who are 'those doctors'?"

"You know, the bossy ones." Lines deepened at the corners of his eyes as he returned her smile. He said, "Thank you."

"You're welcome. And I meant what I said—you need bed rest, and I want to check you over again. What are you doing up and dressed?"

"I'll have to take a rain check on that exam. The boy is going to see me home, and I'll rest there. We've been here too long, and his mother will be worried. You've done enough for now, and it's past time for us to leave." His smile faded. "You and the others, you have bigger and more dangerous concerns to face."

She bit her lip. She had meant to do more than just check Jerry over. She had wanted to tell him how much Nicholas, even as a ghost, had come to mean to her.

She had also been tempted to tell him what they were going to try to do.

But now she rethought that impulse. If they failed—if she failed to resurrect Nicholas—Jerry would mourn his son all over again. If they succeeded, then Nicholas could tell his father in person.

"Hold on," she said. "You're not going to slip away from me that easily. At least let me examine you."

He grumbled, but there was kindness in his eyes and no heat in his complaints. She made him sit at the kitchen table, while she stood behind him and put her hands on his shoulders. Then she sank her awareness into his body and studied her handiwork from earlier.

Finally she pulled out again, patted his shoulder and told him, "You're not going to like me saying this, but you need rest and a low-fat diet. No red meat."

He grunted. It was the most noncommittal grunt she had ever heard.

She nodded and patted him again. "When you feel up to it in a few days, start taking short walks and gradually increase those over time. Build up to at least a half an hour a day. And no more smoking."

He reached to his shoulder and took one of her hands. "On that note, I think it's past time I leave."

She chuckled. "Okay."

He stood and faced her, and to her immense surprise, he gave her a strong bear hug. It startled a smile out of her, and she hugged him back.

"Come and see me," he said. "I'll make deer stew, fry bread and blackberry sauce. It was Nicholas's favorite meal."

"I would be honored," she told him. With any luck, Nicholas would be with her to visit, and they could turn the meal into a celebration.

Jerry nodded and turned toward the door. Nicholas joined her, and together they watched Jerry as he walked out of the cabin. He moved with care but he was steady on his feet, and he appeared to be in no pain.

I will go with them and watch over him, Nicholas told her. *He and I have more to talk about in dreams. It is the only way he can sense me.*

She took a deep breath at the sudden pang she felt. Her

growing affection for Nicholas was the most uncomplicated relationship she had at the moment. "I know he would appreciate that very much."

He put a shimmering hand to her face. She felt the warmth, and the steady strength in his presence. *Like I said, call me if you have any need of me.*

She reached up to his hand, wishing again that she could actually touch him. "You would hear me?"

If you direct your call to me, I will hear you.

Her lips pulled into a smile. "And we are still going to work together to bring you back, right?"

Yes, he told her. Darkness flashed across his features and brought with it a touch of savagery. *I have too much unfinished business in this lifetime not to try.*

If she hadn't experienced everything that she had over the last several days, she might have been much more unsettled at that flash of expression. Still, she shivered.

She said, "Then I will see you soon."

Yes, Mary. The ghost bent and brushed her lips with his in a light, fleeting caress. *We will see each other again soon.*

Her eyes widened. As she touched her lips with her fingers, he melted away.

Chapter Eighteen

MARY STARED AT the space where Nicholas had been standing.

Were there implications in that kiss?

She thought . . . there might have been implications in that kiss, which seemed kind of crazy since only one of them was alive and embodied.

Or maybe she was just still overtired and out of balance. At the moment, she was prone to reading the wrong thing into just about anything.

She scrubbed her face hard with both hands. Implications or not, she had too many other things to deal with, so she set the whole thing aside. She gave the Haokah figure one last glance and resumed her exploration of the cabin.

Most of the items decorating the cabin appeared to be from the indigenous cultures of North America. There was the occasional exotic surprise, such as a small, crudely shaped statuette of a horse that appeared to be Grecian, or an exquisite, simple marble urn. An antique spinning wheel had been tucked into one corner of the living room. It was obviously still used, the spindle and the wheel threaded with wool.

As she acquainted herself with Astra's house, she knew she was really circling around the hot, steady flame of Michael's presence, which emanated from one of the rooms. She did pause when she came to a metal firewall door that was locked with a thoroughly modern, electronic keypad.

The sight of the door was jarring. It seemed starkly out of place with the rest of the house. After eyeing it with a frown, she moved on.

Another door was closed, only this one looked as simple and ordinary as the rest. She could sense Michael's presence on the other side, and she bit her lip, sorely tempted to either knock or crack the door open and peek inside. If he wasn't asleep, perhaps they could talk.

But if he were asleep, her knock would wake him up. He needed to rest as desperately as she, and he had still been working when she had fallen into bed. It wasn't fair to disturb him. She didn't even want to try cracking open the door.

She moved to one of the windows to look out. Astra worked in a large vegetable garden. Her small, thin figure made a compact bundle as she knelt between rows. She pulled weeds from between young, green shoots while a light breeze stirred her white hair.

The chore looked so ordinary, yet Mary could sense a density of spirit activity swirling around the old woman. Astra was doing much more than it appeared at first glance.

Something inside of Mary relaxed. With both Michael and Astra occupied, there was nothing for her to do but rest. She stretched out on the couch and, with a sense of deep relief, let herself doze in the quiet of the afternoon.

A noise brought her awake. As she sat up, she realized that she had heard quiet movement from behind Michael's closed door.

She rose and moved toward his room to pause just outside the door. What if he had just been tossing and turning in his sleep? She hadn't heard any further movement, but she grew convinced that either he was awake, or he was close to it. Something about his energy had shifted and grown sharper.

If he was close to waking, he had rested enough. This time, she didn't back away. She eased the door open a crack to peer inside.

Heavy curtains had been pulled shut at the window, but even though the room lay in deep shadow, she could still see details.

The bedroom's furnishings were minimal. Michael sprawled facedown on the covers of a king-sized bed. He still wore the black cotton pants he had been wearing earlier. His torso and feet were bare, and his dark head was buried in a pillow.

She glanced from his broad, muscular back to the bedside table. It held a lamp, along with the first clock that she had seen in the house, and a gun. The clock's luminous digital face read 2:23 P.M.

She regarded the gun wryly and with a pang of sadness. He wouldn't or couldn't fully relax even here.

She had expected him to roll for his gun as the door opened, or at the very least sit up, but he did neither of those things. Some deep, buried part of him must realize that she wasn't a threat. She wanted to believe that he knew she was present, and that he welcomed her, but cold reason said that more likely his defenses weren't quite as heightened on the island because he knew they were relatively safe for the time being.

She inched across the room to squat by the bed. He was still in a light sleep. He had showered, although he hadn't bothered to shave. She caught the faint, familiar scent of Astra's soap.

In spite of the shadow of beard that darkened his jaw, he seemed younger in repose, his harsh features softened. She felt guilty about studying him without his knowledge and almost turned to go, but then she stopped.

By his own admission, he was a pragmatic man. Astra

struck her the same way. Ruthlessness was one of the traits they shared. Mary had a gut feeling that when he got up, she might find herself at the mercy of his and Astra's agendas.

That was okay. She respected it. Michael and Astra had been preparing for a long time for the danger they faced. They were much more knowledgeable than she, and they had been preparing for a confrontation that had been building over centuries.

But she had her own agenda. If she didn't manage ruthlessness, she certainly achieved stubbornness. Remembering how Michael had connected with her when she had been locked inside her own mind, she laid a hand on his arm and sank her awareness into him. This time she focused on his presence, the ephemeral part of him rather than his physical body.

She had been prepared to fumble her way through something she hadn't yet attempted in this lifetime, but in a fast, catlike swipe, Michael's presence connected with hers.

She lost her physical point of reference, except for a distant awareness of her hand as it rested on his muscled bicep.

What do you need, Mary?

Sorry to wake you.

I'm not awake yet, he said. *My body is still resting.*

That was a neat trick, and something else for her to learn.

She floated in nothingness, with no sight or sound other than his disembodied, measured voice. His telepathic voice sounded controlled and self-contained, like an impersonal voice on an answering machine. Mr. Enigmatic had survived the trip and was doing just fine.

I don't like this, she said. *I feel like I'm floating in an isolation tank. When you connected with me in my head, we had a cave and a floor and light so that we could see each other. How did you do that?*

She could almost hear him sigh. *I'll teach you later,* he said. *You did most of the work. You were trapped in your memories, and the image of the cave was yours. I simply entered the scene. What do you need?*

She said, *I heard you stirring, and I wanted to talk to you in private.*

What did you want to talk about?

The guarded neutrality in his mental voice hurt more than she had expected.

In a flash of intuition, she knew that his disembodied voice was a deliberate ploy to keep their conversation at a distance. She almost told him, *Never mind, I'm sorry.* She almost broke the connection, but then she didn't.

She had been following her gut instinct all her life. When she did, for the most part things had turned out. Whenever she tried to make decisions based on more rational criteria, the results were less than successful. Witness her foolish fiasco of a marriage to Justin. She had parsed that decision down to a cold-blooded nicety, when her gut had known better.

And as Astra had asked earlier, why do things always have to make sense or operate on human logic?

So she followed her gut. She said, *I had a dream. I wanted to show you an image so you could help me identify it. Do you mind?*

A long, undefined moment passed, and a sick feeling began to bloom in the pit of her stomach. He wouldn't reject her. Not her, of all people. Not after looking for her all this time. He wouldn't stay closed off. Would he?

He said, *Reconstruct the image and put yourself in it. Visualize all the details around you like it was in your dream. Do you remember it well enough?*

Yes.

She did as he said. It was remarkably easy. Within a few moments, the complete image settled around her like a tent. She looked around with satisfaction at the old ruins of the chapel. Everything was as clear and immediate, and as rich with sensual detail as it had been the first time.

She told him, *Okay, I'm ready.*

She moved to her altar and sat on it cross-legged. The noon sun poured down like fiery gold rain. Earthy, dark power welled from the altar, and the light and dark energies met again inside of her.

This time she wasn't taken by surprise and knocked out of the image. She found that she could hold her position, although the intensity of the power made the construct of her body shimmer like the mirage that it was.

Michael appeared in the chapel. He was dressed in a black T-shirt, black combat pants and boots.

They were clothes made for fighting. Even now he shielded himself. The realization caused another pang.

He spun on one heel as he cast a swift glance around. Then he looked at her. His expression was grim, unreadable, and his eyes sword sharp.

She kept her voice soft and easy. "What do you think of it?"

His gaze narrowed. "How can you be here and not know what this place is?"

He could have said, How could you be in this place and not know yourself?

"I know what this place is." She ran her fingers along the cool, uneven surface of the altar. "I wanted you to see it."

Astra had said she had needed to connect with some place inside of her. Understanding had blossomed only after she had awakened from her dream.

The chapel didn't exist anywhere in physical form. Although her mind had chosen the scenery, the details of the image didn't matter. They were cosmetic. They provided definition to the eye, symbols of that which was invisible.

This was a place past guards and barriers, cynicism and shortcomings, a place of pure spirit. It was purely private, purely Mary. She would have to be quite broken before she would fail to recognize her own heart. And she was no longer broken.

He jerked away and strode to the opposite side of the chapel, pacing like a caged animal. Unlike a caged beast, he was free to leave whenever he wanted. She was relieved that he did not, at least not yet.

"I don't understand," he said in a clipped voice.

He kept pacing, back and forth, and the force of emotion that emanated from him was blistering.

"What don't you understand?" she asked. She still spoke as gently as she could, for she realized that they had reached this point in other lives. Sometimes they had failed to resolve the fundamental differences in their natures. Those lives had been filled with great hurt.

"You looked at me with such horror this morning," he said between his teeth. His pain was palpable, and it echoed back through time. Back and back, to their beginning.

"You misunderstood me earlier. I didn't look at you in horror," Mary told him. "I think you're beautiful."

Michael stopped pacing but he still stood poised for action. The doubt in his expression said more than any words could.

She kept a stern grip on her own emotions and reached for patience. "This morning I had a flashback. I looked down the guns of those two men who shot me, and then I shot at two people. I could have killed two men who were innocent of the Deceiver's crimes. They might have had families and friends, and they thought they were only doing their job—"

"You've got to be kidding," he said. "You're torturing yourself over them?"

Her back stiffened. "I'm disturbed by what happened, yes."

The first sharp edge of his pain had eased, but he still felt volatile, unpredictable. "Let me put your mind forever to rest," he told her. "You didn't shoot those men. You might have managed to hit the boats once or twice, but that's about all. I shot those men while I was running to get to you."

She paused. "That's not the point."

He tilted his head and prowled close. "You just said it was."

"No." She put up both hands. "Please listen to me. The actual fact that I did not shoot those men is not the point. What I experienced—what I believed—is that I shot those men. That's the point. I picked up a gun, something that I said I would never do, and I pointed it at two human beings. I pulled the trigger, and not once. I didn't stop shooting until the gun was empty."

He spun away. "Now we're back to where we started."

She slid off the altar and walked over to him. "You know as well as I do how much has happened over the last few days. The dragon healed me, but I have still sometimes felt like I've lost my center. This experience was one of those times, and it was wrapped up in the memory of the bullets hitting my body. I was so scared, and I was so sure that I was going to die."

He looked over his shoulder at her, and the lines of his face had tightened again.

She put a hand on his back. "This morning had nothing to do with you. It had everything to do with me. Then Astra gave me this dream, and I went on a journey. I reached my center again, and I know who I am. I'm not talking about discovering new memories." She gestured at the scene around them. "I'm talking about this. That's what this place is all about, and that's what I wanted to show you."

He turned to face her, and he took her hands. Somehow, even though it was the first time he had reached out to her since they had parted early that morning, he felt more distant than he had before.

"That's where I think you're wrong," he said. The gentleness in his voice was even worse than his touch. "Everything that you described—taking the gun, emptying the clip at two other people. That's what I do. That's who I am, and I don't have a problem with that. You have a fundamental problem with it. That means you have a fundamental problem with me."

This conversation had slipped out of her control. She tightened her fingers on his. "No," she said. "I didn't mean that. You're twisting things around."

"Healer and warrior," he said. He touched her face lightly with the tips of his fingers. "We may need each other, but we do not always see eye to eye. We do not always come together."

"What are you trying to say?" She tried to smile but it came out all twisted. "You sound like you're trying to break up with me."

"I could never do that," he said, very low. "After all, we're bound together, aren't we?"

She sucked in a breath. The cadence of his words was both tender and bitter at once, and after everything that they had been through in the last few days, that was what hurt the most. "Maybe this was a mistake," she managed to say. "I was trying to show you that I was doing better and that I got my balance back."

"I'm glad you told me," he said. All his emotion retreated until it was locked behind a fortress again, and Mr. Enigmatic looked down at her.

She shook her head. Suddenly she was furious with him. She didn't think. She just flung words at him.

"How convenient for you that you figured me out so completely, despite everything that I'm trying to say to the contrary. It makes it so much easier for you to erect your walls and live behind them, just like you always have."

The fortress cracked. His eyes flashed, and she saw that she had scored a hit.

He opened his mouth to reply.

A blast of fury and terror hit Mary. It knocked her out of her mental image. In Michael's bedroom, she fell back on her heels, disoriented, while Michael surged out of his bed and slapped the light on.

Nicholas's presence raged in the room. Mary rose to her feet as Michael asked, "What is it?"

The ghost said, *The Dark One is in my father's house.*

Chapter Nineteen

MICHAEL'S EYES FLASHED, and he swore. "Has he taken them yet?"

They are getting close to the mainland. They have no radio, or any way to reach them on the boat. My father cannot hear me unless he is asleep. Nicholas rampaged the room like a cyclone. *I don't know why I ranged ahead of them. Instinct. Habit. I backed away as soon as I sensed the Dark One's presence in the direction of my father's house.*

"Oh, my God," Mary said. "Oh no."

The news hit her like a punch in the gut. That wonderful, stubborn old man, and that sweet, sexy boy. If he took them, he could torture them for information. He could use them the way he had used her ex-husband Justin. The thought made her feel physically ill.

"Is there any way to make phone calls from here?" she asked. "Do they have cell phones with them?"

"We have a couple of satellite phones," Michael said. He reached for a black T-shirt and dragged it over his head. "But they would need one too, and they don't have one. They won't get cell reception out on the water."

He strode out of the bedroom toward the outer door, but before he reached it, Astra walked in. Her face had turned sharp and drawn. "What's happened?"

"The Deceiver is at Jerry's house," Michael told her. "And Jerry and Jamie are getting close to the mainland."

Astra sucked in a breath. "They both know the coordinates for how to reach this island. We're not ready for a confrontation. We've only just reunited. Both of you have been seriously injured in the last few days. You're barely rested, and you haven't gained back all your strength. We have to pack and leave."

"No, wait," Mary said. "We have to find some way to help them. Nicholas said they haven't reached shore yet."

Both Astra and Michael turned to look at her. Michael said, "It's a two-hour trip to the mainland. They may not have reached shore yet, but they are a lot closer to it than we are."

"Our boat is bigger than theirs," Mary said. "It has to be faster, right? We could try to catch them, couldn't we?"

He shook his head. "We wouldn't make it in time. They've gotten too much of a head start."

Astra said bitterly, "I should never have let them go. I knew better, and I did it anyway."

Mary cupped the back of her head with both shaking hands. Jerry and Jamie were doing fine. They were traveling on the Lake on a sunny day. They both believed that she had saved Jerry's life, and all the while, they were traveling toward the worst death imaginable.

"There has to be something that we can do," she said. "A spirit messenger. There has to be someone we can call on the mainland to get a warning to them. *Something*."

"They can't hear spirit messages the way we can," Astra

told her. The wrinkles in her face had deepened. "Sometimes Jerry hears snatches of messages in his sweat lodge or, as Nicholas said, in his dreams." She looked at Michael. "We need weapons, clothes, money, and it wouldn't hurt to have some food packed just in case."

Astra walked to the refrigerator and pulled out food containers, moving more quickly than Mary would have thought possible. She unwrapped a loaf of bread and cut it into slices.

A chill washed over Mary. She said, "Two men are traveling to their deaths, and you've decided to make sandwiches."

"Don't try to lecture me, girl," Astra snapped. The older woman looked up from her task, her gaze hot and black. "This is about survival."

Mary looked at Michael, who hadn't moved. Mr. Enigmatic watched her with a hooded gaze.

"We can't do nothing," she said to him, near to tears.

"Even if there was anything that we could do, if we help them we put ourselves at risk," he said. His voice was cool, calm. It belied the escalating tension that poured off his body in waves. "And then we risk losing everything."

"Listen to him," said Astra as she slapped pieces of meat between bread slices. "We're too vulnerable at the moment. We have to think of the greater goal."

"Screw the greater goal, and screw the both of you too," Mary said. The tears filled her eyes, but she refused to shed them. She said to Michael, "You may have lived behind that wall for most of your life, but you can choose differently. Be somebody better."

His face went blank, his gaze distant. She felt like she was talking to that wall, her words useless puffs of vibration and air.

Nicholas coalesced close beside her. His energy still raged, but he felt as if he had gained control.

She turned to the ghost and looked up into his face. "I can't do nothing," she said to him in a quiet voice that deliberately shut out the other two. "But I don't know what to do. Can you think of anything that we can try?"

The only thing I can think of is the Lake, Nicholas said. *Your boat engine was dead last night, but it still brought you here in the storm, and it did so more quickly than you could have traveled on your own.*

She spun to face the others. "What if you asked the Lake to help us again?" she said to Astra. "Then we might have a chance to reach them in time."

Astra's jaw angled out. She said between her teeth, "I won't do it. It's too great of a risk."

The sickness in the pit of Mary's stomach worsened. She couldn't look at Michael. She walked to the fireplace hearth and grabbed her shoes.

"Mary, stop this," said Astra.

Mary ignored her. She jammed her feet into the shoes and snatched up the poncho.

Michael angled his head to watch her. It was the only part of him that moved. His hands were fisted at his sides.

Astra pointed her knife at Mary, as she said to Michael, "Stop her from doing something wasteful and stupid."

Then Michael moved. He strode to the metal door. He punched out a quick sequence of numbers, opened the door and walked inside a room. The door swung shut behind him.

Mary went beyond pain and turned numb. Of all the things he could have done, he simply walked away. It was incomprehensible to her.

"Come on," she said to Nicholas. "You're going to have to teach me how to start and drive a boat."

The ghost silently followed her outside and down the path to the pier. While the sun was shining, the wind was sharp. It would be colder out on the water. She barely spared a glance at the bullet holes that dotted the side of the boat as she shrugged on the poncho and climbed aboard.

Nicholas's raging energy had subsided. When she was

standing in the cabin, staring at the all the strange knobs and dials, he finally spoke.

Mary, he said gently. *If Astra won't ask the Lake for help, there's no way that you can make it in time.*

She shook her head as she gripped the wheel in both hands. The tears that had been building finally spilled over and streaked down her cheeks.

"I've been on a boat exactly three times," she said. "And that's counting last night. I always meant to make time to go out on the water more. But I was always so busy. Sometimes after a really brutal shift at work, it was all I could do to get carryout on the way home. So you're going to have to tell me how I start this damn thing."

Nicholas's warm presence surrounded her, as if he had taken her in his arms. She could still feel his pain through the contact, and yet he still tried to comfort her. He said, *I should go to be with them.*

"Don't," she told him sharply. She scrubbed her wet face with the poncho. "Don't go. If he senses you, he'll destroy you too."

They're my family.

If she could have physically laid hands on him, she would have. "Sacrifice is one thing," she said. "Suicide is another. Please don't go. Stay with me instead."

The sense of closeness to him eased, as though he drew back, but he still lingered.

How far away were Jerry and Jamie from the shore? The next few hours would be excruciating.

Not that the Deceiver would necessarily kill them in the next few hours. He might choose to hold on to them for days. The thought made her want to vomit.

A streak of movement outside the window caused her to lift her head.

Michael ran down the steep path. He was dressed much as he had been in her dream, in a black T-shirt, black cargo pants and combat boots. He wore weapons—a hunting knife strapped to one thigh, a handgun and an automatic rifle slung over one shoulder—and he carried another heavy black bag, but still his big body conquered the distance with impossible lightness and speed.

She stared as he jogged down the pier and threw the bag onto the boat.

He gave her a pointed look, eyebrows raised. "You weren't going to get very far with the boat still moored to the pier."

She burst out laughing, and she didn't care if it sounded like a sob. "I haven't figured out how to turn it on anyway."

He untied the ropes that held the boat to the pier and threw them onto the deck. Then he leaped aboard and stepped into the cabin. The force of his presence filled the small, enclosed area.

Nicholas retreated further. He hadn't promised her that he would stay, but he also didn't leave. She sensed him hovering at the railing toward the front, as if he could make them go faster by force of will alone.

She stepped back to give Michael room and watched as he opened a panel and connected a few wires together. Only then did she see the ignition keyhole. The boat growled to life. Expertly, he shifted into reverse and they pulled away from the pier.

Then she repeated what Nicholas had said. "We're not going to make it."

"Probably not," he agreed. "But we're going to push as hard and as fast as we can go. We won't stop until we reach Charlevoix, and we have an answer one way or another."

When the boat had pulled clear of the pier, he spun the wheel and gunned the motor. They roared out to open water.

The floor shifted rhythmically underneath her feet, and she adjusted her balance to the dip and swell. When she felt like she could walk, she edged closer to Michael, who stood with his feet braced wide apart. She raised her voice to be heard over the motor. "What made you change your mind about going?"

"I didn't. All I said was that it was a risk. I was undecided, and then I made up my mind." He glanced at her, his keen gaze moonstone bright. “I’m not the only lunatic, you know,” he said. “I’ve followed you before too. And you never could give up on someone that you healed.”

The boat hit a bigger wave than most and lurched. She grabbed hold of Michael’s bicep to steady herself and hung on. After a moment, she said, “About that talk we were having before we were interrupted.”

This time he kept his gaze on the water. “Let’s finish that conversation later, when we have more privacy, and enough time to do it justice.”

“Okay.”

She looked out over the water too as she wrestled with her unruly emotions. She didn’t have time to think about her personal problems when she was treating someone in the ER, so she had some experience at compartmentalizing. She kept the thought of Jerry and Jamie in the forefront of her mind and settled into a clearer focus.

Michael said, “This is going to go one of two ways. Either we try hard on our own but we don’t make it, or Astra gives in and asks the Lake to help us again.”

“How likely do you think that is?” As she asked the question, she checked again for Nicholas’s presence. He was still with them.

Michael shook his head and shrugged. “I have no idea. Her decision will be based on weighing risks. We do have something in our favor that might change her mind.”

“What’s that?”

“When I made my choice, it shifted the balance. If we commit to fighting to keep Jerry and Jamie out of the Deceiver’s hands, we’re in more danger without her help than we are with it. Now she stands to gain more by helping us than by risking the possibility of the Deceiver taking one or both of us too. And she still needs our help.”

The bulk of hard muscle underneath her hand felt strong and steady. “For that to be true, she has to believe that we’re not just trying to force her into helping us.”

His lips pulled into a slight, hard smile. "Astra knows I don't bluff."

She looked back in the direction of the island—or what she had thought was the direction of the island. There was nothing on the horizon but the sun shining on the sparkling water. For all intents and purposes, the island had vanished.

She muttered, "That's a fancy trick."

He caught the direction of her gaze. "That is a much stronger and more effective null space than what I can produce. Astra started it, but over time, the land itself turned secretive. It began to project the null space on its own. It would be good if we could prevent Jerry and Jamie from giving that secret away, but over the years we've developed other contingencies. It won't be the end of the world if we have to leave the island. We have several safe houses scattered across different states."

"I just want to try to save their lives," she said.

"I know."

The sense of the lonely presence at the front of the boat became too agonizing for her to resist. She squeezed Michael's arm. "I'm going to keep Nicholas company, if he'll let me."

Michael nodded without reply.

She made her way out of the cabin and toward the front of the boat. Think nautical. The prow. The edges of her poncho whipped in the wind, and she was grateful that she had grabbed it.

Nicholas's energy was stretched so thin, he was barely present. She felt him straining in the direction of his father and nephew. She tried to think of something to say, but in the end, she remained silent. She simply stood at the prow with him. His presence grew stronger, and he wrapped around her, as if holding on to her helped to keep him anchored in place.

After several minutes, the boat tipped drastically as the

water swelled underneath them. The swell turned into a high, narrow wave that built in size and speed, until they hurtled forward much faster than they could have ever hoped to go by themselves.

Hope surged, along with their speed.

Astra had convinced the Lake to help them again.

Chapter Twenty

THE MINUTES SCROLLED past. Each one was filled with an agony of waiting.

They raced across the water much faster than Mary would have believed possible if she hadn't experienced it for herself. Her hands and face grew wet and cold, but she refused to go inside. If Nicholas needed to be out here, then she would stay with him.

A shadow grew on the tip of the horizon, and Nicholas stirred. *That's the mainland. I need to find out how close they've come to land.*

His energy had changed. Now he felt sharp and eager.

She said out loud, "Be careful."

I will. I'll be back as soon as I know anything.

He vanished.

Shivering, she turned to make her way back to the cabin, taking extra care because they were traveling at such a crazy speed. A fall into the water at this pace would almost certainly kill someone.

Michael gave her a sharp look as she stepped inside. The tough lines of his face had settled into grim lines.

She joined him at the wheel. “What is it?”

“You’ve grown quite attached to him, haven’t you?”

She used the excuse of wiping off her hands and face with the dry underside of the blanket, so she could think about how to reply.

Were there nuances in his question? She thought there might be nuances.

But they had no time to explore nuances. They had no idea what they would be facing over the next hour, so in the end she chose to keep her answer simple.

“I have,” she said. “He’s a special man.”

“Yes, he is,” said Mr. Enigmatic.

Nicholas exploded into the cabin. *They are close to shore. There are two drones stationed at the dock.*

“Time to get ready,” Michael said. Mary jumped as he hooked an arm around her. He hauled her in front of him. “Take the helm, and keep it steady on course. The Lake might be shoving us in the right direction, but if we angle too sharply to either side, we could capsize.”

“Okay.” When she took hold of the wheel, power vibrated up her wrists. It was harder than she had expected to hold the wheel steady. She widened her stance and leaned forward, bracing her body to take the strain.

Michael stepped outside and made his way to the prow. The railing around the boat was simple metal fastened directly onto the deck. He knelt, took the rifle and braced the barrel on the top railing.

Adrenaline strung out her nerves until she felt tight as a wire. They hurtled forward at an impossible pace, toward the Deceiver, and toward more drones with guns. She clamped down on her fear. Her mind shut down until the only thing that existed was the race over the water, and her battle to keep the boat on a steady, straight path.

The shadow on the horizon expanded with dizzying rapidity. Motorboats and sailboats dotted the water in all directions. She broke out in a sweat as details on the mainland became visible. Tree-covered hills swooped along the shoreline, and she caught a glimpse of houses through the trees.

Nicholas whirled onto the boat. *There—do you see them?* he demanded. *They're just ahead. The drones are waiting in a black SUV at the end of the road by the dock.*

She looked down the faint shimmer of Nicholas's arm as he pointed, and then she could see the old motorboat with two people in it, chugging unhurriedly through the water. They were perhaps a hundred yards away from the dock.

She could also see the black SUV, parked in a wide gravel area at the end of a neighborhood road that ran up an incline into a cluster of trees and houses.

Michael? she asked telepathically. He was too far away to talk to verbally.

Hold steady, he said.

His shoulders tightened as he bent his head over the barrel of the rifle. Whatever Michael was aiming for, it was an impossible shot to try to take. The boat bucked rhythmically and they were still a good two hundred yards away from Jerry and Jamie's motorboat. They were even farther from the shore.

A sharp sound cracked the air. It was only after the passenger window of the SUV exploded that she realized Michael had taken his first shot.

All the while they raced closer, straight at the shore.

The passenger door of the SUV opened at the same time someone leaped out of the driver's seat, crouched behind the vehicle and aimed a gun over the hood in their direction.

Here we go, she thought. She started to shake.

The drone that had been in the passenger's seat jumped out and raced to the back of the vehicle. Another crack sounded as Michael shot again. This time a spray of water kicked up beside the other motorboat.

She whispered to Nicholas, "Was that a shot from *Michael*?"

He's trying to get their attention, the ghost said.

The scene on the shore grew bigger as they drew closer, and she could pick out more details. She could see the glint of sunlight winking off the sunglasses of the drone behind the hood of the SUV. After opening up the back door, the second drone ran behind the vehicle and joined the first with a rifle.

The wave that had been propelling them forward died down, and so did their hectic speed. The intense vibration eased at the wheel, and the sound of the boat's motor grew louder as it engaged.

Part of the window blew in. Dots of pain flared along the side of her face. She twisted away from the flying glass with a gasp and lost hold of the wheel. When she straightened, a spiderweb of fractures had exploded over the rest of the glass, obscuring her vision.

Michael leaped into the cabin, rifle held in one hand. He punched out the glass with the rifle's butt. He barked, "There's blood on your face. Are you hit again?"

She wiped the side of her wet face. There were three points of pain. Mentally she probed at the areas. They were all shallow cuts.

"Glass shards," she said. She grabbed for the wheel. "I'm fine."

He raced out, knelt at the railing again and fired off a few more shots. More windows shattered in the SUV. One of the drones had disappeared from sight, but the one with the rifle was still shooting.

Only this time the drone shot at Jerry and Jamie's motorboat. She saw that they had begun to turn away from shore. Splashes of water arced around them.

"Come on," she whispered, willing their boat to move faster.

How long would it take for them to get out of gunshot range? And where was the Deceiver? For Nicholas to be so panicked, he couldn't be too far away, and he would be drawn by the gun battle.

We have to draw fire away from them, Michael said. *Take us in a circle between their boat and shore.*

She fit her foot to the boot-sized gas pedal and gunned it. The engine roared and the wind whipped her face as the boat leaped forward, while Michael kept up a steady spray of gunfire, pausing only to exchange his empty clip for a full one.

Nicholas had left her again. They came abreast of the other boat, which was headed in the opposite direction. She could only spare a worried glance for them. Jamie had slumped to one side, and Jerry had taken the seat at the helm. Red sprayed the open interior of their boat.

Oh, no.

Then they blew past Jerry and Jamie. She spun the wheel, feeling the tension as the boat turned in a wide arc, spraying a tall wave of water. Out of the corner of her eye, she saw another black SUV roar down the hill of the neighborhood street toward the dock.

Her stomach lurched, and she forgot to telepathize. She shouted, "Do you see them?"

I see them, said Michael. He didn't lift his head from the rifle or stop shooting. *Take us out again.*

She kept the boat in a tight arc until they were headed away from shore. Then she aimed for the other boat. When she looked over her shoulder one last time, she saw the approaching SUV swerve sharply to the left and crash into a clump of trees and bushes.

After another few moments, Michael stopped shooting and ran into the cabin.

"We're out of range," he said. "I disabled as many boats on the pier as I could, but there were a couple toward the shore that I couldn't draw a bead on. They could try to follow us."

Her chest had tightened, and she forced herself to take in deeper breaths. She said through gritted teeth, "Tell me he was in that SUV that crashed."

"I think he was, although they weren't going fast enough

to kill anybody. More's the pity." Michael gripped her by the back of the neck. She thought it was as much to steady him as it was to steady her.

"I could say that's got to be the craziest thing I've ever experienced, but I've already been saying that for several days now." She gave him an anguished look. "I think Jamie's hurt."

His expression tightened. "We need to get them transferred to this boat and leave the area as quick as we can." He stepped behind her to place his hands beside hers on the wheel, and he nudged her foot off the gas pedal.

As he took control, she sagged back against him. He held the wheel with one hand, slipping another around her waist to hug her tight against his torso as his cheek came down on top of her head.

Leaning back against his strong, steady body felt so good. She cupped the hand that he flattened against her waist and tried not to think too far ahead to their next conversation. If this moment was all she would get, she was going to soak up as much of it as she could.

She squinted against the spray of wind and water, watching as they drew close to the others. "Do you think he'll follow us?"

"I don't know. It depends on how much reinforcement he has with him. He'll weigh the risks just like Astra did. I can maintain the null space around us, which should discourage him. We'll be a lot more difficult to track in the open water than we would be traveling down predefined highways on land."

They had approached within hailing distance of the other boat. Jerry looked over his shoulder and waved at them. He shouted, "Jamie's been shot!"

Michael eased them into a slower speed. He shouted back, "Cut your motor."

Mary took the wheel again when he nudged her. The other boat slowed to a stop, rocking gently in the waves. "Just hold it steady," he said. "Don't use any gas. Let us coast up to them. I'll get them on board, then take the helm again, while you help Jamie."

"All right."

She tried to hold them on a steady course. They came up alongside the others. Their hulls scraped as the waves rocked them together. Michael threw a rope to Jerry who caught and swiftly tied them together. Then he tossed a rope ladder to the older man.

"Can you climb aboard on your own?" he asked. "I'll get Jamie."

Jerry said, "Yes."

Mary twisted to watch what was happening. She was in time to see Michael gather himself and leap like a great cat from their bigger boat to the smaller one.

Jerry's head appeared as he climbed the ladder, his face scored with deep lines and his eyes stark. With the boats moored together, she let go of the steering wheel and rushed to help him climb the rest of the way aboard.

When he straightened, she put an arm around him and nudged him toward the galley. "Are you shot?"

"No." The pain in his eyes was palpable. "The boy is bad off."

"I understand." She took a moment to scan his heart. The spike in stress hadn't helped him at all, but her earlier handiwork held. She told him, "We had a rough trip last night, and things are a mess down below. Make a place where we can set Jamie when Michael gets him aboard, will you?"

"Of course." Jerry ducked his head and stepped through the hatch.

In the other boat, Michael had bent over Jamie's sprawled form where she could also see that Nicholas's presence hovered. Blood was everywhere, down Jamie's head and all over his front. Michael gathered the boy in his arms, squatted and lunged into the air.

He cleared the railing with inches to spare, landed at a crouch and straightened. "It's a head wound."

"Take him below," she said.

Jerry had cleared the tangle of blankets off the pile of mattresses by the time they got downstairs. He stood and flattened against the wall to give Michael enough room to ease Jamie's body prone on a bare mattress. Mary wriggled between the two men and knelt by Jamie's head. Nicholas knelt on the other side.

Jerry asked Michael, "How did you know to come for us?"

"Nicholas told us," Michael said.

She ignored him and the others, and focused solely on Jamie. She parted his matted, wet hair, looking for the wound. Her fingers found it before her eyes did. Gently she probed at the area.

Her heart sank as she realized the bullet had penetrated his skull. Mortality rates for penetrating brain injuries were over ninety-two percent. Still, she tried to hold out hope as she sent her awareness into his body.

Jamie was brain-dead.

She saw that immediately. The gunshot wound was simple but fatal. The damage to his brain stem was too severe. She absorbed the details of the injury almost reflexively and knew that if it were only a matter of healing the flesh, she could cause the damage to heal.

The problem was his spirit had already departed, probably within a few moments of the bullet hitting him. There was no psychic scar, as she had seen in the drones that had their spirits ripped out of them. Jamie was a smooth, quiet blank. His body still functioned, but that wouldn't last long without life support. His blood pressure had already plummeted. Within the next half hour, his organs would shut down.

She closed her eyes and bent her head as a storm of reaction overtook her.

Outrage, grief, guilt. Fury.

This is our fault, she thought. Her mouth worked.

As soon as any of us had heard that Nicholas had been killed, we should have thought of it, especially Astra and Michael but even me as well. He went after my family. Look at what he did to Justin. Of course he would think about looking into Nicholas's family too.

We were too wrapped up in our own quarrels and dramas to even think about Nicholas's family. So sad, too bad, you just got in our way, because we've always got to think of our greater goal.

She wiped her forehead on her forearm and realized that Michael and Jerry were still talking. Michael must have asked about any supplies on the other boat, because Jerry was talking about bottled water and packaged snacks.

"We're low on fuel," Jerry said.

"I don't care about that," Michael said. "We used hardly any fuel on the way over, and we have nearly a full tank."

She said in a hoarse voice, "Would you please talk outside?"

They stopped immediately and stepped out on the deck, closing the door to the hatch softly. She looked down at Jamie's handsome face. He looked so peaceful, as if he had just stepped out for a little while. It was maddening to know that she could heal his body and yet lose the fight to save his life.

The growl of the boat's engine started, and they lurched into movement. She ignored it. At the moment nothing mattered outside of this small room.

She looked up at Nicholas, who remained, intent on her. His dark, transparent gaze was the most distinct thing about him. She said, *I'm so sorry, Nicholas. He's gone.*

Pain blazed at her. *Is there nothing that you can do?*

There's plenty that I can do, she said bitterly. *But none of it will bring him back.*

The ghost bowed his head.

Nicholas, we have to have a hard conversation, she said. *Jamie's body is beginning to shut down. I can stop it. I'm pretty sure that I can physically heal the damage done to him, but his spirit is already gone.*

She already knew he was a clever man. He knew where she was going, and he shook his head against it. *No. I will not take my sister's boy.*

She nodded. *I thought you might say that. It's a natural reaction, when family members face some kind of issue of organ donation. Usually in a hospital, there's a little more time to talk about it, and people can work through their emotions with a counselor. But we don't have that option here, and we don't have life support to keep Jamie's body viable.*

No, he said again. This time he sounded almost pleading.

She couldn't look at him. His pain was too hard to watch. She looked down at Jamie.

I can't tell you what to do, and obviously there aren't any rules of ethics to follow in this situation. I just know two things. One is that we face so many risks, we may not get another chance for you. Look at what happened just this afternoon. There's no guarantee we'll survive from one day to the next. She paused then said as gently as she could, *The other thing is, it isn't fair that your father and sister have to lose both of you.*

That brought his head up. Moments trickled by as he struggled in silence.

Finally he said, *How long before I have to make a decision?*

She averted her face and concentrated on Jamie again. She said, *Twenty minutes.*

Nicholas vanished from sight. She lost all sense of his presence.

"Goddamn you," she muttered.

She wasn't even sure whom she was cursing. The Deceiver, certainly. Herself, Michael and Astra, yes.

And fate. She definitely cursed at fate.

She didn't wait twenty minutes. There was no clock in the room, and she had no way of telling time. She had wanted to give Nicholas as long as she could, but she was afraid that she had cut things too close. She wasn't sure she could wait twenty minutes and still repair the damage to Jamie in time to prevent major organ damage.

So, sick at heart, she sank into Jamie's body, stabilized

his blood pressure, stopped the bleeding and began to work on repairing his brain stem.

God help her, if Nicholas came back and said no again, she was either going to have to stop Jamie's heart herself, or ask Michael to help her. Otherwise his body would continue to function until it starved to death.

She finished sending basic commands to his brain stem and started repairing the rest of the wound. She worked on the skull next. There was so much damage she plunged into an entirely new area of healing as she tried to coax the bone into regenerating.

And it did.

Slowly, very slowly, the bone began to grow back over the jagged holes left by the bullet. Tears blurred her eyes. She didn't know if she cried from gratitude or grief. She wiped her face on the rough sleeve of the poncho.

The last thing she did was focus on the skin at his scalp, both entry and exit. She didn't take a real breath until the wound had sealed over. Then she slumped.

Nicholas formed in front of her again. She looked up at the ghost, her eyes raw.

Yes, he said.

Chapter Twenty-one

AFTER RETRIEVING JERRY and Jamie's blue and white cooler of water bottles and packaged snacks, Michael untied the cords that held the two boats together and pushed away from the smaller one. He shoved a water bottle at Jerry, who looked shell-shocked.

"Drink," he said.

The older man obeyed. His hands shook.

Taking the helm again, Michael accelerated away. In the back of his mind, where he kept a tally of estimates, he guessed they probably had been stationary for around five minutes. "The simplest thing will be if you and Jamie come back to the island with us."

"No," said Jerry. "Thank you, but we need to get to Sara and make sure that she's all right."

Sara, Jamie's mother, lived and worked in Muskegon. Michael's jaw tightened. Jerry was right to be concerned. He thought through their options, came to a decision and turned toward Charlevoix. Jerry lived roughly twenty minutes outside of the city, traveling by car, but they could reach it a lot quicker by boat.

"Here's what we're going to do," he said. "We'll get close enough to Charlevoix that I can swim the rest of the distance into the docks. You'll pilot out to deep water. I'll get my boat and meet up with you. Then you and Jamie can take this one. I have weapons, money and a sat phone." He nodded to the black canvas bag that he had set in the corner. "You can go to one of our safe houses and wait there until you hear from us. You're not his main focus. He's too busy to spend too much time searching, if we make it difficult enough to find you. And in a week or two, we can hope that it won't matter anymore."

Jerry's gaze focused on the bag. "Sara's probably on her way home from work at the bank. I need to call and tell her not to go home."

"Keep the call brief. Don't explain or identify yourself by name. She'll recognize your voice. Just set a place to meet. Make sure it's somewhere that you are both familiar with, but don't mention it by name or talk about directions. Then hang up."

Jerry knelt and dug through the bag until he found the phone. Then he paused as he held it. "What about Charlevoix? Won't they be watching the ports?"

"They are," said Michael. "But they should be focused on watching the shore. They won't be expecting me to swim in alone underwater. I'll slip onto the boat and take it out before anybody notices."

Probably. Projecting the null space would help with his chances. It was always a matter of weighing risks.

Jerry called his daughter. Michael tuned out of the brief, frantic conversation. Instead he thought about what was happening below. Mary hadn't contacted him or surfaced, which meant that Jamie was in a bad way but hopefully salvageable. With luck, she would be done with healing him by the time they had to split up.

If he were a kind and generous man, he would give Jerry and Jamie his sleek, fast cigarette boat.

He wasn't a kind and generous man. He had helped to rescue them from certain death, and he would give them a fighting chance. That would have to be good enough.

The late afternoon was beautiful on the lake. The silver-topped sapphire water looked limitless, as did the sky. Violence and gun battles seemed a lifetime away, whereas he knew better. They were never a lifetime away. They were always in this lifetime. He carried them with him wherever he went.

When they were about a third of a mile out from the city, he said, "This is as close as we should get. Take the wheel and head out exactly due west. Keep the speed steady, but don't go too fast or do anything else that might call attention to you. If I don't catch up with you in a half an hour, go straight to the island. Understand?"

Jerry nodded, his craggy face determined. "Just get back to us in a half an hour."

"I will." He unlaced his combat boots and toed them off. Then he took several deep, rapid breaths, held the last one and dove over the side.

The water was bitingly cold. He ignored it and swam hard, keeping the null space firmly around him. After a few minutes, his body temperature spiked from the exertion, which made the cold swim much easier to tolerate.

The psychic realm felt as unsettled as it had yesterday. Things ghosted along the periphery of his senses, and he felt creatures roaming up ahead. After swimming roughly half the distance, he eased to the surface for a fresh breath of air and a quick look around. He adjusted his course to aim straight for the docks and slipped underwater again.

He rented a slip for the boat in the Charlevoix City Marina under a fictitious name. The slip lay close to the marina exit. While he was certain that watchers had been stationed at

Charlevoix, their job was made more challenging by the fact that the day was so sunny and beautiful.

Traffic was heavy on the water with all kinds of pleasure craft. The most dangerous part of the swim was making sure that he kept well below the hulls and propellers of passing boats and Jet Skis.

Also, he belatedly realized, it was Friday of Memorial Day weekend. All of that conspired to work in his favor.

He stayed low in the water until he reached the slips. Then he surfaced underneath one, alongside a metal railing. He had come in close to his boat, just three slips away.

The rest of the maneuver went as smooth as butter. When he reached the correct slip, he climbed up the railing and eased over the side of the boat. He untied it, started the engine and accelerated gently out of the marina. The whole thing took less than three minutes.

When he reached open water, he increased his speed until he traveled at a carefully sedate pace. The wind sliced through his wet clothes, cooling him rapidly from the heat of his swim, until his body tightened into a miserable knot. The farther out he maneuvered from the other craft, the faster he accelerated, until he hit over 120 mph and the boat skimmed along the top of the water with a high, smooth growl.

The sight of land slid away behind him. He adjusted his course to travel at a slight northwestern angle while he scanned the horizon. With Jerry's trajectory, they should come in sight soon.

They did. As soon as he spotted a likely speck on the horizon, he headed straight for it. The speck grew rapidly. Soon he could make out identifying details on the other vehicle.

He didn't relax until he knew for sure it was them. Then the tight snarl of tension between his shoulders eased. He grew aware all over again of how cold he had become. Shudders wracked his body. He kept extra clothes, plus other supplies in the tiny cabin space below, but he didn't want to stop until he had reached the others.

Jerry had been keeping an eye out for his appearance, because the other boat slowed to a stop as he came closer. He shifted down and approached them slowly. Jerry left the cabin to catch the ropes that Michael tossed to him. Together they hauled the two boats close together. Michael leaped aboard the other boat.

"Your lips are blue," Jerry said with a frown.

The other man started to shrug out of his lined jean jacket. Michael waved at him to stop. "I have clothes I can change into in a minute. We need to finish this and separate."

Mary and Jamie sat close together on the deck. Jamie had a blanket wrapped around his broad shoulders, and Mary had her arm around him. Her face was smudged from recent tears, but she looked calm enough.

Michael was pleasantly surprised. She had found some way to wash some of the blood off of Jamie. His clothes were still bloody, but his face and neck looked somewhat cleaner. So did his long, dark hair, which spilled loosely down his back. Dark hollows etched the skin around Jamie's eyes, and the rich copper tone of his skin carried an ashen hue, but he looked a hell of a lot better than he had earlier when he had been covered in blood and unconscious.

Jamie lifted his head and met Michael's gaze briefly. Michael paused at the power and intelligence in those dark, too-old eyes. He had underestimated the younger man.

That was good. That meant Jamie would be a real asset to Jerry and his mother with the challenges they would face over the next several days.

Precious time was ticking away. Michael said to Mary, "Ready?"

She nodded, turned to Jamie and they came together.

Michael had intended to turn away and sort through what he would give to the other two men, but the sight of Jamie and Mary's tight embrace held him in place. Jamie put a hand at the back of Mary's head, closed his eyes and bowed his greater frame around Mary's shorter, slender body.

"I have no words for what you've done for me," Jamie said, very low. "Simply no words."

"Not everybody gets a second chance," Mary said. "It was the right thing to do. You can do this. It'll be hard, but it's going to be okay. Remember, be sure to protect your head for at least a couple of weeks. It's going to take a while for the bones in your skull to finish regenerating."

Michael's eyes narrowed as he listened to them. What was the right thing to do, and why would it be hard?

"Poor kid's been rattled since he came to," Jerry muttered to him. "Near death experiences can do that to a body."

Jerry's words brought Michael back to his purpose. He knelt in front of his canvas bag and pulled out an envelope of cash, two handguns and printed directions to one of their safe houses. He handed everything to Jerry.

"This house is in northern Illinois, about a half an hour outside of Joliet," he told the older man. "It's quiet and rural. You should pick up supplies at one of the strip malls just after you exit I-80. There's a thousand dollars in the envelope, which should be more than enough for five to eight weeks of food for all three of you, if you're frugal. You'll have to figure out transportation once you reach land. Don't use your IDs to rent a car."

"I understand," said Jerry. "We'll get there."

"You have a cell phone?"

"Yes. Astra has the number."

"Good." Michael grabbed his combat boots and shoved them into the bag. Then he grabbed four bottles of water from Jerry's cooler and shoved those into the bag as well. He zipped it shut and straightened. "We will call you when it's safe for all of you to return home again."

He didn't bother with any further instructions. If they didn't call Jerry, it meant that they had failed. Jerry, Sara and Jamie would have to figure out the rest of their lives on their own.

Mary and Jamie joined him. She gave Jerry a hug, while Michael looked at Jamie. He said, "Look after your grandfather and your mom."

Jamie's young, sensual face set into uncharacteristically hard lines. "I will."

Michael climbed into the cigarette boat first and held out a hand to help Mary. They cast off. Jamie raised a hand to them as they pulled away.

Mary looked at Michael with concern.

"You need to change into dry clothes right now," she said.

"I know," he said. He was shaking violently, and he couldn't feel his fingers or toes.

He couldn't fumble the hatch key into the lock, and she had to help him. He ducked his head to enter the small space and tore out of his wet, freezing clothes. "Be sure to keep an eye out. Let me know if any vessels approach."

"I am," she said from above. "I will."

The minuscule cabin was very simple. It held a bed, with storage space underneath and shallow cabinets along the walls. He forced his shaking limbs into jeans, woolen socks and his boots, a T-shirt and a sweater and a wind-resistant jacket.

He had expended massive amounts of energy over the last two days. He hadn't eaten since earlier that morning before he had gone to bed, and he couldn't remember the meal he'd had before that. Desperate for some quick calories, he opened a plastic storage container that held a box of protein bars and bags of trail mix, and he didn't stop until he had bolted down four of the protein bars.

Finally he was able to slow down. He hadn't stopped shaking, but he felt as if the worst had passed. He climbed back onto the deck.

The afternoon had melted into evening. Golden color blazed across the western sky, while the blue toward the east had deepened. Mary sat with her makeshift poncho wrapped tightly around her torso. She looked as exhausted as he felt.

"There's food and warm clothes down below," he told her. He started up the boat again, compulsively calculating again how long they might have been at a standstill. He guessed not quite fifteen minutes. It could have been worse. "It's going to be a chilly ride to the island. You should put on a few more layers."

She nodded, her expression distant as she looked off in the direction that Jerry and Jamie had gone. She asked wistfully, "Do you think they'll make it now?"

He wasn't one for uttering meaningless reassurances. "I don't know. The Deceiver hadn't gone after Jerry's daughter yet. You were able to heal Jamie, which frankly I didn't think was possible when I first laid eyes on him. They've got a fighting chance, which is all any of us can hope for right now."

She turned to look at him, her gaze turning grave. "That wasn't Jamie."

THE TRIP BACK to the island was uneventful and, thanks to their vastly improved boat, as quick as possible.

After retrieving one of his long-sleeved thermal shirts from the cabin, Mary offered only a brief explanation about what had happened, her words slow with exhaustion.

"I can't even describe what I did. It was part of what you did when you taught me how to give energy, and part of what the dragon did when it healed my spirit wound. I . . . fused Nicholas's spirit with Jamie's body."

"It's goddamn amazing," he said. They were traveling at such high speed, he could only spare quick glances at her. She did not look triumphant. Instead, she looked incredibly saddened.

"It was a terrible decision, of course." She shook trail mix into one hand. "Brain stem injury. Jamie had died almost instantly, except that his body had not yet shut down. Nicholas had to decide quickly. At first, he didn't want to, but I told him, it wasn't fair for his dad and his sister to lose both of them. And he gave in, I think, more because he thought he should than because he really wanted to. He's hurting pretty badly right now."

"I knew something was different, but I didn't even think to connect it to that." He wiped spray off his face. "You do realize what you did, don't you?"

She just looked at him, her gaze a tired blank.

"Not only did you give a dead man a second chance at life," he told her, "but you might very well have thought of a way to save one of us if we get killed. If our ghosts hang on and the others can find a drone, we don't necessarily have to pass on to another life. That potentially changes *everything*, Mary."

Life came back into her expression. "You're right. I hadn't thought that far."

They spent the rest of the journey in silence. The last of the daylight was fading into night when they reached close enough to the island's coordinates that Michael had to slow down. They crept forward at a cautious pace, apparently moving toward nothing but open water, until from one moment to the next, they passed through the veil of the null space that the island projected.

Land appeared before them. The entire island lay not two hundred yards away.

"If I hadn't just seen that for myself, I don't know that I would believe it," Mary said. "Of course, I've been saying that a lot over the last several days."

"I know what you mean."

He eased the boat near to the old pier and cut the motor to coast the rest of the way. Then he released the anchor, and both he and Mary worked to moor it in place.

Together they both looked at the path.

"I don't think I don't have the energy to walk up that hill," she muttered.

"We don't have to." He put an arm around her and steered her toward the tiny cabin. "We can sleep right here."

She didn't object, but she asked, "Shouldn't we let Astra know we're back?"

"She already knows. She knows everything that happens on this land."

He kicked the door shut behind them. The cabin was chilly and in deep shadow as the last of the daylight fled, but the bed was right in front of them and he had plenty of thermal blankets.

He helped her to undress, and then she turned and helped him. With the matter-of-factness of the immensely exhausted, they climbed naked into the bed. He reached out for her, and after only the slightest hesitation, she came readily into his arms.

The feeling of her slender, warm body against his was the most amazing thing he had ever experienced. It was a haven that he couldn't have known to imagine before they had come together, and it felt like salvation. He meant to tell her all of that, but his overtaxed body hauled him into darkness.

No. His spirit rebelled and fought back to awareness.

He was not done yet, and he would not accept his body's limitations.

Mentally he assessed Mary. Like he had, she had fallen deeply asleep, nestled against him with her head on his shoulder. He eased into her mind. She had not yet started dreaming but lay drifting in darkness.

Mary, he whispered.

Mm, she grunted. Her body nuzzled closer to his, and his arms tightened around her.

You can let your body rest while we talk, he said, keeping his mental voice easy and quiet. *Remember when I did it earlier?*

She murmured, *Don't know how to do that.*

Just follow my voice and let go.

Still sounding mostly asleep, she asked, *You sure?*

He had to smile, in spite of himself. *I'm sure. We need to finish our earlier conversation. Come with me. Please.*

He felt her spirit rouse, and as she joined him, he created a scene around him.

A great hall in an early Norman castle appeared, with a long, scarred wooden table, a massive fireplace and suits of armor displayed at various points around the room. The castle was from the first strong memory he had recovered of a lifetime he and Mary had spent together long ago. This was the life that had taught him the simple, powerful lesson of happiness.

After he formed the image of the great hall, he created a mental construct of his physical self. This time he chose to wear a simple gray T-shirt and jeans.

Mary was learning fast. When the scene appeared, she formed a construct of her body too. She still looked sleepy, and she was wearing checked flannel pajamas and fuzzy slippers. Her tawny hair lay loose on her shoulders, curling in crazy directions. He almost laughed out loud when he saw her.

She looked around the great hall, blue eyes wide. "I know this place," she breathed. "I've been here before."

"Yes, you know this place," he told her. "We lived here once. I wasn't going to say anything about it. I meant to wait and see if you remembered it on your own, but I changed my mind."

"I'm glad you did." Her face filled with wonder. She wandered over to the table to touch it with the fingertips of both hands.

He walked up behind her and put his hands on her shoulders. "You were trying to tell me something earlier, and I did a bad job of listening. I'm sorry."

She turned around to face him. "What changed your mind?"

"Your growing closeness to Nicholas."

Her expression filled with wary confusion. "I don't understand."

"I was jealous as hell, but that's beside the point." He

touched her cheek, her lips. "You said earlier that you thought I was beautiful, but I couldn't hear you. But then today I watched how you were with Nicholas. It's remarkable how much the two of you have bonded, even though he's a warrior too, and I realized that I really had put up a wall between you and me. Astra had told me repeatedly over the years that while we might hope to reunite with you, twinned souls don't always come together or see eye to eye. I . . . listened too well to her warnings."

"Of course I think you're beautiful. How could I not?" She clasped his wrists gently. "Killing is an ugly thing, but that doesn't make you ugly. If you enjoyed the killing you would be ugly. If you killed for ugly reasons, that would make you ugly. You don't, do you?"

He stroked that fabulous hair off of her face as he thought through his reply. He wanted to get their talk right this time, so he chose his words with care. "I enjoy the physicality of a fight, the intellectual challenge and pitting myself against a worthy opponent. I enjoy winning and exacting justice—no, that goes beyond enjoyment. I need that. Do I enjoy killing someone, or watching their life drain out of them? No. I can see how I might become twisted that way, though."

"But you're not twisted that way. I've seen so much of you these last several days. You're not just a warrior." She gave him a smile. "You are a champion. Don't you see? That's one of the reasons why you're so beautiful to me. Part of healing is the knife. Sometimes you have to cut the cancers out."

"Yes," he said.

Her smile faded. "Please listen carefully to what I say. It's important to me that you don't misunderstand this either. Astra's warning carried some weight. We've been here before, you and me, haven't we? I don't mean this place." She gestured around at the great hall. "I mean at this kind of juncture in our relationship. We haven't always understood each other, or been successful in resolving the differences that lay between us."

"Yes, we've clashed and walked away from each other. I refuse to do that this time."

Her expression eased. She nodded. "I don't want to either. This life is too precious to waste. So I want you to know that what I say next is about me, not you."

He stroked her cheek. "I'm listening."

Her bright, blue gaze shadowed. "I am making a choice not to pick up a gun again. If I take that path, I feel like I would become someone else, someone that's not me. I would have to grow callused in ways that I'm not right now. I think some parts of me would have to die and I wouldn't be the healer I need to be, because I don't have your spirit, Michael. I'm not a fighter. Maybe I'm making a selfish decision. I know it means I take certain risks in our fight, but if that's the case, so be it—"

He shook his head and put his arms around her. "Hush. You'll take no more risks than I do."

"Well, that's not exactly true." Her voice was dry. She slipped her arms around his waist. "You're freakishly fast."

He started to laugh, and it felt good and healing. "I guess I am."

He sank to his knees and rested his face against her flat abdomen, basking in her warm, vital energy. She bent over him and ran her hands down his wide shoulders and strong back, and stroked his short, dark hair. For a while they rested against each other in silence.

Then he stirred and lifted his head. "If fighting—my type of fighting, anyway—is a kind of healing," he said, "then would you say that healing is a kind of fight?"

"Makes sense," she said. "Yin and yang. Two sides of a coin." She touched the tip of his nose with her finger.

He captured her hand and kissed her finger, then stood. "I've calmed down and I'm listening to what you said, but this isn't a simple either/or kind of topic."

She bit her lip. "What do you mean?"

"You're not comfortable with guns, and I can respect that. But just as being afraid to do something doesn't make you a coward, you can't look at what I do and then say that you're not a fighter. I don't think that's the right way to think of this issue. You may not be a fighter like I am, but you still have a lot of fight in you. Look at how hard you've fought over the last couple of days. Jerry should have died twice over, and he didn't because of you, and of course there's Nicholas."

"Okay," she said slowly. "I get what you're saying."

"I think you might enjoy some of the martial arts I know, especially the disciplines that are defensive in nature."

She ducked her head and scowled. He cupped her face with both hands and tilted it back up. "Keep an open mind. You promised."

Grimacing, she said again, "Okay."

"You're so sexy when you're sullen," he told her.

He bent his head, and his mouth covered hers. She closed her eyes, draped her arms around his neck and kissed him back, and he lost himself in the raw, animal physicality of the moment.

He pushed her back and lifted her so that she settled into a sitting position on the table. Then he nudged between her legs and wrapped his arms around her, holding her tightly.

She linked her legs around his hips, hugging him with her whole body.

When he pulled away, Mary rested her head on his shoulder. She fingered her swollen lips and said in a drugged voice, "Wait. That was all just inside our heads, right?"

He nuzzled her ear with a husky chuckle. "Yeah. Think of how good it will be again in the flesh."

She stroked his hair, and it felt better than before. It felt better than ever, passion and completeness, yin and yang.

"I haven't had a chance to say thank you," she said. "Jerry and Nicholas are alive because of you too."

"They are alive because of what we both did." He took her hand and kissed the tips of her fingers. "About your image of the chapel that you showed me earlier. I have an image I want to show you too."

She smiled up at him. Everything about her had lightened until she glowed, her spirit burnished bright. "Do you?"

"Yes." He looked around at the great hall. "It's here, deep inside the fortress."

Chapter Twenty-two

SO THIS WAS supposed to be a new day.

He had read all of the most successful self-help books. He had been determined to turn his frown upside down and keep a positive attitude. Cultivating a positive attitude was supposed to create a positive outcome, wasn't it?

What had that glass half full of bullshit got him?

Nothing. Nada.

He had scrambled so hard to get his traps in place along the coastline. For a brief time, at Jerry Crow's pathetic little hovel, he had felt on top of the world, ahead of the curve and in control of the game. He just knew he was onto something good.

Until Michael and Mary intervened, he *had* been onto something good. Jerry Crow had almost come home . . . from somewhere. Then Michael and Mary swooped in . . . from somewhere . . . and his monkey suit still ached from when Michael shot out the front tire of his and Martin's SUV and sent them crashing into a tree. Only his seat belt had saved him from hitting the windshield.

By the time he had been able to get people searching that specific area of the Lake, everybody had vanished again. The only thing his people had located was a drifting, rusty motorboat, full of blood and bullet holes.

He was spending a king's ransom on manpower and equipment, and the expenditures no longer came just from state and federal resources. Now they poured out of his own bank accounts, along with those of his wealthier drones.

He was, by far, the richest man in the world, because not only did he have his own wealth, but he also had access to all the wealth that his drones had amassed.

(He adored Swiss banks and electronic access to numbered accounts. It made life so convenient as he moved from host to host.)

But many of those assets were dispersed through various individual, business and government accounts, and those funds took time to access. Because the situation was developing so fast, he was forced to fund the more esoteric aspects of the manhunt for Mary and Michael out of his own pocket.

He was spending his own money.

That offended him mightily, but even then, he spared no expense. He was willing to squander every cent he had acquired over centuries of plundering. He would be willing to bankrupt several small nations as well—if only he found out where Michael and Mary were hiding.

He was also willing to destroy major cities if he could just be assured of their destruction too, but what ultimate use was nuclear or bioweapons when they could return—and return—and return? They were a plague maddening him to the point where he could howl like a dog, a fugitive pestilence he would gouge out of his own flesh if he could only get his fingers on it.

WHY COULDN'T THEY LEAVE HIM THE FUCK ALONE? He only fought for the right that was every creature's, to live his life on his own terms and do what was in his nature. He ground his teeth and growled in fury.

The worst of it was he didn't dare call off any aspect of the manhunt—just in case.

So his drones drove along the coastal roads of Michigan, Illinois and Wisconsin, just in case. Armed federal agents worked in coordination with the Coast Guard to comb the waters of the Lake. Just in case.

Authorities from all three states were canvassing every bed-and-breakfast establishment and every last squalid roadside motel. His creatures from the psychic realm had orders to fly over every inch of the landscape.

Early that evening, he took to the air in a private helicopter in order to travel quickly between Michigan's Lower and Upper Peninsulas. Every minute that trickled by was uselessly weighted in gold.

Because Mary and Michael had vanished, and they did it not once, but twice.

People didn't just vanish, not even his people. If they were alive they were corporeal. Like all physical creatures they could be measured and weighed, captured, imprisoned, dissected, tortured and killed. Their spirits were damned slippery and infuriating, but while they were embodied, they were bound by certain physical properties and limitations.

Last night, he had actually wondered if Michael and Mary might have been killed by the storm that had roared along the Michigan coast.

But they weren't at the bottom of the Lake. They were hiding really fucking well, which led him back to the need to squander his fortune.

They were either waiting for the search to die down before they moved again or—and this was the kicker, this was what had him suffering from indigestion and would have given him nightmares if he could have afforded the luxury of sleep—they had met up with Astra.

If they had united with Astra, they would have no need to travel anywhere, because they had already arrived at their destination. And if that happened, all of his frantically complicated efforts to tighten a search noose around Michael and Mary had failed.

Each puzzle piece had a name. He whispered them over and over again. Nicholas Crow. Jerry Crow. Michael and Mary. Astra.

How could Michael and Mary have known to come to Jerry Crow's aid, except through Astra?

He had a bad feeling, and it wasn't based on any conclusive evidence. It was purely based on the need to assume the worst-case scenario, because making that assumption was what had kept him alive for so long.

So he prowled through the air in his private helicopter, tracing and retracing the same pathways in gigantic loops, as he sniffed for the slightest sign of any of the three. The day passed into evening, and still, he gained nothing.

No scent of Astra.

No sign of Michael.

No hint of Mary.

That last clinched his bad feeling into a graveyard's certainty. He should have picked up something from Mary by now, some kind of indication of what the little shit was up to. She didn't have the skill to hide with complete efficacy from him. She hadn't had the time to remember how, and Michael couldn't have had time to teach her.

For the last several days, Mary had been trumpeting through the realms with all the finesse of a brain-damaged elephant, but ever since yesterday, she had grown very quiet, almost as if a powerful, dexterous hand had come down over her to muffle her noise.

The only time he had really sensed Mary was earlier in the afternoon, just after she and Michael had rescued the old Crow and the boy. Then her presence blazed powerful and bright, escalating in intensity until it reached some unknown conclusion. He wondered if that had something to do with all the blood they found in the old motorboat.

After that, again there was nothing.

Time drained away and silence told a tale. If the three of them had joined together, then Astra's hiding place had to be accessible from the Petoskey and the Charlevoix marinas in Little Traverse Bay.

The old bitch was close, very close. He couldn't smell her on the airwaves, but he could feel it in the bones of his current body. He knew she was there, like a spider, lurking right across the next hilltop, around the bend, down the road.

One day he was going to look over his shoulder, and she would be standing there, smiling, as she plunged a dagger into his back. Her very presence on this planet had turned it from a playground into a prison. So many of the people he had slaughtered over the millennia had died as poor substitutes because he couldn't manage to get his hands around her goddamn neck.

Millennia ago, back on his home world, he had researched the properties of spirit until he had thrown open the cage of his existence in one of the greatest alchemical acts his people had ever seen.

He had transformed himself and left the universe of his birthplace forever. He had expired in a transcendent blaze of power, and rose reborn from the ashes, all so that he could free himself from the perpetual nightmarish connection with his soul mate.

He had hoped his transformation would destroy her. No such luck.

He had broken free, but mutating his spirit had changed hers too. His greatest triumph had carried the seed of potential failure, for by studying his accomplishment, she and the rest of the group had learned how to follow him.

One fact remained that provided both comfort and warning. He cuddled that fact close throughout the long years. At least now they lived independent of each other's existence. At least he had achieved that much. Congratulations, ladies and gentlemen, the operation was a complete success. The conjoined twins survived the separation.

That meant he could destroy her and survive. She also

had the potential of surviving his destruction, but that didn't mean anything to him. When she followed him to Earth, he knew she was prepared to destroy herself if that was what it took to bring him down.

If he could find her, if he could only just find her.

She was the opposing queen on the chessboard, the most powerful piece in the shadow game. Mary and Michael weren't strong enough to defeat him on their own. If he took the old bitch out, he would achieve checkmate. Destroy her, and he would have conquered this world. Then it would only be a matter of time before the inhabitants of the Earth realized it as well.

The endgame was so close.

The helicopter completed another massive circuit.

"Do it again," he said to his pilot.

They hovered over the rugged south coast of Michigan's central Upper Peninsula. The area spanned four million acres of protected state and federal forestland.

One could wax poetic about the panoramic beauty of the sky on that late afternoon. The storm had left nature lovers a present in its wake, for they were going to have a spectacular sunset.

One was not in the mood. He curled a contemptuous nostril.

"Sir?" the pilot said, glancing at him sideways.

For this trip, he hadn't brought one of his drones. He thought he might need a pilot who would be able think with more creative independence. Now he wanted to pull his hair out, only his monkey suit, with the hairy knuckles and hairy ass, didn't have enough hair on his head, just a receding hairline and that wretched, army-style buzz cut.

He said icily, "What part of 'do it again' did you not understand? Oh forget it, just put us on the fucking ground."

"Certainly." The pilot spoke with smooth courtesy and an impassive face. "Where would you like to land?"

The interior of the helicopter felt too close. He was

passionately sick of confinement. The pressure building in his head was intolerable.

He whispered, "Find a spot."

The pilot found a spot. He settled the helicopter down on a high bare outcrop of rock on the eastern shore of the Garden Peninsula, which overlooked Lake Michigan. They landed a comfortable distance back from the cliff's edge.

"Wait here," he told the pilot.

He removed his helmet and climbed out of the helicopter on stiff legs. He sucked in deep draughts of clean, chilly air and jogged in place to wake the meat up. Then he paced the length of the short cliff. White-capped waves churned against the rocks at the foot of the outcrop forty feet below.

He looked over the water as he paced back.

Wisconsin lay south and west. Michigan's Lower Peninsula lay southeast. He spun north, a slow narrow-eyed pan that encompassed the wilds of the Upper Peninsula.

Where are you, bitch?

An early evening sky smiled down at him.

He pressed monkey fists to his forehead, concentrating ferociously. The psychic landscape was as bare, open and peaceful as the windswept hilltop view.

I know you're out there, he thought at her. *I know it.*

Silence told a tale of her laughing at him.

"Sir," said the pilot from behind him. "I thought I'd remind you—"

A body could only take so much. He snapped, and the pilot died in midsentence.

After he recovered from the convulsions of the migration, to his startled pleasure, he realized what he had been too preoccupied to notice before.

The pilot was a beautiful male, as graceful as a dancer with lean, whipcord strength, coffee-and-cream-colored skin, a clever aristocratic face and black almond-shaped eyes. He paid more attention to the pilot now than he had when the young human had been alive.

He stretched and looked at the long, dark fingers with satisfaction. Now that was more like it. He booted the body of his old host over the edge of the cliff and stood staring over the Lake, hands planted on slim hips.

So the bitch wouldn't show herself. She probably thought she had things under control.

It was time he stopped indulging in temper tantrums and shook her out of that control, and past time he reminded her of whom she fought.

For thousands of years and countless battlegrounds that spanned the realms, she had refused to even speak any of his true names. She called him by the shabbiest of nicknames, the one that was both insult and lie, for he was no Deceiver. He lived true to himself. He refused to bow down to her mores and strictures, or to submit to any society's rules or judgment.

His oldest and truest name—that was the one she feared the most. Morning Star he had been called when he had been the King of Babylon, but his dark radiance had never been like her white, pitiless glow.

Light Bearer.

The ancients had not meant it as a compliment.

Lucifer smiled a wicked smile, spread out his beautiful hands and called on his oldest, primeval power.

Fire rained down on the land.

Chapter Twenty-three

JUST AS MARY did, Michael had a place of the heart that existed past guards and barriers, cynicism and shortcomings.

It was the image of a large bedchamber. A fire blazed in a stone fireplace, chasing away the shadows and the chill of the night. The bed was massive, with a rope frame and a thick mattress stuffed with feathers, and a pile of luxuriant, embroidered woolen blankets and soft furs.

As soon as she set foot inside the room, Mary knew the place. The heavy wooden door was reinforced with iron, and it could be barricaded with a thick oak bar from inside the room. The chests that were filled with his possessions lay against one wall, while the chests that were filled with hers were set against another. It was an intimate scene filled with peace and safety.

Two chairs were positioned in front of the fire. A lady's embroidery lay on one seat of the chair.

Mary walked over to the chair and picked up the embroidery. It depicted a woodland scene with colorful flowers and wild animals. “I remember this piece,” she breathed. “I worked on it all winter long.”

Michael walked up behind her. He buried his face in the hair at the nape of her neck. “Recalling details of this lifetime saved me, I think,” he said. “I couldn’t feel any real emotion when I was younger. I couldn’t connect to anything, until I remembered this place.”

Mary turned in his arms. She nestled against him. “We were happy here. I was so happy.” She paused, searching the dim, distant impressions that had surfaced. “It wasn’t perfect. There was always something to worry about, wasn’t there?”

“War.” He ran his hands up and down her back. “There was always the threat of the Deceiver, and war. We could never risk you getting pregnant, and sometimes, when there was a drought, we worried about the harvest. But we remembered who we were. We were together and completely present, and in this room, nothing else mattered.”

“Yes,” she whispered. For an enchanted time in this place, they had shared peace, love and safety, three of the most powerful words in any language. “Thank you for bringing me here.”

“I had to.” He pressed his lips to her temple, and they stood together silently for a time. Then he sank a fist into her hair and tilted her head back to kiss her, in a deep, thorough exploration of her mouth. He said against her lips, “When I make love to you again, we won’t be exhausted and caught in the images of distant memories. We are going to be completely present and in our bodies.”

She tightened her arms around him as she whispered, “Promise?”

“Nothing on earth could keep me from it.” He kissed her again, and his warm lips were hard and demanding. He pulled away with obvious reluctance. “But for right now we can truly rest.”

“And wake up together,” she said.

"Absolutely." He eased her gently from the mental image and with obvious reluctance pulled away from her presence. Then nature took over, and she joined her body in a deep sleep.

A formless time later, cold air wafted over her cheek, and she surfaced out of the peaceful dark to discover that she was on the move. Michael had wrapped her in a blanket and he carried her up the steep hill to the cabin. Overhead, the moon winked through the trees, and the night sky was crisp and clear.

"What happened?" Her voice was blurry with sleep. "What time is it?"

"I'm sorry I disturbed you," he said quietly. "It's around two or three in the morning, and I'm ravenous. I can't get back to sleep until I eat something, and we don't have any real food on the boat. I didn't want to leave you down there by yourself in case you woke up and wondered where I had gone."

"I'm glad you did," she murmured. Michael had slipped on his jeans and the sweater. She nestled into his chest, tucking her face into his neck. Not only was she naked underneath the blanket, she was barefoot too, and she remembered all too well how rough the path was. She was entirely happy to let him do all the work.

When he strode across the clearing and reached the cabin, she shook an arm out of the blanket to open the door for him. Astra was either asleep or at least resting, for the cabin lay in deep shadow, but Michael was still surefooted and certain as he carried her quietly into his bedroom and deposited her on the king-sized bed.

She discarded the blanket and slipped underneath the covers, while he disappeared. In the kitchen, the refrigerator light came on briefly as he rummaged for food. She turned on the bedside lamp, and a few minutes later, he walked into the bedroom carrying a plate of sandwiches and two tall glasses of water. He pushed the door shut with one foot.

Now that she had awakened, she realized just how hollow

and empty she felt. He set the plate on the bed, undressed and slid under the covers with her, and they ate in companionable silence. The sandwiches were Astra's handiwork from earlier, made with homemade bread, individually wrapped and quite delicious.

She finished before Michael, and lay down to curl against his long, muscular legs, drifting until he set the empty plate on the bedside table. He switched off the light and slid down to lie beside her.

They turned to each other at the same time. She wound her arms around his neck while he rose over her and settled between her legs, and the weight of his long, powerful body covering hers was the very best thing that had happened to her all day.

He kissed her, hardened lips moving sensuously over hers while he explored the moist, private interior of her mouth. She relished the slight abrasion of his unshaven cheek and lost herself in sensual pleasure. He leaned his weight on one arm while he caressed her breast and plucked gently at her nipple, and his erection pressed against her inner thigh.

Then his body stiffened. He broke off the kiss, leaned his forehead against hers and swore under his breath.

Frowning, she stroked the back of his head. She loved him so much. She murmured, "What is it?"

"Our supply of condoms are in a police evidence room," he growled. "Along with your purse and my backpack that we left behind in Petoskey after you were shot."

The corners of her mouth drooped in disappointment. "Oh, no. And you don't have any here."

She didn't say it as a question. He wouldn't be so frustrated if he had any condoms here, and she already knew that he had never been with a woman in this life, before her. He had chosen instead to wait and look for her.

Still, he shook his head wordlessly. He began to roll off of her. "We can always make love in other ways."

She gripped his shoulder. "Wait."

He stopped, settled his weight again comfortably on her, stroked the hair off of her forehead and waited.

Just as she couldn't risk a pregnancy in that lifetime long ago, she couldn't risk one now.

She also had more resources available to her than she had when they had stopped to rest at the cabin near Wolf Lake. She sank her awareness into her body and realized almost immediately that they weren't in any danger. Her monthly cycle wasn't viable for conception.

"We're safe," she whispered. "We don't need to worry for at least another week."

He took a breath. "You're sure."

He didn't ask that as a question either, but still, she smiled. "Quite sure."

She slid her fingers through the short, dark hair at the back of his head, coaxing him down to her. He came readily, and his mouth slanted over hers in a kiss that blazed along her nerve endings.

He cradled her, mind, body and spirit. She could feel it. There was no part of him that held back. He was totally engaged, totally present and open. It set her alight. She arched upward against his long, muscled torso, rubbing her body against his and reveling in the sensation of being skin to skin, of feeling the fluidity of his powerful muscles flexing and shifting on her.

He broke off the kiss, muttering something that she didn't catch, and trailed his lips along her skin as he slid down her body with delicious, agonizing slowness. He stopped to suckle at her breasts, tugging strongly first on one nipple, then the other. She gasped and cradled his head in both hands while white-hot pleasure shot arrows down her limbs. It settled into an escalating need at the intimate juncture of her pelvis.

He put a hand between her legs and pressed at the exquisitely sensitive nubbin at her center. She tilted her pelvis up and pushed against him. The wetness of her arousal slicked his hard, clever fingers, and pleasure turned into a keen, bright spear that stabbed her so sweetly, a sharp, involuntary sound broke out of her.

He buried his face against her flat stomach. "Feeling nothing is worse than blindness," he whispered against her skin. "When you're blind, you can still experience a wealth of sensation. Feeling nothing is the worst kind of starvation you can imagine, only you don't know it. You don't know it until you start to feel something. That's what happened to me when I started to remember what it was like to love you. I looked for you for so long. I needed you, and I knew that I was starving."

"You know I love you, don't you?" she whispered back to him. She stroked everything she could reach of him—his hair, the side of his lean cheek, his broad shoulders. "I just love you. I love you."

"We don't leave each other alone ever again," he gritted. He gripped her hips in a bruising tight hold. *"NOT EVER AGAIN."*

"Never," she told him. "I swear it."

Her body housed too much extreme emotion. She ached for his centuries of pain, and she was aroused and so damn happy. She couldn't hold it all in, or hold still. She wiggled down the bed, running her hand down his lean torso until she found his thick, stiff penis. He sucked in a breath as she caressed him. She relished the velvet skin covering the hard length of his cock, stroking the tips of her fingers along the beautifully shaped tip until he jerked in reaction to her gentle caress.

He grabbed her wrist. "I can't take too much teasing right now. I'm so fucking close to spewing all over you."

"Not yet, you don't," she told him. She took him in a strong grip. "Come here."

He followed her urging, shifting his position until he lay over her again, his weight on both elbows while she held him poised at her swollen, wet entrance. She rubbed the thick tip of his cock against her, moistening him and heightening her own pleasure.

He sank both fists into the sheets on either side of her head, shaking all over. "Goddamn," he hissed. "Goddamn."

"Don't you come," she breathed in his ear. "Don't you do it."

Listen to them. They almost sounded like they were arguing. It was the best kind of struggle, the best argument, unbelievably sharp and delicious. He bit at the delicate curve of her ear, the light, stinging nip conveying his urgency.

She raked the fingernails of one hand down the wide, tense curve of his powerful back. At the same time, she lifted her hips and groaned, "Now."

He surged into her, swearing a low litany in her ears, and he didn't stop until he was buried to the hilt inside of her. Then he froze.

She made a disappointed sound and wriggled against him, longing to reach for that sharp spike of pleasure again.

He gripped her hip and said sharply, "Mary."

She exploded into laughter, threw her arms around him and hugged him tight. "It's okay. Just do it."

He growled, cut loose and fucked her, driving in long, hard strokes. She slammed back against the mattress, and the wildness was so exhilarating, she stretched both arms over her head and whined high in the back of her throat. She used to have absolutely no interest in sex or making love. How she had ever thought she might be frigid, she had no idea, because this was so bloody fabulous, she could barely stop from screaming.

Then he put a hand between them and found her sweet spot. Still fucking her, he worked her with his fingers, and she lost all vestige of control. She bucked underneath him and clawed at his shoulders. There was light shining in her eyes.

No, that wasn't light, it was Michael's spirit. The tiger that lived in his human body roared at her in a wild frenzy.

She convulsed into the most savage climax she had ever experienced. The peak hit her—body and mind—and she froze in incredulity. It was the whitest, purest light. It rolled out of her and into him.

Then he twisted and bucked on her, and his own highest point doubled back on her. They fed it back and forth to each other as they rocked together. It was very slow to die away.

"What the hell," he whispered in awe.

She was shaking. He was shaking. They were wrapped around each other so tightly, she didn't know where her skin left off and became his.

Love. In love. The words simply didn't encompass the reality of this.

"I just have no words for what you mean to me." Tears spilled out the corners of her eyes.

He covered the back of her head with one big hand, and gripped her even tighter. "Jesus, woman," he said from the back of his throat. "Neither do I."

Chapter Twenty-four

AFTERWARD, MARY DIDN'T fall back asleep so much as plunge into blackness.

She was the first one to awaken, and awareness felt pure and new. She opened her eyes to discover light streaming in through a crack between the dark, heavy curtains. The digital alarm clock said that it was close to noon. They had slept the morning away.

Michael lay sprawled on his stomach beside her, his arm lying across her torso. She settled her pillow into a new position and scooted up the bed until her head and shoulders were propped against the headboard.

Michael roused long enough to curl around her body. She tucked the covers around his shoulders, noting the red scratches she had left on his skin. He fell back to sleep, this time with both an arm and a leg draped over her, head pillowed on her narrow shoulder. Alert and at peace, she rested with her arms around him.

She could hear Astra moving around the cabin. Cabinet doors opened and closed in the kitchen.

Then, very quietly, the knob on their door moved. The door eased open, and Astra peered inside. The light from the large central common room shone through the thin white nimbus of hair around her head. There was something poised about that shabby, skinny figure, an alert listening attitude in how she held her head.

Mary led her eyelids fall. She watched the older woman between the veil of her eyelashes with a potent cocktail of emotions.

Astra looked like a shadow puppet, held together by pins and wishes. Was there also a forlorn, wistful air about the little old woman? Or did she project an extrapolation of her own self onto Astra?

Behind that shadow puppet was an entity Mary thought she loved, or at least it was someone she had loved once. Now she needed, respected and pitied the older woman, but she also couldn't quite bring herself to trust Astra.

I don't know how you can bear to be who you are, Mary thought, taking care to keep the thought locked within the privacy of her own head. She wondered if Astra could see that her eyes were open. The thought unsettled her even further. If so, they were staring at each other in silence, like two opponents sizing each other's strengths and weaknesses. A chill washed through her.

Michael's head rested against the bare curve of her collarbone. She felt the whispery brush of his eyelashes as he opened his eyes.

In a quiet move, Astra closed the door and walked away from the bedroom.

Mary expelled a shaky breath. Michael's arm tightened around her. He put a finger at the racing pulse in her neck. He whispered, "What's wrong?"

She shook her head. "I'm being too imaginative."

"Okay. What's wrong?"

She discovered another new experience, an impulse to

smack him, and strangled it. Instead she confessed in a bare thread of sound, "Astra scares me sometimes. I don't know why. Like I said, I'm being too imaginative."

"No you're not." He rolled away from her, perched on the edge of the bed, reached for his shirt and dragged it over his head. "You should be scared of her."

"Why?" She levered up to sit beside him.

He reached for his wristwatch and strapped it on. "She cares for us, enjoys our companionship and misses us when we're gone. I don't doubt any of that. But she is not our ally. Not in the final reckoning of things. If she suspects that we might get in her way, she wouldn't hesitate to kill or destroy us." He rubbed the back of his neck and sighed. "But I like to think she would be sad about it."

Disappointment shadowed the peace she had felt when she had awakened. "We're all she has left here of her people. We're her family. We came here to help her."

"We did," he agreed. He braced a hand on the mattress behind her spine, half-twisted to face her. "But the fight has gone on for too long. We've gotten heartsick and soul-scarred and out of patience. She has watched the Deceiver destroy most of us, and there will be no reinforcements from home. Nobody else is coming. That was decided before the group left."

She looked up into his shadowed face and blew out a breath. "I don't want to die. We just found each other. We've just gotten good again."

He kissed her forehead. "I don't either. Yet our purpose is not to fight for survival. We're here to destroy the Deceiver, and we promised to do whatever it takes. One of Astra's tasks is to make sure we remember that. If she can't hold us to that purpose she's got to clear us out of the road."

She gritted her teeth against a surge of rebellion. Why would Astra have to clear them out of the road? Why couldn't she just leave them in peace?

Then she thought of the life she had lived nine hundred years ago, and how the Deceiver had preyed upon her and her human family. Astra couldn't leave them in peace because as long as the Deceiver existed, there was no peace to be found for them anywhere on Earth. She rubbed her eyes.

"I don't know how can she live that way."

"She's been under an intolerable pressure for a long time. The thing is, I'm not sure what it has done to her sanity." He frowned, put an arm around her and pulled her against his side. "I don't remember enough about our original life, but she seems changed somehow from who she originally had been. She's different in a way that I haven't been able to pinpoint."

She searched his face. "What do you think it is?"

"I don't know. I just don't want you to trust her blindly because of who she once was to us. We've all changed in ways I don't think any of us understand, but you and I have become the most human." He paused. "We should get dressed. We all have to talk."

She nodded. "I know."

He shifted to face her and sank his hands into her hair. She held still as he rubbed his face in the thick, curling mass. Then he lifted his head to smile at her. He whispered, "I love your hair."

She leaned against him, feeling warm all over. He was such a settled, mature man. In many ways, he was more worldly and informed than she was. The wonder that filled his expression in that moment made tears well in her eyes.

"It's a pain in the neck at the best of times," she said softly. "I keep it long enough so that I can pull it out of the way, but after everything that's happened this last week, I think it might be better if I just cut it short."

"Please don't. It's gorgeous."

"All right."

"Thank you." He smiled, cupped her face and kissed her, his lips lingering over the shape of hers. She stroked his cheek, kissing him back. He pulled away and gave her a grave look. "Now we talk."

She grimaced. "I hope we at least get a cup of coffee first."

Michael pulled on his jeans and boots. "Wait here. I'll scrounge up something for you to wear."

"Thanks."

While he was gone, she searched for something she could use to tie back her hair. He didn't seem to have any simple rubber bands anywhere in the room. Finally she stole a shoelace from a pair of shoes. She finger-combed her hair, braided it with practiced fingers and tied the ends as tightly as she could.

After a few minutes, Michael returned with the pair of jeans she had worn yesterday. Astra had washed them. He had also gone down to the boat to retrieve her shoes and the long-sleeved thermal shirt she had borrowed. The ends of the shirt came down to her thighs, but the clothes were comfortable and that was all that mattered to her. She rolled the sleeves up until they hung at her forearms.

They left the bedroom to find Astra sitting at the dining table, eating a bowl of leftover chicken and dumplings. Mary was very aware of Astra's cool, blackbird eyes watching them move around the kitchen.

A white-speckled blue pot on the stove held more chicken and dumplings, and the coffeemaker at the counter held a full pot of coffee. Two empty mugs sat on the counter. Mary poured coffee while Michael ladled chicken and dumplings into two bowls. Then they joined Astra at the dining table.

Astra nursed a glass of tea while Michael and Mary ate their meal. Michael's bowl of stew disappeared fast, and he polished off a second helping before Mary had a chance to finish hers. Meanwhile, the silence stretched out between the three of them, and it was not a calm, peaceful one.

Astra was the one who spoke first. "You're a pair of damn fools. And the risk you took yesterday was inexcusable."

Mary set her spoon down on the table and met the older woman's hard, angry gaze.

Somehow she managed to wrestle her own anger under

control. She kept her tone soft and even as she said, "We didn't agree on this subject yesterday, and we're not going to agree today, so let's just cut to the chase. Do you want to waste time going over who should have done what? Or do you want to talk about something relevant? And by the way, Jerry's just fine, but Jamie's dead. Thank you so much for asking."

Astra's expression underwent a drastic change. "What are you talking about—Jamie's dead? I called Jerry this morning, and he said Jamie was just fine."

Mary sat back in her seat. She and Michael exchanged a look. Michael said, "That's not Jamie. It's Nicholas."

Astra's gaze narrowed on Mary. "Well, that's unprecedented," she said, almost to herself. "And potentially very, very useful."

Mary closed her eyes and pinched her nose. "Just don't go there. Nicholas gets to do whatever he wants with this second chance. He's already lost his life once. I hope he stays the hell away from all of us."

"He won't," said Astra. "He'll come back, and when he does, I'll make use of him again."

She knew better. She knew she shouldn't engage, but she just couldn't help herself. "People are not your tools to use as you see fit."

Astra leaned forward, slapping her flattened hands on the table. "Do you know what you did yesterday? You and Michael risked your lives for two people. Two people. Do you know what the Deceiver did yesterday? He killed at least twenty that I know of. And that is *NOTHING* compared to the kind of destruction he has wreaked on this earth."

Mary blinked. "What are you talking about? Who did he kill yesterday?"

This time it was Astra and Michael who looked at each other. Astra said, "She hasn't heard the news."

She looked from the old woman to Michael, who leaned back in his seat. His pewter gaze darkened, one of his hands resting beside his empty dish. His hand balled into a fist. "I haven't had time to tell her."

Mary's stomach clenched. "Whatever it is, I think you'd better tell me now."

Michael's mouth tightened. "He massacred eight people in a restaurant not far from the cabin and framed us for it. That was how he mobilized the authorities to look for us."

Mary felt the blood leave her face.

Astra watched her closely. "Those weren't the only people he killed. The body that he left in your old house was that of a computer salesman. The man had a wife who was searching frantically for him. The Deceiver took that man like he took your ex-husband, and he makes drones as casually as other people make scrambled eggs."

Michael said, "Astra."

"No, I'm not going to shut up." Astra's expression turned ruthless. "Meanwhile you two chose to risk your lives on just two people. Don't get me wrong. They are nice people. But they are just two. If the Deceiver had destroyed you, everybody else that he would kill would be *your* fault."

Michael slammed his fist on the table. "Stop it."

Mary stood and listened to the echo of her chair as it clattered backward onto the floor.

"I'm going to take a few minutes," she said. The words scraped her throat raw.

"Mary," Michael said. He reached for her.

She threw up her stiffened hands as if to push away the news or keep Astra's words from hitting her, but she couldn't reverse time, or save any of the people, or erase anything that Astra had said. All she could do was stop from hearing more.

"Stop," she said. "I'm going to take a few fucking minutes."

He rose to his feet as she headed blindly for the door.

Astra said, "Let her go."

"You had to push it, didn't you?" Michael's voice was savage. "What the hell is the matter with you?"

Mary didn't wait to hear anymore. She wrenched the door open and ran outside. But she couldn't run away from what was already inside her head.

MANY LONG YEARS ago, Astra had made up a pretend mate who cared.

See, she said to her pretend mate. This is why I keep wondering if I have to kill them.

If they are not with me, they are against me in a thousand ways that matter. They distract me. They drain my energy. They keep me up late at night, sleepless with worry, when I should be working on other things. They present targets to the Deceiver for manipulation and corruption, and they might possibly turn into outright enemies.

She couldn't kill them just because they drove her crazy, could she?

No, she could not. That was something the Deceiver would do. Not her. If that was her line in the sand, then so be it.

She and the Deceiver had once been young. Yes, she remembered the early days of their first life all too well. As all mated pairs of their kind, they had been born together, and they had known each other from early childhood.

Echoes of their raging fights still played in her memory. Even now sometimes in dreams they got in each other's face and cut loose in screaming matches fit to wake the dead.

How many times had she told him? Ask, don't take. Give back sometimes. When are you going to grow up? Why do you have to destroy everything you touch? The hell's the matter with you?

She made Michael tell her the details of what had happened when they had gone after Jerry and the boy. Then, for a wonder, she got him to agree to let her talk to Mary alone.

She couldn't believe he had given in. It wasn't from anything clever she had done. He had flared and snorted like a highbred stallion gearing up for a kick-ass fight, just as she'd known he would, and utter exhaustion had seeped into her old bones. She wondered if she had the energy to take any more.

For a mercy, he had seen it in her face and curbed his temper. Much to her surprise she found herself out the door and looking for the other idiot.

Give back sometimes. Oh, Lord.

She found Mary kneeling in the vegetable garden, and she shuffled near to see what the young woman was doing. This far north, the growing season had not truly set in, but the land on the island loved to produce. Mary was weeding the garden in the early afternoon light.

The younger woman said, "It seems like the more I recover of my memories, the more I've been calling on God. I wasn't a particularly religious or spiritual person before this week. Did our people believe in God?"

"Some did," Astra grunted. She shrugged, though Mary didn't see it. "Some didn't. Maybe you've just had a bad time and need to hang on to something bigger than yourself."

"Is that why you call on a Creator?"

"Guilty as charged," she said.

Mary's head came up and her red-rimmed eyes were hot. "I just want to know one thing. If God exists, how could he have created something like the Deceiver?"

Astra exhaled in a silent snort. This was why she was neither a philosopher nor a poet. She didn't have the god-damn time. Acid corroded her words. "That is not a new or original question. Believe me, it has been asked countless times before."

Mary's expression hardened. "I don't give a damn about new or original, or what somebody else has asked. These are *my* questions."

Astra rubbed her face and sighed. "How we got placed in this universe is beside the point. The real questions are, what are we going to do about it? How do we live our lives? How do we die our deaths? We are all creators. We are responsible for creating our own identities, our own realities. You can't blame the Deceiver on the Creator. He wasn't victimized by an immutable nature that some deity inflicted on him. He didn't have to become the person he became. He made choices. He and I could have balanced each other in half a dozen different ways. He could have been . . ." Her throat locked. She had to force herself to go on. "He could have been the highest Prince of our people. Instead he became our worst criminal."

Mary ground the heels of her hands into her eyes. "Why didn't we destroy him when we had him imprisoned?"

Astra's gaze was steady. She said, "Because destroying him would have meant destroying me. Our ruling council decided instead to imprison him. From that point on, every murder, every atrocity he committed is on my shoulders as well as his."

Mary's hands fell away. "How can you say that? You just said he's responsible for his own choices, his own crimes."

"True, but we had already discovered the extent of his crimes at home," Astra said. "And we had him imprisoned. Then we made a choice. We didn't destroy him because I didn't want to die, and the council didn't want to kill me. We wimped out. I won't make that mistake again. There have been too many Northside Restaurants, too many gas ovens and beheadings, and famines, and political assassinations and wars. This poor world has enough to deal with without the Deceiver adding to its burdens. You have to understand something. Destroying him is worth everything we've paid, everything that we will pay. Never forget, he is doing do *everything* in his power to destroy us too."

Mary sat back on her heels, and her eyes went wide. "I thought when one twin died, the other one did too. Can he survive if you're destroyed?"

"I think so. Probably," Astra said. "He wants to badly enough. He did something to alter us when he escaped and came to this world. As a group, we all changed something of our nature when we followed him to become at least partly human. We are literally no longer the people we once were."

She watched as Mary slowly shook her head, her gaze unfocused. "What really happened to Ariel and Uriel? He told me that he destroyed one, and the other just unraveled."

"I think he was able to destroy them both, partly because one didn't want to survive without the other. That mattered more to them than why we came here." She paused, then repeated with slow emphasis, "It's all about choices."

"Whatever you're trying to say to me now, I wish you would just say it." Mary's voice turned weary.

"I'm trying to say that we're still making choices right now that will affect the outcome of this struggle." Passion made Astra's voice shrill. "We need all of our dedication focused on winning this battle. Remember the sacrifice you made when you chose to come to this world. That sacrifice is still relevant and necessary. Destroying the Deceiver is not just worth my life. It's worth all of our lives."

"Don't preach at me anymore right now, damn it." The younger woman dashed the back of her hand across her eyes. "You've done nothing but push at me since we've become reacquainted. I don't want to hear platitudes about making choices or making sacrifices, or about living or dying well, or reasons why we came here. I've already lost the life I had. I just lost someone that I loved very much. And as you pointed out in excruciating detail, I've lost count of how many people have died just in this week alone."

"Kinda makes you want to run away from it all, doesn't it?" Astra said.

She had gone probing for a nerve and found one.

Astra's shoulders sagged when Mary's gaze fell away. Even now, Astra thought, after all this time and all that has happened, Mary cannot wholly commit to this battle. How many more Justins will it take to end this? How many more blood-filled decades would they have to witness or sacrifices would Astra have to endure?

Sadly, she bent over Mary's kneeling figure and reached out a hand.

"Astra," Michael said from behind her.

She looked over her shoulder, then straightened.

Michael stood a good fifteen feet away from her, and in one hand he held his gun.

WHEN ASTRA HAD gone outside to talk to Mary, Michael had prowled the confines of the cabin while he wondered how long he should let them to talk.

The tired expression on Astra's face had been enough for him to step aside and let her go out to Mary. But the decision left him feeling uneasy.

And so he prowled.

Why was he so uneasy?

Possible answers came quickly. He was losing his perspective. After lifetimes of increasing self-isolation, he had allowed someone inside his fortress. He had become invested. In some ways, it was easier when everything was pastel. One could make hard decisions without having one's thinking skewed by fear, grief and pain. Just look at how those emotions tore at Mary.

He paced the length and breadth of the cabin while his patience grew thin. He looked out at the women in the garden and studied them with a scowl. What were they saying to each other?

Astra's posture was eloquent with emotion. Tension vibrated from Mary's kneeling figure.

Mary, who had confessed that Astra scared her.

Astra, who had said yesterday that she didn't have time to mother-hen them. Yet she had been so quick to follow Mary outside.

Danger breathed gently on his internal antenna.

He never questioned his instincts. Questioning took time that could all too often turn fatal. Instead he lunged for his gun and sprinted outside.

He stood on the balls of his feet with the gun held at his side, the muzzle pointing to the ground. He kept far enough away that Astra couldn't reach him, and he noted with icy precision just how easily she could put her hand on Mary's shoulder.

"Astra," he said.

She turned and straightened. She caught sight of the gun and disappointment deepened the lines on her face. Like he gave a flying fuck.

Back away from her, he warned her telepathically. *Now.*

Michael, Astra said. *This isn't going to work. We have too much at stake. Let's diffuse the situation while we still can. Let me send her on to her next life. It would be peaceful. You can follow her if you like. We can start fresh in your next life and we'll fight the Deceiver as a united force. I swear she won't feel any fear or pain.*

I would, he said. He raised his gun.

Mary didn't notice the razor's edge she walked. Astra's body blocked Michael from her line of sight, and she was still focused on their previous conversation.

Mary said, "Why is it such a crime to want to run away from this nightmare? It's a reasonable reaction when you don't have a death wish. You're not just prepared to die, Astra—you want to. Well, I don't, and I'm still here. That counts for something, damn it."

"It counts for a hell of a lot," Michael said. "Especially when what you want more than anything in the world is to spend a summer on the beach." His swordsman's gaze slashed with Astra's.

After a moment, Astra's gaze dropped. "Of course it does." She looked shaken. She rubbed at her face. "I'm sorry. Don't mind me. I'm just so tired."

"That kind of tired can make an ugly situation worse." Michael bit out the words.

"Don't push it," Astra gritted. "I said I'm sorry."

Mary stood to brush the dirt off the knees of her sweatpants. Michael noted she still didn't seem to notice the strain between him and Astra. Her face tilted up to the northern sky. She took a few heedless steps forward.

"What's that?" In a voice that had gone small and scared, she repeated, "What is that?"

He looked up. A bare rocky patch of ground broke the line of trees, through which one could catch a glimpse of the silvery Lake. The sky was sunny and cloudless, but the northern horizon was covered in a sulfurous black haze.

Michael sent his attention winging north. Astra was already ahead of him, her expression stricken, straining.

Astra breathed, "The Upper Peninsula is on fire."

Chapter Twenty-five

WILDFIRES ARE THE very definition of running amok. They can move at incredible speeds as they consume everything in their path.

The evening before, he had radioed his people from the grounded helicopter, then walked along the southern coast of the U.P. He called lightning down several more times to be sure the fire took hold. It roared into gorgeous, ravenous life.

Its birth was helped by the fact that the main strength of last night's storm had struck along the shores of the Lower Peninsula. The Upper Peninsula had received a mere sprinkle of rain, and that had come after a long, dry spring.

As a consequence, the land was dry as a bone. A steady northeasterly breeze blew off the Lake and provided a perfect fan for the growing flames.

What a prodigious bonfire he would have.

He continued along the shore and called his creatures to come to the holocaust, until trees exploded from the brilliant heat of leaping red flames while black-winged shadows danced in the psychic realm.

He had come to this earth to start a new life. They just had to come after him, didn't they? Every time he tried to build something, create his own empire, reach for a new beginning, either she or one of her group was there to get in his way. He had never been able to escape her presence, not once in his excessively long life. He was always aware she lay in wait for him somewhere.

She pushed him to reckless acts of destruction. She made him who he was.

He was sick to death of this cat-and-mouse game. She had a talent for hiding. Very well then, he would smoke her out.

Because people didn't just vanish. Like all physical creatures they could be measured and weighed.

She could be captured, imprisoned. She could be tortured, killed.

He just had to find her. He had to be clever and take extreme care.

He had another advantage over her. He had remained strong whereas she had grown weak. One good thing had come from chasing Mary and Michael up north. He had been forced to gather most of his servants together. The bitch was close—closer than she had been in a long, long time. She could be measured, dissected.

Destroyed? Would he finally get to taste that elusive freedom?

Oh, he had to be very clever.

He had to push until her iron control cracked. He had cracked her before. He could do it again. He had to make her slip, drop her cloak. Then he would be able to sniff her out, along with the warrior and that elephant-loud clown.

"Come on," he whispered into the wind that grew ash-tainted and noxious with sparks. His people worked through the night to spread the blaze as fast and as far as they could. Humans and animals burned, and news services called it terrorism, and the green land turned first red, then black as it died.

"Show me where you are," he murmured as he searched the psychic realm. He arranged the positioning of various creatures and servants and drones, and they all poised ready for an attack.

Just after noon it happened.

She cracked. Grief welled on the air, as fine a flavor as any aged wine. For a marvelous, magical moment her cloak slipped. He couldn't sense anything more from the bitch than that. But he sensed the warrior's blade-sharp presence. Most especially he sensed the clown. He dove toward them and inhaled every clue he could with obsessive greed.

The fire hadn't smoked them out in a literal sense. They were safe, stationary and on an island.

An island?

Then Astra resumed control. Her cloak came back down, but by that time it didn't matter. He hadn't gathered much information, but it was enough to take to his army of experts for a consultation, and to study satellite pictures and maps. They searched every graphic representation of the area they could find.

It took hours, but he finally noticed an anomaly between the human-created maps and the satellite pictures that his human servants showed him. He tried to point it out to his human servants. They had an annoying tendency to forget what they saw, no matter how many times he showed it to them.

Victory sang in his stolen veins.

He breathed, "Gotcha."

Chapter Twenty-six

MARY HUDDLED IN her overlarge, borrowed shirt and rubbed her face. The muscles around her eyes ached from the strain of staring so hard at the hellish black smoke that spread like spilled ink on the blue horizon.

It looked like the earth itself had sustained some unimaginable injury and had cracked wide open. The smoke stretched as far as the eye could see in either direction. How large would the blaze have to be to make the entire northern skyline that dark?

She wanted to shout at it. *No, no, heal.* But she could only heal the body, not the land. The horizon still darkened, and the land still burned.

"I'm going to see what information I can gather." Michael's face had settled into grim lines. He strode inside.

Astra stood in the middle of her vegetable garden, hugging herself as she stared north. Mary hovered beside her, until a bitterly sharp wind started to blow off the Lake. She jogged inside, dragged one of Michael's sweaters over her head, grabbed Astra's battered jean jacket and went back out.

Astra stood as she had left her. Mary draped the jacket gently over those thin shoulders and held it in place until Astra moved to grasp the edges of the denim.

Astra's wrinkled face gleamed with damp streaks. There was nothing left of menace, no cheerful malice, no brusque kindness, no furious manipulator, nothing but an old woman bearing a weight of sadness that went so deep it could have broken apart the world.

When Astra spoke, her voice was a thin, dry thread of sound. "He did it."

"Are you sure?"

The old woman nodded. "I'm sure. You would think that he would get tired too sometimes."

Mary put an arm around Astra's shoulders and hugged her close. She whispered, "It's so senseless."

"He's certainly capable of that. Usually, though, there's a motive if you bother to look hard enough for it." Astra took the edge of her jacket sleeve and scrubbed at her cheeks. "Is it any wonder I would give anything to stop him?"

"We're going to stop him," Mary said. She injected a flat certainty into her voice.

A ghost of a laugh made Astra quiver against her side. "You're good, kid. You should be onstage."

Mary hugged her again and looked up at the sky. She said, "You know, after this whole thing is over, my summer on the beach is going to be the best vacation anybody could have. There will be lobster salad and crab pâté, a discreet waitstaff and pristine white sand just outside the hotel room's French doors. Michael is very enthusiastic about the red string bikini I'm going to buy."

She glanced sidelong at Astra. A corner of the old woman's mouth lifted in a reluctant smile. "I'll just bet he is."

Mary told her cheerfully, "We'll get one for you too. Yours will be very chic. How about black?"

Astra's blackbird eyes cut over to her, and this time her smile turned real. "Get thee behind me, Satan."

She grinned, glad that they were no longer arguing and that Astra showed signs of returning to life. "What's wrong with that? I don't see why not if you want to."

"It would guarantee all kinds of privacy," Astra said wryly. "You wouldn't have any waitstaff left, or any other customers either. They would run off screaming. These days my boobs dangle around my waist." She sighed and rubbed her arms. "I've got chores, and it's getting colder. I've got to feed the chickens and pen them in their coop. Then we'd best go inside until Michael can tell us what he's learned."

Mary nodded. "He'll be wearing his bad-news face."

"Bad-news face, huh?" Astra grunted. "Until you arrived, I didn't know that he had any other kind of face."

She followed Astra to the pen, helped her to feed the chickens and shoo them into the coop. Afterward, they retraced a path back to the cabin. Astra went straight to the kitchen, washed her hands and started to pull out baking ingredients.

Mary followed her. She picked up a light-colored package of quick-rise yeast. "What are you doing?"

"You two ate all my sandwiches." Astra gave her a grim smile. "And I used all my bread."

Mary left her to her baking. The locked metal door was wide open. She peeked inside. Metal, army-style lockers lined one wall. Michael sat at a desk in front of a computer. His fingers flew over the keyboard. She went back into the kitchen and washed their lunch dishes while Astra kneaded the bread dough.

Astra had set the dough to rise, and she had just put away the last of the clean dishes when Michael joined them.

Mary realized something as she watched him stride with tiger-like grace across the room. Every time he was mentally engaged with an opponent, he moved differently. There was something extra about him that came alive.

"I'll make more coffee." Astra's grim expression had never eased.

Mary sat at the dining table, planted her elbows and covered her mouth with both hands. Michael joined her.

"You already know it's bad," he said. "Apparently the fire started sometime last night, and it has already covered almost sixty miles along the southern coast of the U.P."

"Sixty miles," Mary whispered. The pit of her stomach bottomed out. The size of such a blaze was inconceivable.

Astra walked over to the table and sat down.

Michael rubbed his face. "Firefighters are being flown in from across the nation, and towns and settlements are under a mandatory evacuation. Because of the fire pattern, arson experts have put out statements that it's been artificially accelerated. A couple of news websites are claiming it's a terrorist attack."

"They're right," said Astra quietly. "If not quite in the way they envision."

Mary listened until her mind, already stretched from dealing with the events of the last couple of days, couldn't absorb anymore. Then she simply gave up, walked into the kitchen area and focused on pouring three cups of the freshly brewed coffee.

"He could have located his base of operations as far north as Marquette," Michael said. His eyes were sharp and his expression clear, even tranquil. "But I don't think so. I think he's operating from a mobile base stationed on the U.P., so that he can keep an eye on his handiwork."

Astra tapped gnarled fingers against her mouth. "I agree."

Mary put a cup in front of Astra and another in front of Michael. He captured her hand to squeeze her fingers in brief, silent thanks.

"Several of the news reports claim that a couple of hikers saw lightning strike from a cloudless sky yesterday evening. So," Michael continued, "we know it's him. In order to avoid being evacuated, his base has to be disguised as official somehow—either the police, or the National Park Service, or maybe the National Guard. The President is expected to declare Michigan a state of emergency sometime by midnight, so his base may be disguised as a mobile army unit."

"Sounds logical." Astra sipped coffee.

"Let's take the offensive." Michael said it with the casual tone one might use to suggest taking a walk. "We're together, and Mary and I have had a chance to rest and eat. Let's do what we came here to do and go hunt him down."

Mary had grown used to a pulse of dread at regular intervals. This time, it was mingled with an anxious excitement. She gulped hot coffee and burned her tongue. She healed the small burn absentmindedly as she looked from Michael to Astra and back again.

Astra's blackbird eyes were narrowed in thought. She appeared to be studying the handwoven blanket adorning the opposite wall. "We're not quite ready to move yet."

Michael lost his tranquility and leaned forward. "What do you mean, we're not ready? You know he's fanning that blaze to get a reaction out of us. If he doesn't get one, he is going to set the whole damned peninsula on fire."

Astra nodded. "I know."

"So let's give him a reaction. We haven't been in this strong a position in over a thousand years."

"I didn't say we should sit back and do nothing," the old woman said. "You're smart. I'm going to turn this back on you. Like you said, he's fanning the blaze because he wants to get a reaction out of us. Means he's waiting for it. Means he'll have traps set up. Now maybe you're bad and sneaky and strong enough to get through them. But maybe you're not, because he's bad and sneaky and strong too."

Michael looked at her from under lowered eyelids. "I could get through."

Astra rubbed her forehead. "Then there's Mary and me to consider. We each have our own strengths, but she and I do not have your physical attributes or skill set. So the best thing to do is to think things through before we make a move. Gather as much information as we can. Let me see what I can find out."

"We can think and move at the same time," he said. Mr. Enigmatic had gone expressionless.

Astra nodded. "We could. But I can't gather information, move and still cloak us nearly as well as I can while we're here where the island is helping me."

"I don't like it," he said, almost to himself.

Astra waved a gnarled hand. "Forget about the fire spreading. It's already beyond our control. That's for the humans to fight now. You've had your turn at gathering information. Now it's my turn. Take the evening to refuel that fancy boat of yours and pack everything you want to take with you. I'm going to lie down, and while I do, I'll see what I can find out." Then Astra pointed a finger at Mary. "You."

Mary startled. She had settled so deep into the role of a spectator she was surprised to be included in the discussion. "What?"

"Finish baking the bread, will you? In about an hour, the loaves need to go in the oven. Bake them at three hundred and fifty degrees for thirty minutes. We're going to want more sandwiches. Whatever information I can get, I'll have it by dawn. Then you two will be feisty enough to take it from there."

Michael stayed silent but the stubborn line of his jaw spoke volumes.

Astra added in a sharp tone, "I didn't get to be as old as I am by flying off the handle. We will make our move, but we must do so carefully. I would go to bed early, if I were you. Dawn is not that far away, and I'm going to wake you sooner if I get any solid information before then."

Michael's moonstone gaze lifted to Mary's. He raised his eyebrows. She realized he was silently asking for her opinion. She cleared her throat and said tentatively, "I'm a physician, not a tactician, but taking the time to prepare and gather all the information we can does sound sensible."

"All right." It was clear by his short tone that he still wasn't happy with the decision.

Astra pushed herself to her feet. "I'll see you later."

She disappeared into her room and shut the door with a decisive click.

Michael stood as well. He bent to give Mary a swift, hard kiss. "I'm going to fuel the boat."

She lifted her shoulders. "I guess I'm going to bake bread."

Michael left the cabin. Since she had a good forty-five minutes to wait while the bread dough finished rising, Mary went to the bathroom and relished brushing her teeth thoroughly. It was one of those small parts of life she could no longer take for granted.

She grimaced at herself in the mirror. The sum total of her worldly possessions had narrowed down to a pair of shoes, a pair of socks, nylon panties and a toothbrush. Oh, and her jeans, which, while clean at the moment, were stained so badly that a thrift store would reject them.

Making a mental catalogue of her current possessions made as much sense as trying to keep track of anything else in her life. The details of the week had begun to run together in a continuous, surrealistic stream of information.

My teeth are clean. I have a pair of shoes. The Upper Peninsula is on fire. I have six bullet scars on my chest. I resurrected a man. I gave another man a heart attack.

She supposed she sort of killed somebody. On purpose. It didn't matter if Justin was already dead and the Deceiver survived. She had taken a healthy man's heart and torn it to shreds.

How was that any different than shooting a gun? It was worse, sneakier and in some ways, it was more powerful. As soon as her life was in danger, she had thrown her Hippocratic oath out the window. Twice. At least the gun was an honest weapon. She had used her healing skills to kill someone.

Close to overload again, she turned on the shower,

stripped and scrubbed herself under a hot spray of water. She shampooed her hair twice. It was another one of those small parts of life that she could no longer take for granted.

When she was finished getting clean, it was time to put the bread in the oven. She brushed and braided her hair while the bread baked. When the bread was finished, she set four beautiful, golden brown loaves on the counter to cool. Whatever else she might say about Astra, the older woman was a hell of a good cook.

After Michael refueled the boat, he stocked it with a variety of weapons, which was when Mary found out what was stored in all the army-style lockers in the office-like room. She helped him carry loads down the path. By then, the bread had cooled enough that she made sandwiches, wrapped them and stored them in the fridge, just as Astra had done earlier. While she did that, Michael showered and shaved.

It was eight o'clock by the time they had finished. The sun had not yet set, and long evening shadows lay across the clearing.

Michael said, "We should go to bed, just in case she does end up waking us at three in the morning."

She followed him into his room and sat on the edge of the bed.

He sat beside her and took her hand. "What has caused that look on your face?"

She didn't try to dissemble. "I'm okay. I just have a lot of things to reconcile in my head. Things that have happened. Things that I've done. Things aren't going to magically settle into place after a conversation or two. It's going to take me some time. In the cosmic scheme of things, it's not that big of a deal, and I don't want to expend any energy on it right now."

"There's nothing to reconcile," he said. "You did whatever you did in order to survive. End of discussion."

"Easy for you to say." One corner of her mouth lifted. She noticed he was still frowning. "What's wrong with you?"

He shook his head.

It was her turn to be stubborn and pry. She persisted. "What's wrong? Tell me."

"I'm not trying to hide anything." His mouth tightened into a grim line. "I don't know what's wrong. Something."

Dread didn't pulse through her body as much as breathe a delicate chill on the back of her neck. She thought back over the afternoon and evening and slid closer to him until their thighs pressed together. He put his arm around her, pulling her close against his torso. She rested her head on his shoulder.

Aloud she asked, "Is it something I've done?"

He shook his head again and tightened his arm. "Absolutely not." He paused. "Everything Astra said made sense, didn't it?"

She thought back over their last conversation and nodded. "She's been focused on this task for so long. If she says to wait, there must be a good reason for it. It's to our advantage to have her find out what she can before we act, and in the meantime, we were able to get the boat prepared and see to some of our other needs."

"Yeah." He scratched his lean jaw. "Yet something's niggling at me."

"What do you want to do about it?"

"We do the sensible thing and rest. Tomorrow's going to be a bitch. We should sleep in our clothes in case we have to move fast."

"That sounds wise."

"Yeah," he growled. "Too damned wise."

He tilted her head up and kissed her with such passion, she felt like she went winging out of her body just to be closer to him. She ran her hands compulsively down his body. He yanked up her thermal shirt, urging her arms over her head so that he could pull it off. She could barely stop kissing him long enough to comply. He tore off his own T-shirt and kicked off his jeans while she wriggled out of hers.

He shoved her back onto the bed and fell on her. He muttered, "I'll never get enough of you."

He would never be the type of man to say pretty things. Everything he said came straight from the gut with a kind of raw honesty that meant far more to her than pretty things. And she knew he would guard her passionately, with all the considerable force of his being.

"I'm here," she whispered. She bit along his jaw, small, quick nips. "I'll always be here."

"Swear it," the tiger said. He pulled her braid out and pinned her down, gripping her by the hair, eyes blazing.

"Yes, of course. I swear."

He took her, harder than before, until she rose out of her body with the force of her climax. Her pleasure spilled out of her, into him and doubled back, until together they reached one soaring, pure note of vibration.

She still had no words for the immensity of the experience. They existed, spirits entwined together, until reluctantly they fell away, back into their own bodies.

After resting for a time, he stirred and pulled away from her to gather their clothes together. They dressed and settled back on the bed. She took the side by the wall. Michael wrapped his arms around her.

She rested her head on his shoulder and stared into the dark, and tried so hard to hold on to what they had just shared, but after several minutes, dread crept back and darkened the pleasure.

No, she thought. I can't lose this so soon. Her fingers tangled in his shirt.

As if he had read her mind, Michael covered her hand with his and whispered fiercely, "We will make it through this. We will get more time. I swear it."

She nodded and hid her face in him. He was the first to

fall asleep, one hand buried in the soft, loose mass of her hair.

She supposed his being horribly pragmatic had its moments. She tried to follow his example. After she faked it for a while, she managed to fall into an uneasy doze.

All of her dream images were filled with fire.

Chapter Twenty-seven

MICHAEL WOKE UP.

He couldn't put a finger on why, but he was patient as he tried to pinpoint the reason. Pragmatism had certain benefits. It meant he never did anything without a reason, not even waking up.

He hadn't awakened because he felt refreshed. Tiredness had accumulated to the point where he could use a week of good sleep. No, something else had disturbed him, something like his earlier niggle. Easing away from Mary's sleeping figure, he climbed out of bed.

The digital alarm clock read half past three. He slid one corner of his curtains open and looked out the window. Moonlight flooded into the room, gilding him with silver. He could see a portion of lawn, the dark edge of the bordering forest and a corner of Astra's chicken coop. The night sky was draped with sullen gray. He guessed that ash made up a good portion of it.

Mary had curled into the space he had just vacated, one

hand on his pillow, but she hadn't awakened. Careful not to wake her, he ran his fingers through the soft, loose ends of her wild, sexy hair. He sensed the trouble in her spirit and knew she wasn't completely at rest.

But that wasn't what had awakened him either.

He left the room, silent as moonlight and shadow.

The cabin's large common area was empty of both physical and spiritual creatures. He glided from doorway to doorway, pushing doors open to scan the contents inside each room. All was quiet, dark and peaceful. Just as it should be.

When he reached the door to Astra's bedroom, he hesitated only a moment before easing it open.

Her bedroom was empty.

Usually when she roamed the psychic landscape for information, she let her body rest in bed.

Michael didn't like it when things weren't the way he expected. He didn't care for surprises. In his harsh life, surprises had hardly ever turned out to be good.

What are you doing, Astra? he thought.

Moving to the center of the cabin, he stood for a moment with his hands on his hips. He glanced at the stairs to the loft but didn't bother to climb them. He could already sense that the darkened room upstairs was empty.

Barefoot and shirtless, he strode outside. The spring night air bit into his skin. The cold heightened his sense of urgency. He scanned the clearing, then made a swift circuit around the outside of the cabin. Astra's presence wasn't in any of the outbuildings.

He frowned. The clearing was only a small part of the island. Astra literally knew every inch, every broken rock, every nook and cranny of land. Going in search for her physically would take time and energy that he wasn't willing to spend.

Centering himself, he expanded his awareness. He touched Mary's presence in the house, the sleeping fowl in the henhouse, chirruping nightlife in the tangled foliage beyond the clearing. His awareness swirled through the forest, over the wetlands at the southern end, a ghost riding on the wind.

His senses kept trying to tell him that everything was as it should be. Astra was in bed. He knew that was an illusion. She wasn't in the house. He could find no sign of her energy's signature anywhere else on the island.

But he did detect other human presences.

Many human presences, in every direction. They quietly poured off several boats moored around the island, and moved fast toward land.

Shock gripped him in iron jaws. While his body stood frozen, his mind raced to the inescapable conclusion.

Astra was not on the island. She had either been taken or she had left. And she couldn't have been taken without him knowing it. So she had left voluntarily, without telling him or Mary.

She might have discovered something she needed to act on. She might have decided to make a grand, self-sacrificing gesture. If so, he would have said, Okay. You sure you don't need help? Good luck then. Make it count.

And she had known that. The old bitch had known that.

She should have awakened him so that he could resume watch on the island. She didn't do that. Staying silent had benefited her in some way. She was like him. She never did anything without a reason.

And she would do anything if she thought it would take the Deceiver down.

She was making a grand gesture, all right, but he and Mary were the sacrifice.

"You Judas," he breathed.

He found that he had room to be amused, both at the ruthlessness of her decision and at himself. While he had known she was capable of something like this, he had still been fool enough to trust her a little too much. He must have, to feel this sense of betrayal.

He hoped that she would make damn good use of the sacrifice. He, for one, had no intention of going out like a lamb to the slaughter.

He lunged inside the cabin and to his armory.

At the same time, he said telepathically, *Wake up, Mary. It's bad.*

He heard her cranky mutter from the bedroom as well as her voice in his head. *Of course it is. It's always bad.* He knew the moment she realized he was not with her and came fully awake. Her telepathic voice speared him. *Michael?*

He didn't bother to be quiet. He flipped the light on, threw open lockers and armed himself. He called, "I'm in here."

She appeared in the doorway. She held one shoe in each hand, her face crisscrossed by the pillow, her eyes wide and stricken. She sucked in a breath when she saw him. Her expression settled into a doctor's calm. Her voice turned brisk. "What can I do?"

He smiled at her. "God, I love you. I love your scent and silliness, your too fine sense of ethics and your crazy, sexy hair."

She returned his smile with a joyous one of her own. "We're not going to talk about my silliness. I'm glad you think my crazy hair is sexy. My ethics are not too fine, no man should tell a woman she smells, and I love you too."

He laughed. "Fair enough." He grabbed items from a locker and flung a Kevlar vest in her direction. She dropped her shoes to catch what he threw at her. He bent to finish yanking his bootlaces tied. "You're not that much bigger than Astra. That vest should fit. Put it on."

"Where is Astra?" She stomped her feet into her tennis shoes without untying them and pulled the Kevlar vest on, all her actions designed for optimum speed.

"Astra's gone." He tossed a black hooded mask at her. "Cover your face and hair." He jerked one over his head as well.

She obeyed. Her shocked face disappeared. "Gone?" she said, her voice muffled. "I don't understand."

"She left us, Mary. The island's surrounded."

He slapped an explosive, complete with a timer, on his computer tower and keyed it to detonate in five minutes. He didn't want anybody getting their hands on the contents of his hard drive, especially if he and Mary managed to make it off the island alive.

The explosive was designed to do maximum damage in a five-yard radius. When it went off, it would ignite other items in the armory. He straightened and swept the room to make sure he had everything he wanted, because they weren't coming back. He turned his attention to Mary.

Worried blue eyes blinked at him from two lopsided holes in a black mask. He wrapped an arm around her shoulders and steered her through the darkened cabin. She asked, "Why would she just leave?"

"She didn't see fit to inform us." He forced his voice to remain calm and even, to keep his rage contained. He paused in the doorway to scan the clearing. "But I think we're bait. We have to make our decisions based on what we know, and I've fucking had it. I'm voting us off this island. I don't see any reason why we should die without knowing why. Do you?"

"Hell no. Let's get out of here."

"They're going to have night-vision equipment," he whispered. Precious seconds trickled away so he spoke fast. "But the equipment has to be monitored by human minds, and we can fool those. I'm going to cloak us. Stay right with me and as quiet as possible. You can help me avert their attention if you focus on something inconsequential and natural. Pretend you're a mouse, or a squirrel, and keep that image fixed in your mind. All right?"

"Does it help you to know what I'm pretending?"

Pleased, he squeezed her tight. "Yes."

"I'm a mouse."

"Good. No talking and no telepathy," he warned. "Remember, mice don't talk." He paused to think of his hawk friends and the pack of wolves that had been guarding Mary when he had found her. "Much."

She shook a little. Incredibly, it was a chuckle. "Got it."

He took a few more seconds to fix the null space around them. Then he pulled her out the door. He thought through their options. One of their boats had been moored in the small bay, so taking the path to the pier was impossible. Within the next few moments, the path would become the setting for an ambush, or at the very least, they would have disabled—or sabotaged—the boat.

The island was shaped like a human foot without the toes. West and south would take them to wetlands that covered the heel of the foot. Not ideal, but then again, it wouldn't be ideal for their enemies either.

He steered Mary across the open area of the clearing, grateful she responded without question to his silent prompting, her small, compact body moving in concert with his.

They reached the forest. He let his arm fall from her shoulders and took her hand. Then he continued at a slower pace, picking a path through the dark.

Mary gripped his hand so tight the tips of his fingers throbbed. She tried to move with his stealth but couldn't quite manage it. He slowed further to help her pick her way more quietly.

The cluster of pines bordering the clearing gave way to deciduous trees. They reached a large tangle of underbrush and fallen tree limbs. They would have to circumvent it. A couple of stealthy figures approached and were sneaking around one side of the tangle. He touched Mary's mouth with a light warning finger and pulled her in the opposite direction.

He thought ahead to their next challenge. The men came to the island on boats, and they could no longer use theirs. They would have to commandeer one from their uninvited guests. There would be one or two guards left on the boats for just this kind of eventuality.

The cabin exploded. The night roared with a concussion of heat and light.

He had accounted for the explosion and had dismissed

it. It had already become a part of his past, so he didn't react other than to note that it blew right on schedule.

But what he hadn't accounted for was Mary's untrained reaction. He had forgotten to warn her.

She gasped and stumbled.

For want of a nail, the shoe was lost.

Michael had loved that old fourteenth-century poem as a small boy. He had discovered it when he had written a school report on Ben Franklin, who had quoted it.

For want of the shoe, the horse was lost, and so on, in an escalating series of catastrophic events, from horse to rider, to message, to battle, to the war being lost, and all for the want of a nail.

Just like the poem, Mary's stumble was really a small thing. But what she stumbled over had deeper connections in the pile of rotted tree limbs, ivy and sticker bushes. Something rolled and shifted. An entire four-foot section of ivy jerked in a way that was not at all natural or mouse-like, and suddenly where they were standing became the subject of intense scrutiny.

One man straightened. As he brought up his assault rifle Michael flung a throwing knife that embedded in his eye.

The second man had stayed crouched behind cover. That was unfortunate.

Michael dropped Mary's hand and launched toward him. Even as he broke the man's neck with a perfectly executed kick, he knew he was too late.

Because if they had night-vision equipment and too many men surrounding the island, then they probably had . . . He bent to grope at the dead man's blackened face and found what he was looking for, a small wire and earpiece now mangled by his kick.

Shit. Shit.

They had a comm link. With so many in their group, they would have a centralized communication point, one person to coordinate maneuvers and relay orders, often nicknamed

"God." That person would be tucked safe away from any fighting, probably on one of the nearby boats.

Shit.

As he spun back toward Mary, he caught sight of something streaking through the air toward her. He thought, I can't believe it. Did she just get shot again?

He was both right and wrong. Even as he took comfort in her bulletproof vest, the something unfurled into a nylon net that settled over Mary's head and shoulders, and she reacted in the most natural way in the world. She fought to get it off of her. The net had been designed to tighten more as the captive struggled.

He threw himself forward as another net streaked through the air. In that flash of an instant, he knew he couldn't get to her in time. He would risk them both getting tangled in the nets.

He had to stay free to maneuver. He switched course and dove. The weighted edge of the second net brushed his thigh as he rolled.

A third net shot through the air. It wrapped python-tight around Mary's staggering figure. She groaned, lost her balance and fell to the ground.

Michael's attention snapped to the person who shot the nets. He shot the man twice in the neck.

He loped over to the dying man. After reaching down to carefully remove the man's slender headset, Michael shot him in the temple to give him a cleaner death.

From twenty feet away Mary said in a quiet, flat voice, "I am not okay with this turn of events."

He kept his reply easygoing and reassuring, the quality of which alone should win him an Oscar. "Don't worry. At some point we would have had to stop sneaking around and fight."

He slid the headset on and adjusted the earpiece.

A strange young man said, "She'll have something to worry about soon enough. Hello, Michael. If I can hear you, I'll bet that you can hear me."

Michael knew who was at the centralized communication point. Well, who else would it be? How it must amuse him to play God.

"Hello, Lucifer," he said.

At the same time, he thought, if I get my hands on Astra, I'm going to kick her ass. Why the fuck couldn't she have warned us?

For want of the message, the battle was lost.

Chapter Twenty-eight

ASTRA LIKED SOME of Earth's modern vernacular.

The sixties and seventies had been a great time for slogans.

Give peace a chance. Make love not war.

That tall chick with the great nose and long, dark hair and her short, goofy-looking husband with the mustache—they had come up with some of the silliest ones she'd ever heard.

The beat goes on. What the hell did that mean? What was another one? Oh, yeah. I got you, babe.

Jerry had a slogan that she really liked. Don't push the river. There was a lot of sense in that one. How, in God's name, could you possibly push a river? You couldn't. A river flowed where it would. It was an act of insanity to even try.

Her translation of that? The universe was an easier place to live in when you stopped kicking against how things were going, and you made use of what you were given.

Or in other words: go with the flow. She liked saying it.

It made her feel hip and snappy. Groovy, as it were. Never mind how Michael would laugh himself sick at her when he was a boy. She sniffed.

For instance she had known exactly the moment her cloak had slipped. The Deceiver had not just been waiting for it to happen. He had been pushing to make it happen. She had sensed him sneak past her guard like the thief that he was.

Instead of lashing out to drive him back, instinct stayed her hand. Just for a moment. Not for too long. She had to make it look good.

When she resumed cloaking the island, she had known he had gained information about their location. So she went with the flow.

Long ago, she had chosen an island as her sanctuary for a lot of reasons, and all of them involved its remote location. She could cloak the area and make it difficult to locate. If men forgot the island was there, they couldn't draw it on any map.

Also, it was a perfect place to do battle. The only victims would be the various species that lived on the island and, of course, the land itself. She and the island had several good, long talks about that. She had wanted to be certain it understood the danger before she took up residence.

So Astra had waited until Michael and Mary went to bed. Then she got to work. For the first time in years, she went into Michael's armory/office to gather the materials she would need. She wasn't as strong as she used to be, and she had to make several trips down to a secluded area.

The only safe place to dock a boat was the little bay with the pier. The water around the rest of the island's shoreline covered an uneven rocky terrain. She particularly liked the area of shore that she chose for that night. For a good fifty yards out from land, half-submerged boulders made the water treacherous to any boat larger than her small, handmade bark canoe.

After she had gathered what she needed and carried her canoe down to the water's edge, she sat waiting in the shadow of an outcrop of rock.

The fox she had healed some time ago joined her. She allowed his companionship. He was a sensible little fellow and knew the value of hiding in silence. He curled around her ankles. She stroked his fur while she drew the tightest, most impenetrable part of her cloak around them.

Several hours after nightfall, large, dark boats surrounded the island. Men, dressed in black wet suits and armed with water-protected assault rifles, slithered over the sides of the boats and swam to shore.

One man passed by so close to Astra's hiding place she could hear his breathing. The fox trembled under her stroking fingertips, but he remained silent and stationary.

The battle at the cabin erupted. She sat unmoving. Neither Michael's shock and outrage nor Mary's hurt and fear caused her to shift. She did nothing as fire destroyed her home. She waited while Mary was netted, and by virtue of Mary's immobility, their attackers had Michael trapped.

I am a stone by the water, she thought at the night. Astra is hiding inland.

She stirred only when a sleek, dark powerboat purred into the small bay and the Deceiver stepped onto her island.

Then she lowered her canoe into the water and stacked her supplies into it. She picked up the fox and deposited him in the canoe as well. If he had stayed with her this far, he could come along for the rest of the journey.

Mary and Michael might die. She experienced a pang that faded almost as soon as it had come. If they died, they died. At least she would be done with all the drama. She no longer had room for anything else but the one task she had waited her entire existence on this earth to complete.

She was tired of being scared. She was tired of living with guilt and heartache and loneliness. She had called in all her favors. She had to go on trust that help would be available when she needed it. If she failed and the Deceiver destroyed her, well, somebody else would just have to take up the intolerable burden of this fight.

She bent over until her mouth hovered just above the

gentle lapping water, and she whispered in a voice so soft even the mosquito hovering near her ear couldn't overhear.

"Hi, Lake? He's here. Can you swallow any more swimmers that try to get to land?"

The Lake radiated placid innocence but a small finger of water plopped up to kiss her lips.

Astra breathed, "One last thing. It's important. Would you mind taking me real quiet-like to all the other boats around the island so I don't have to use my paddle? I've got to stick these newfangled explosive things to their sides."

There was a certain peace to be found in finality. The only people getting off this island would be the victors, and possibly one or two extraordinarily lucky innocents. She kept her spine straight as she sat in her bark canoe and rested her paddle across her lap. Her little fox friend sat at the prow with his bushy tail curled around his feet. His large ears swiveled and twitched at the sound of nearby gunfire.

Their patience was rewarded as a curl of intention rose underneath the canoe. They began to slide through the water in the dark.

Like she had yelled at that damn Deceiver so many times.

Ask, don't take.

Chapter Twenty-nine

MARY SPRAWLED ON the ground, trussed like someone's holiday dinner. She listened to the sounds of battle surrounding her. Her mask had skewed when she tried to free herself from the net. Her nose still poked out of a hole but she could no longer see.

She growled. Aside from the dignity factor, it was hard to hear what was happening. What she could hear was violent and disjointed.

Footsteps pounded past. Someone gave a breathless shout. Gunfire spurted. Her body flinched each time she heard the gunfire. She waited for bullets to tear into her flesh. Shivering caused her skin to ripple in trembling spasms. Locked helpless inside darkness, she began to understand how someone could die of fright.

Then she overloaded again, and her mind detached from the battle. Intimate sensory input began to preoccupy her. The ground was cold and wet with dew. Dampness seeped into her clothing. The detritus of forest underneath her, comprised of dead leaves, new plant growth and earth, smelled rich and loamy. She caught a hint of acrid smoke.

She hoped the cabin wouldn't set the rest of the island on fire. She hoped she wasn't lying in poison ivy. She had to go to the bathroom, only Michael had blown up the toilet.

I have nylon panties, socks and shoes, she thought. I have a Kevlar vest and a damn inconvenient mask.

I have two nets. No. I guess two nets have me.

I have a headache. I have a bad feeling.

Her mind settled into cool focus. Michael fought because he wouldn't leave her. He didn't snatch her up and carry her away because he couldn't. There were too many men that had converged on their location. He hadn't killed her yet because he still had hope he could get them out of this alive. Their opponents hadn't touched her because she was the least of their worries, with Michael loose and running at full throttle.

She realized something else as well. It was actually possible to be terrified and bored at the same time. She sighed. It was time for her to see what she could do to help.

Slipping out of her body really was a clever trick. She sat up and glanced down at her body with a grimace. From the hips down she was still connected to her physical self. She could still feel the binding of the nets cutting off the circulation in her legs, and the cold dampness of the ground. Apparently she was only partly astral.

She looked around, surprised to find the psychic realm clean of dark spirits. It carried hints of Lake, and forest, and healthy land, all of what she would have expected to find. Perhaps Astra's influence still lingered. Whatever the reason, Mary was grateful Michael didn't have to battle spirits.

She sought out Michael's presence. He hadn't gone far. He was in the process of stalking two men.

Three more were stalking him.

She pulled the rest of the way out of her body and rushed

at the three men. Concentrating mightily, she managed to scoop up handfuls of leaves to throw in their faces. Two of them flinched in surprise. The third tapped at his headset as if it had suddenly stopped working.

She paused, cocked her head and watched the man. Did her presence cause static?

Suddenly Michael was there. In a flurry of action too fast for her to follow, he killed all three men. His body bore a light sheen of sweat. He had removed his mask. She could see the calm executioner in his face and noted with relief he had yet to take any wounds.

What are you doing? he asked.

Unable to resist the hot illumination of his presence, she flitted toward him, a moth to the flame. *I got tired of waiting for you. I thought you could use some help.*

He laughed softly. *I'll try to be a little faster, shall I?*

I wouldn't mind. He crouched and sprang somewhere. Disoriented, she looked around. She found him standing high in the limbs of an old oak tree. As he surveyed the shadowed area for oncoming attackers, she floated up to join him. *Michael, I think my astral presence disrupts radio signals. Do you want me to try to mess up their communications?*

His head snapped up. His eyes flared with what looked like panic. *NO!*

The force of his reaction blew her like a feather out from him. She didn't gain control of her position until she had drifted down several branches, and she concentrated on floating back up beside him. *Why not?*

He listened intently at his stolen headset, tapped the earpiece, then he whispered out loud, "Mary, the Deceiver is controlling their communications. If you can disrupt the radio signals of the men in our immediate area, fine, go ahead and do it. For pity's sake, stay close to your body, and remember he might overhear telepathy."

I understand. She floated back down to the ground.

Searching the immediate area, she found armed black-clad men and rushed at them. She caused their headsets to erupt with an unexpected crackle of static, or startled them with an explosion of leaves, or made them flinch at strategic times when she trailed ghostly fingers along their bare skin. Once she managed to rock the aim of one rifleman who had Michael in his sights. That took a gargantuan effort.

After several minutes of frenetic activity, she shook with strain. She knew she couldn't continue for much longer, yet she was unwilling to give in to exhaustion. Their attackers tightened in a circle around her and Michael like a hangman's noose.

Their fight felt hopeless. There were so many attackers. Michael had killed, what, fifteen already? There had to be over a hundred or more.

But she had thought their battle at the cabin was hopeless. She had been convinced at Petoskey that she wouldn't live to set foot on a boat. She had no real sense of Michael's limits. When he had run up the side of the building at Petoskey's marina? Boy howdy, she hadn't seen that coming.

She turned her attention back to her body. She could affect the physical realm if she concentrated hard enough. Frantic to get rid of the hood, she threw everything she had into pulling at it. With an immense effort, she managed to yank it off her face.

Then she attacked the tight nylon bonds, plucking fiercely at the stubborn strands. If she could loosen the loops around her arms, she would have some freedom of movement once she slipped back into her body.

How long could she afford to stay out of her body? Would it kill her if she remained astral for too long, or would she simply snap back into her body?

Then something reverberated through the psychic realm that struck past faith and hope, and filled her with unreasoning terror.

The black diamond man stepped onto the island.

She lost control of her astral projection and slammed back into her body. Deprived of physical movement, drained of psychic strength and helpless, she whimpered, a panicked animal sound.

I have just one question for you, Mary, Mary, said the Deceiver. *How can one small person make so much noise?*

Sweat trickled down her ribs. Michael was caught in battle. God only knew where Astra was. She couldn't do anything. She had no more magic tricks to pull out of her hat. She could only wait and watch while hell approached.

Something struck her back. She jerked and cried out. It took her a moment to realize that the blow had not hurt her. Something had fallen and bounced off her back.

It's a present, Michael said. *Work fast.*

Michael had thrown something at her. Work fast at what? Rolling over, she landed on something cold and hard. Arching her body and twisting, she groped for the cold, hard thing and closed her fingers around a handle. It was some kind of tool.

She rolled back onto her side, careful not to wriggle and cause the nets to tighten again. She had managed to loosen the nets. It wasn't much, just enough so that she could touch her hands together. Forcing her breathing to remain deep and steady, she ran shaking fingers along the tool as she tried to figure out what it was.

It felt like a thick pocketknife, a fancy, complicated one. Maybe it was a Swiss Army knife. She dug her fingernails into one of the grooves and pulled on it. A blade emerged halfway before her hold slipped, and she sliced open a finger. Damn.

Mary? Michael said.

"I'm working on it," she gritted.

The black diamond man strolled up the path to the clearing where the ruins of Astra's cabin still blazed. Half a dozen bodyguards ringed him. He spoke into his headset. More guards joined his group. He was taking no chances with this meeting.

She resumed a frantic exploration of the knife, digging

for grooves and pulling parts of it out. Where was that damn blade?

What was that one? Shit, it was a corkscrew. What she wouldn't give for a stiff drink right now. In safety. She shoved it back in and pulled something else out.

What was that? Her questing fingertips found a sharp hook at the base of the section. She reversed the handle in her hands, located a strand of the net and sawed at it. She sliced through the strand.

Eureka. She grabbed another strand and attacked it.

As she worked, an upsurge of activity yanked her attention back to Michael. He fought a couple men, trying to work his way back to her. He seemed to be moving more slowly. Several more fighters raced to join the battle.

Why was Michael moving so slowly?

A couple of the newcomers shot him. The percussion of their weapons sounded strange. Michael didn't seem to react with much pain. He shot one man point-blank in the face, kicked at another and lurched closer to her. More men poured into the space between them.

What is it? she shouted.

Drugged darts, he said. Even his telepathic voice sounded slurred.

She froze, breathing hard. Should normal human medication affect him like that? Michael had a finely developed sense of separateness between spirit and flesh. Tranquilizers might bring his body down, but psychically he should be as alert as ever. Something was terribly wrong.

At last she got her arms free. She turned onto her side and curled into a ball to attack the bindings on her legs. Inside she was screaming.

Slowed, drugged, Michael continued to fight. He remained lethal and on his feet long after a normal human would have collapsed. In a lunge, he came within a few yards of her. Two men tackled him and brought him down. Even as he twisted to stab one in the neck, more darts struck his neck and hands.

I'm sorry, he slurred.

You have nothing to be sorry for, she told him. *Nothing.*

He didn't reply. His prone body went still.

Two more men darted forward to bind Michael's arms and legs. The black diamond man waited in the clearing with his guards until they were finished. Then he strolled toward her, his elegant figure silhouetted by the blazing cabin behind him.

She froze. Could he see that she had cut partway through the tangle of net? She was lying on one of her arms. She shifted the knife to that hand and, using just her wrist, she surreptitiously worked at sawing through the strand of net that bound her calves.

"Hello, cookie," said the man.

His voice was young and male. She had never heard it before but it still held a terrible familiarity. It was the voice from all her night terrors.

Still talking, he drew closer. "Michael's body count is already at twenty-three. The amount of money and manpower that bastard has cost me is unbelievable. Well, it could be worse. Thank God for modern pharmaceuticals, huh? The drug in those darts is one of my own concoctions. I created it specifically for just such an occasion, and I'm glad to see it worked."

"Did you kill him?" Her mouth shook. She didn't recognize her own voice and she couldn't sense Michael's energy. She had almost cut through the strand.

"Not yet. The amount of sedative he took would have knocked out a giraffe. I would have preferred talking to both of you at the same time, but it is impossible to reason with Michael. There's nothing you can do except shoot him like a rabid dog. Sometimes that can be kind of sexy, but it's so damn infuriating. Personally, I always thought you could do better. Just because he's your soul twin doesn't mean he has to be your lover." His footsteps stopped by her head. "Know what I mean?"

She froze, her breathing coming in quick, shallow pants. She clutched the knife in a death grip. During my summer on the beach, she thought, my summer off . . .

The black diamond man bent over her. The unspeakable nightmare whispered in her ear, "All right, cookie. Where is the bitch?"

She said in that stranger's raw voice, "She left us. She was gone when we woke up."

"I think she's still close," he said. "What do you think?"

"I swear I don't know anything," she gasped. "I swear it."

Something exploded in the bay.

The black diamond man leaped to his feet. Five others in quick succession followed the first explosion. Deep booming concussions shook the trees, all sounding from different points around the island. Light flared from beyond the tree line, an incandescent necklace of destruction.

"Jesus *fuck*," someone said.

"Report!" the Deceiver bellowed. "Report now, goddamn it!"

And another man's voice: "There were six. Six explosions. Somebody just blew all our boats."

In the tiniest breath of a whisper in her mind, Astra said, *Buy me some time. Just a few more moments, cookie.*

At the same moment the Deceiver turned on her. He roared, "*TELL ME WHERE SHE IS!*"

Time.

A kind of insane fury took her over, built on centuries of struggle. It was clear and cold like freezer-chilled vodka, and it sliced away all of her terror. She barked out a laugh. "Right. I'm so motivated to do that."

He kicked her. "Tell me, you sack of shit!"

"Fuck you," she gasped. "Oh wait. You're already fucked." Still laughing, she curled tighter to protect herself from the blows.

Just a few more moments, cookie.

He continued to kick at her. A crescendo of pain swept

away her laughter, until she began to disconnect from her physical body. She fought to stay present and connected.

No, she said to her body when his steel-toed boots slammed into her. *Heal.*

Dampening the pain, she managed to snag another groove on the knife with her fingernails, and she pulled out a thin, sharp blade.

Then she noticed an oddity in the tableau of forty or so watching men. A small, skinny shadow puppet, held together with pins and wishes, stumped up to an army of alert, trained guards who didn't appear to notice anything. Astra.

Shots rang out. Mary had no idea who was shooting, but two men fell and didn't move again, and another one writhed on the ground, screaming. The rest erupted into frantic movement, most of them running toward the trees. The Deceiver whirled with a roar to face this new threat. He didn't appear to see Astra either.

Part of healing is the knife. Sometimes you have to cut the cancers out.

Mary rolled and pushed to her feet. She aimed for his cervical spine at the back of his neck and drove the blade in deep. She wasn't picky. Anywhere between vertebrae C1 and C8 would do. She sent her awareness spearing down the knife's edge to make sure she struck her target—and she severed his spinal cord.

The Deceiver's bellow of rage choked into silence. His head fell back and his back arched, and his body collapsed to the ground. Almond-shaped dark eyes blazed with a nuclear-hot fury, but his body was now effectively a quadriplegic. He was trapped as long as he couldn't touch anyone else to leap into another body.

"Asshole," Mary said, still in that stranger's ragtag voice. Ignoring the rapid, staccato sound of gunfire, she wiped the blade on her thigh, snapped it shut and shoved the knife into her pocket, sucking in deep draughts of the cold night air as she stared down at him.

The black diamond man sat up, out of his paralyzed body. His head tilted back as he looked at her.

Well, shit.

She whirled and lunged for Michael's body, fell to her knees and swept her hands over him. She grabbed every dart she found. Come on, damn it. There—several darts had stuck in his Kevlar vest. They couldn't have discharged the drug into his system. She snatched at them and whirled, just as the black diamond man bent over her kneeling figure. He wrapped his arms around her.

Time to say good night, cookie.

A discordant humming dug bitterly sharp talons into her mind. Pain scalded her. She fell to the ground, her back arching. The talons ripped at her. She heard herself start to ring like strained crystal.

"Oh no, you don't," she gasped. She concentrated on crawling forward toward his body. She managed to claw forward a few feet.

Was she close enough? She had to be. Blinded with pain, consumed by the lethal noise that threatened to shatter her mind, she reached out as far and as hard as she could and stabbed downward with her fistful of darts.

She connected.

The black diamond man screamed in her face. With a groan she twisted away, straining to get distance from his malignancy.

His presence flickered and weakened. Gathering her energy, she shoved at his spirit with the full force of her revulsion. His hold on her slipped and fell away.

The sound of gunfire came closer. She didn't look around. Her eyes refused to focus, and her ears kept ringing.

Only one thing mattered. She crawled back to Michael, running her hands up his body until she found his neck with shaking fingers. His pulse was slow, strong and steady. She pulled out her new best friend, the pocketknife, and opened up a blade to cut through the bindings on his arms and legs.

"Sorry, lover," she muttered. "Time to wake up."

She had lost the ability to finesse a long time ago. She shoved her awareness into his body, located his adrenal glands and punched them into the next week.

Michael's back arched so violently his torso left the ground. She lost her hold on him. Her ear itched. She scratched at it, and her fingers came away slick with wetness.

Michael grabbed her, and he held her so tight her bones creaked in protest. He was dragging in deep breaths as though he had just run a marathon. Apparently he had lost the ability to finesse as well, because his bright, golden presence pierced her like a spear of light as he scanned her.

Her senses were too bruised and abraded. She gasped and flinched away from his touch.

His hold loosened and he shifted suddenly. As she squinted at him, he snatched at his rifle and snapped it to his shoulder.

"Ease up, Michael," a familiar voice said sharply. "I'm friendly fire."

Jamie was here?

Not Jamie. *Nicholas.*

"What are you doing here?" Michael rolled to his feet. "You're supposed to be with your father and sister."

"I saw them to the safe house and came back to see if there was anything I could do. I got here as fast as I could."

Mary struggled to stabilize her senses so that she could see. Her head throbbed as her vision remained blurred, and she kept seeing double. She swiped at her eyes. Where had Astra gone? She could have sworn that she had seen Astra earlier.

Nicholas stood nearby, his long hair bound tightly off his strong, sensual face. He had found black jeans and a black sweater somewhere, and he still wore Jamie's silver and leather bracelets and held a semiautomatic in one hand. Michael strode over to him. Figures raced across the clearing toward them, and both men lunged into a brutal counterattack.

The black diamond man huddled in a sullen cloud over his prone body, the crystalline force of his presence weakened. If there hadn't been enough of the drug in the darts to knock him out, the effect wouldn't last long.

She groaned at the thought of moving, forced herself up on her hands and knees and groped along the ground. There were bodies all over the place. Someone had to have dropped one of those dart guns somewhere.

She could barely see anything beyond three feet in front of her with any clarity, which was why she didn't see the figure that slipped past Michael's and Nicholas's guard to reach the Deceiver, until it was too late.

No, no, he couldn't migrate to another body and escape. The figure bent over his body, and she sucked in a breath to scream.

Then she realized the small, shabby figure was Astra. Astra reached out a hand and touched him.

The Deceiver roared. Power surged, like the dark stone-like power from her altar. Only what had happened in her dream was a small mote compared with the force that poured from the ground like Mount Vesuvius erupting.

She cowered to the ground and covered her whirling head with her arms. We caused the end of the world, she thought. I don't think we were supposed to do that.

A figure appeared out of the formless roar. It was a most elegant shape, a black diamond figure overlaid with a shining web of white radiance. The pattern reminded her of a harlequin, beautiful and deadly. It bent over her.

Perhaps she made a terrified noise. She was beyond noticing. With glowing hands, the figure gathered her close.

She could feel physical arms holding her body, but the power in the psychic realm was so gigantic it overwhelmed all her other senses. The power washed over and through her, until she felt tumbled head over heels by an enormous wave. All she could see was the harlequin's black-and-white face in front of her.

It had a bright blackbird's gaze. She cried out and clutched at it.

"There, there." The figure spoke with Astra's briskness as it patted her shoulder. "I've already healed you. You took some psychic damage, a ruptured eardrum, bruised ribs and a bad scare. It could have been worse."

"We thought you left us," Mary said. "I thought you left."

"That would have been most foolish," said the harlequin, who pressed a kiss to her forehead. Mary distinctly felt physical lips on her skin. "Because I wasn't supposed to leave until right now."

"I don't understand."

The figure laughed, and it was a carefree sound. "There isn't much to understand. The land is lending me strength so I can hold him prisoner while I say good-bye."

"Good-bye?" She clutched harder. "You don't have go. You can choose to live without him. You said you could."

"But I don't want to," it said.

"Then let go of this life, rest for a while and be reborn," she said. "You can start over in a new life."

"I'm too tired to start over. I'm ready for a different kind of ending." It passed a hand over her hair. "I am so proud of you. Thank you for all of your years of exile and sacrifice. Thank you for everything. Your obligation is finished. Make your future bright and new." It paused and cocked its head. "Oh, and one last thing." A bright blackbird eye winked at her. "Remember, my canoe is in my favorite place."

"Your canoe? Wait." She reached for the figure again, but this time she couldn't seem to touch it.

The harlequin stood. It reached into its chest with glowing, white hands. The black diamond energy roiled and emitted a howl of despair and rage.

The harlequin said, "Michael, it's time."

Michael joined the black-and-white figure. His radiance shone as golden as the sun. A clarion sound belled from him, as sharp and piercing as an angel's sword.

Astra's white energy picked up on the vibration and

intensified it until it stabbed through the fabric of reality and rang with unearthly purity.

It shattered the black diamond.

The harlequin flung out its hands and scattered the black energy, dissipating it completely. At the same moment, the harlequin broke apart. As the white energy faded, it seemed to give a peaceful sigh.

The roar of the land faded from the psychic realm. Mary lay curled on the ground. After a time, she became aware again of her physical surroundings, the cold night, the cabin's fading fire and men shouting in the distance. She ran her fingers along the quiet, unbroken ground in amazement.

Nearby, Astra's frail body lay beside the body of the Deceiver's last victim.

The nightmare is over, she realized. The Deceiver is gone. They were both gone.

Strong arms snatched at her and turned her over. Michael gathered her up and held her with bruising force. She wrapped an arm around his neck, holding him tight as he ran shaking lips along the curve of her cheek.

Michael said in a rusty voice, "Are you all right? She said you're all right. She better not have been lying, or I'll piece her back together just so I can kick her ass."

Mary stroked his hair. "I'm okay," she said. "You had a chance to talk to her too?"

"Yeah." He kissed her temple and rocked her. "She said she loved me. She said I fought well."

"You did. But I'm awfully glad you didn't get a chance to kill me," she told him.

His gaze darkened, and he held her tighter. "I am too."

Nicholas walked up to them, his semiautomatic pointed toward the ground. His slim, rangy body moved with lithe animal grace. His strong, copper-toned features still held the younger man's sensuality, but Mary's mind kept trying to see the tall, mature man. "That took care of the last of them. The body count is pretty extreme." He looked down at Astra and the Deceiver, and whispered, "Haokah."

Mary looked down too at the young man and the old woman. By some trick of chance, they had fallen so that they curled around each other like lovers. The young man was dark and beautiful, the old woman pale and so very frail. They made a perfect contrast to each other.

She huddled against Michael's chest. "This was never about us. We were always just secondary players."

"Maybe we were more like foot soldiers," he said, his expression shadowed. He smiled down at her, and the shadow faded. "Now it is our time."

An unknown future stretched in front of them. It was right across the next hilltop, around the bend, down the road, too enormous, beautiful and frightening to think about.

She touched his mouth. "I just realized something. I don't even know your last name."

"My last name will be anything you want it to be." He cradled the back of her head in one hand. "You choose."

She put her head on his shoulder. "I'm wanted for multiple homicides. I have to go to the bathroom and you blew up the toilet. We still sound like lunatics."

His chest moved as he chuckled. "Setting up new identities won't be a problem. I have a backup electronics system at another safe house." He looked up at Nicholas. "I can set up a new identity for you too, if you want."

Nicholas rubbed the back of his neck, his head bowed. "Mary was right," he said after a moment. "My father and Sara shouldn't have to lose both Jamie and me."

"I'll set one up for you, anyway," said Michael. "You should have a backup in case you need it." He glanced down at Mary. "We need to figure out our next steps."

Nicholas said, "The Dark One may be dead, but his drones aren't. They're scattered everywhere, and they will continue to follow his last orders until they die."

Michael stood and held out a hand for Mary, who took it and stood. "The drones are a problem of a generation," he said to Nicholas. "In less than a hundred years, they will all be dead and gone."

Nicholas's jaw tightened. "They can do a hell of a lot of damage in that time."

Michael shook his head. "That may be your fight, Nicholas, but it's not ours. We've been battling for six thousand years. I'm done."

Nicholas looked at Mary. She took Michael's hand and laced his fingers with hers. "Michael has been fighting for a lot longer than either you or I have. If he says he's done, we're both done."

Nicholas sighed. "I'm disappointed, but I understand."

"I will do this for you," Michael said. "Now that Astra is gone, she doesn't need the money in her bank accounts. I'll transfer the total over to an account in your name. It's a good sum. You'll go a long way on it."

"I'll take it," Nicholas said. "With thanks."

Michael looked at her. He gave her a small, private smile. "Now we have a date on a beach, and a whole summer ahead of us. All we have to do is figure out how to get off the island."

She stirred. "I know where Astra's canoe is. She told me."

"Not that little bark canoe." He groaned. "It'll barely hold my weight, let alone take the both of us."

"Astra told me about it for a reason," Mary told him. "I think it will be okay."

He looked at Nicholas. "I presume you arrived after Astra blew up all the other boats."

"Yes, I'm moored at the south end of the island," Nicholas said. He blew out a breath as he looked around the clearing. "I was going to stay and clean up here."

Mary looked around. The cabin fire still burned energetically and bodies littered the clearing. She slumped. "We'll stay and help."

Nicholas touched her shoulder. "It's okay," he said gently. "I want you to go. I could use some time to myself."

"Are you sure?" Michael asked.

Nicholas nodded. "When you get to the mainland, just call my dad and let him know I'm—Jamie—is okay."

"We will," Michael promised.

Michael did indeed know where Astra kept the canoe and he led the way. Nicholas came along with them. They found a small, anxious fox sitting in the canoe. Nicholas clucked soothingly at the animal as he scooted it into his arms.

"I haven't seen you for a while, little man." He scratched the fox behind its ear, then set it on the ground, and it stayed close to his feet.

Nicholas turned to Mary and held out his arms. She went readily into them and hugged him as tightly as she could. He whispered in her ear, "If I had a snowball's chance in hell with you, I would give him a run for his money. Don't let the bastard take you for granted."

She smiled and grew teary. "I won't. Take care of yourself, will you?"

"You too." He brushed his lips against her cheek, her mouth. Then he let her go and stepped back.

She turned to Michael to find him watching them both, his mouth drawn into a thin, jealous line. She said, "Oh, don't even be that way."

He cocked an eyebrow, then seemed to make a decision and throttled back. "Fine."

He climbed into the canoe and guided her as she climbed in too. Mary settled between his legs. The water came to just below the canoe's rim.

"Do you know how many miles it is to Beaver Island, let alone the mainland?" Michael asked. "With the canoe riding this low in the water we're going to get exactly three yards."

She glanced at Nicholas who stood nearby with his hands on his hips, watching. Even the angle of the fox's ears was doubtful.

The eastern horizon had grown lighter with the promise of a new dawn. The northern horizon was smudged with clouds of ash, but elsewhere, the sky was crystal clear and the stars were fading. It was going to be a beautiful day.

Mary took a deep, cleansing breath of fresh air as she

looked around. Astra sent us here for a reason, she thought. And the Lake likes me.

Well, it couldn't hurt to ask.

She leaned forward, stared into the black water and whispered, "Excuse me. Hello, Lake?"

Epilogue

ONE NIGHT IN late August, Nicholas had a dream.

He had buried all the bodies from the battle on the island. Then he had worked to clear away the debris from the cabin fire.

When the clearing was readied, he spent the long, hot summer days building a new house. Now the frame was finished, and some of the flooring, but he had a lot to do before it would be ready for winter.

He reveled in the hard, physical work. Through it, he grew acquainted with the young, strong body that he had been given, and it filled out the promise of power in his wide shoulders. It also helped to heal the parts of him that needed healing.

In his dream, he lounged in the shade of his new porch, watching the small corner of the world that he had claimed for himself. Even though it was morning, the day was turning into a scorcher. The fox lay at his feet, panting like a dog.

Mary walked up the path. She wore sunglasses, and she

was tanned to a warm honey brown. A tangle of thick, layered, wavy hair floated around her slender shoulders. She was casually dressed in cutoff jeans, a hot pink tank top with spaghetti straps and matching pink flip-flops. Her toes were painted a bright pink too.

Pleasure welled in Nicholas. When he had first met Mary, she had been too thin, her face carved from stress. Now she was a healthy weight and vibrant with color. As she approached, he rose to his feet and put his arms around her in a tight hug.

He said, "I know I'm dreaming, but it's still good to see you."

She laughed. "It may be a dream, but that doesn't make it less real. Michael is teaching me how to do it." She pulled her sunglasses down her nose to look at him with bright aquamarine blue eyes. "I've been thinking a lot about you. How are you?"

He nodded. "It took me a while, but I'm good. I needed to be alone to think. I've made peace with what we did, and I've thanked Jamie for the immense gift he gave me."

"I'm so glad to hear that." She tilted her head up to look at the house. "This is amazing. How many bedrooms is it?"

"Four," he said. "I always wanted to build my own house but never had the time, so I've gone a bit overboard. The island is never going to stop cloaking itself from the outside world, and it's not like I'll have many visitors here. There's a lot of work still to do, but I'll have it insulated and ready for winter."

"It's beautiful," she told him. "How are Jerry and Sara?"

"They are doing okay." He gestured an invitation for her to join him on the porch, and she climbed the steps to sit on the swing beside him. "Sara doesn't know. She thinks Jamie is working in Marquette for the summer. I call her every week, and we talk. It makes her happy. My dad suspects something, but he hasn't said anything yet, and neither have I." He took a deep breath. "I have to decide soon what I'm going to do about that. For now I'm being who I need to be, and I'm letting them call me Jamie because that's what they need to call me."

Her expression shadowed with compassion. "I'm sorry, that's so hard."

Gently, he echoed the words that she had said to him months ago. "It will be all right." They sat for a while in companionable silence. Then he asked, "How are you and Michael?"

"We're good," she said, giving him a quick smile. "We're better than good. We're happy, and we're not afraid. There's no longer any war on our horizon. We're actually talking about getting pregnant."

"I'm very happy for you both," he said. "Where did you decide to go?"

"We're in Puerto Rico for now and taking things easy. I'm reading a lot. He's tinkering with cars. We may settle there permanently, but neither one of us feels the need to make any long-term decisions in a hurry."

Nicholas looked across the clearing. He heard himself say, "You're never coming back to the continental U.S., are you?"

She shook her head. "I don't think so. Our descriptions have been too publicized. We could have plastic surgery to change our appearances, but . . ." She shrugged. "Neither one of us feels the need to do that. What about you? Have you made any plans?"

"Actually, I have made plans," he said. He gave her an easy smile. "I'm going to finish my house, and I'm probably going to have a talk with my father. Then I have a murderer to catch. Someone killed me, and I'm going to find out who that was. And after that, I'm going to start hunting drones."

There was war on his horizon, and he was at peace with that.

Mary put a hand over his. "Please promise me you'll be careful."

"I will." He raised her hand to his lips. "Don't worry about me. You concentrate on being happy."

"We are." She turned to look in the distance. "Michael is calling me. I need to go." She smiled at him. "May I dream with you again from time to time, to make sure you're okay?"

He stood when she did. "I would love to see you again."

She hugged him and looked deep into his gaze. For a moment, Nicholas saw a flash of something alien in those jeweled eyes, something ancient and radiant. Then he blinked, and the image was gone.

"You should get out of the heat," she told him. "And I really must go. Be well, Nicholas."

"And you."

He watched as Mary slipped off her flip-flops and raced barefoot down the path. A few moments later, a slim, white boat pulled out of the bay.

Nicholas lifted his hand in a wave, just in case either Michael or Mary could see him. Then he went inside the house to cool off.

Look for the next book in Thea Harrison's *USA Today* bestselling Elder Races series

When Midnight Strikes

Coming from Berkley Sensation in September 2014

FROM *USA TODAY* BESTSELLING AUTHOR

THEA HARRISON

Rising Darkness

A Game of Shadows Novel

In the ER where she works, Mary is used to chaos. But lately, every aspect of her life seems adrift and the vivid, disturbing dreams she's had all her life are becoming more intense. Then she meets Michael. He's handsome, enigmatic and knows more than he can say. In his company, she slowly remembers the truth about herself…

Thousands of years ago, there were eight of them. The one called the Deceiver came to destroy the world, and the other seven followed to stop him. Reincarnated over and over, they carry on—and Mary finds herself drawn into the battle once again. And the more she learns, the more she realizes that Michael will go to any lengths to destroy the Deceiver.

Then she remembers who killed her during her last life, nine hundred years ago…*Michael.*

theaharrison.com
penguin.com

M1328T0613

He will watch over her . . .

FROM *USA TODAY* BESTSELLING AUTHOR

THEA HARRISON

ORACLE'S MOON

A Novel of the Elder Races

When Grace Andreas's sister, Petra, and her husband are both killed, Grace inherits the Power and responsibilities of the Oracle of Louisville, as well as her sister's two young children, neither of which she is prepared for. Then Khalil, Demonkind and Djinn Prince of House Marid, decides to make himself a part of the household—as guardian, as counterpoint to Grace's impudence towards the Elder Races, and as the man who holds her heart.

Praise for the Novels of the Elder Races

"Black Dagger Brotherhood readers will love this!"

—J. R. Ward, #1 *New York Times* bestselling author

"Thea Harrison is definitely an author to watch."

—Anya Bast, *New York Times* bestselling author

facebook.com/TheaHarrison
facebook.com/ProjectParanormalBooks
penguin.com

M1141T0712

"A dark, compelling world. I'm hooked!"

— J. R. Ward, #1 *New York Times* bestselling author

FROM *USA TODAY* BESTSELLING AUTHOR

THEA HARRISON

The Elder Race Novels

DRAGON BOUND

STORM'S HEART

SERPENT'S KISS

ORACLE'S MOON

LORD'S FALL

KINKED